I've travelled the world twice over,
Met the famous: saints and sinners,
Poets and artists, kings and queens,
Old stars and hopeful beginners,
I've been where no-one's been before,
Learned secrets from writers and cooks
All with one library ticket
To the wonderful world of books.

FLASH OF SPLENDOUR

In a quiet Warwickshire village in 1848 live Anne Torrance and Doctor Hugh Radlett. Into their lives come two men—Godfrey Bullivant, a man obsessed, shattering the peace of the countryside with his railway and his band of unruly navvies; and Laslo Bathory, an exotic, mysterious figure, involved in revolution. Against a vast canvas of upheaval and change, surrounded by fascinating characters such as the Hungarian Countess Sophia, the prim Esther Wharton, the intolerable Carrington, the pathetic Toms, they work out their individual destinies.

ANNE STEVENSON

FLASH
OF
SPLENDOUR

Complete and Unabridged

ULVERSCROFT
Leicester

First Large Print Edition
published November 1983
by arrangement with
Collins, London & Glasgow

British Library CIP Data

Stevenson, Anne
 Flash of splendour.—Large print ed.
 (Ulverscroft large print series:
 Historical Romance)
 I. Title
 823'.914[F]   PR6069.T449

 ISBN 0-7089-1048-3

Published by
F. A. Thorpe (Publishing) Ltd.
Anstey, Leicestershire
Printed and Bound in Great Britain by
T. J. Press (Padstow) Ltd., Padstow, Cornwall

To
Pat, Joan and Liz

1

IT was a very hot day when they buried Dr. Torrance. They buried him on a day in June in the year 1848, in the churchyard of the village of Rivington in Warwickshire. The parson began the service about eleven o'clock before a crowded congregation, but it was not until after twelve that Hugh Radlett arrived.

He had walked a long way. The white dust of the Warwickshire lanes clung about his trousers and marred the fine polish of his boots. His hat felt too hot and heavy and he had taken it off long before he reached the church.

At the lychgate he paused, waving away an intrusive fly. The church stood on a slight eminence, the ground rising gently from the gate. On the highest part of this ground, a flat plateau at the left hand side of the church, the burial party was standing, grouped in their mourning clothes like fat black crows on a fence. Beyond them the sky was densely blue. At their feet the scythed grasses nibbled at the sunken stones of other deaths. In the damp shadow of the boundary hedge the grass grew long and thickly green; wild flowers, pink and white and yellow and blue, edged near. Only the two yew trees guarding the church door, seemed on a day ripening with heat, lifeless enough for a funeral.

"Ashes to ashes. Dust to dust." The sonorous voice of the parson came to Hugh reduced to a sinister murmuring of bees; his gesture, as he took a piece of earth and crumbled it between his fingers on to the hidden coffin beneath, seemed, with its symbolism of decay, vaguely obscene.

The widow raised a black-gloved hand and pressed a handkerchief to her mouth. The parson stooped towards her. He began to guide her away from the grave. There was a general stirring and movement. The ritual was completed. The procession came towards Hugh down the path. In a moment, one figure alone remained by the grave; the figure of a young woman.

Hugh spoke her name aloud. "Anne."

She had not changed. He could not see her face clearly, but she had still the same proud carriage he remembered. She stood with her head held high, looking, not down at her father's grave, but away into the distance, absorbed in some private thought. But she was not quite alone. A man had stayed behind from the crowd. He approached her, spoke, offered his arm. She glanced at him, moved past, ignoring him, and walked quickly after the others.

"Hugh, my dear." Mrs. Torrance, her face pale with strain, was greeting Hugh, stretching out her hand to him. He took it quickly between both his in an instinctive attempt to comfort.

Mrs. Torrance was a small woman of no great distinction of feature; but the plainness of her face was softened by the pleasantness of her nature and the impression she left behind her was always surprisingly deep and lasting. Surprising because her husband was apparently the dominating force in the marriage. He had been a large, ebullient man, loud-voiced and opinionated, a competent physician who had cured as many people by his supreme self-confidence as he had by his medicine. Beside him Mrs. Torrance had seemed subdued and self-effacing, but her influence had run like an undercurrent through her husband's life. Hugh had often wondered if the help he had received from the doctor had not been inspired and guided by his wife.

"I am sorry I arrived so late," he said to her.

"It does not matter. You are here. It was good of you to come. I was not sure when I wrote to you . . ."

"Of course I would come," he said gently. "There was never any doubt of it. I was very fond of him."

"And he of you." Her voice trembled on the words, but her grief was disciplined and she recovered without pause. "That other matter I mentioned in my letter. The real reason I wanted to see you, Hugh."

"We can talk of it when you please. Later."

"No, no. I should like to get it settled. The sooner it is discussed the better for my peace of mind. It is you who must not be hurried into a decision."

Hugh became aware that, standing as they were in the centre of the gateway, they were creating a slight confusion. No one could get past them and no one wished to be the first to disturb the doctor's widow. The mourners had withdrawn to a respectful distance, talking together in low voices. Behind Mrs. Torrance the parson waited, a tall, lugubrious man, with high forehead and balding head. He affected a trivial growth of whiskers in a vain attempt, Hugh surmised, to add dignity and wisdom to his appearance. Hugh though he looked a canting fool. He met the clergyman's glance and nodded briefly.

"Forgive me. You do not know each other," said Mrs. Torrance. "Mr. Carrington was not here in your day, Hugh. Mr. Carrington, this is Dr. Radlett, whose family once lived in the village. How are your parents, Hugh?"

"Very well."

"They moved to Lincolnshire a few years ago," Mrs. Torrance explained, "and Hugh has not been back since then."

"You practise in Lincolnshire, Dr. Radlett?" the rector asked.

"No. I have been attached to a London hospital for the past two years."

"Indeed." Mr. Carrington bowed his head. "I salute your devotion. A noble profession. Dr. Torrance will be sadly missed, sadly."

"Perhaps we should move on?" Hugh suggested to Mrs. Torrance. He glanced back and saw Anne standing silently at the back of the crowd, the man he had noticed before,

5

beside her. He wondered why she did not come forward to her mother.

"Yes, of course, we must go on." Mrs. Torrance was mildly flustered as if she had been caught out in a breach of good manners. "Hugh, will you walk with me to the house?" She took his arm and they stepped from the churchyard into the main street of the village.

Rivington was a village of moderate size and moderate wealth and this moderation was reflected in its life. There were no squalid hovels sheltering starving labourers in its environment and no aristocratic families holding court in crenellated mansions. There was one aristocrat living in the district but she was a foreigner and therefore did not count. The majority of the inhabitants of the area were prosperous farmers, tenant or independent, who lived in comfortable contentment and a certain degree of smugness. The storms of a turbulent century passed them by. Or had done, as yet.

Hugh Radlett had been born in the village thirty years ago and Anne Torrance ten years later. He was the third son of the local solicitor, the youngest of a large family. Anne was an only child.

When Hugh was fifteen years old, he fell

off a horse and broke his leg. The men who carried him home said they could see the bone through the flesh and warned him to be prepared to lose the leg. When Dr. Torrance arrived the boy raised himself from the pillow and begged him not to cut off his leg.

"Why should you think I would?" he asked.

"They say you'll have to. They say it will go rotten in three days and kill me if you don't cut it off."

The doctor swore vigorously. "What the devil do you want to go listening to that pack of idiots for? What do they know about it? Do I tell them how to plough their miserable fields or milk their damned cows? Let them look to their own affairs and leave me to manage mine. Now take a gulp of this and close your eyes."

Doped with laudanum, Hugh endured the setting and dressing of his leg. When it was finished, Dr. Torrance took Mrs. Radlett on one side and put the prospects to her.

"If he's lucky the wound will heal clean. If gangrene sets in, I'll have to have the leg off. We'll know within the week."

She was aghast. "But you told Hugh . . ."

"Of course, I did. What's the point of

7

worrying the lad to death? If it comes to the worst he'll have had a few days peace of mind, and an easy mind is a good aid to healing any day of the week. But better warn your husband."

For the next week Dr. Torrance was a constant visitor. He watched over the damaged leg with an almost furious dedication. He hated, he told Hugh's father, the thought of turning a healthy lad into a one-legged cripple and he had no intention of doing so. As it proved, the necessity did not arise. Hugh was one of the lucky ones. Mortification did not set in. The torn flesh healed, the broken bone knitted together, leaving him without even a limp.

"You must have cured it by will-power," Hugh told Torrance many years later.

"We cured it by leaving it alone," the doctor replied. "Too many arrogant little butchers calling themselves doctors go about interfering with the natural processes of healing in the mistaken belief they know better. Their patients soon discover the truth."

"We all have to be butchers now and again," Hugh remarked.

"I'm a physician," the doctor said. "The

knife should be the last resort, not the first."

During Hugh's long convalescence, Dr. Torrance developed a great affection for the boy. He liked his curiosity. Even in his worst moments, he noticed, he was always asking questions. Why are you doing such and such? What is happening now? What will happen next? What would happen in such and such a case?

The doctor would explode in exasperation. "We don't know!"

"Why not?" asked Hugh.

When he was able to walk again, the doctor encouraged the boy to visit him. No one was more delighted by this than Anne Torrance. Occasionally, to distract and amuse his patient, Dr. Torrance had brought his five-year-old daughter with him to the Radlett house. She used to run around the room, climb up on the high bed and fall off it again, full of laughter. She was enchanted with Hugh and chattered to him endlessly, claiming his constant attention, pulling at his arm impatiently if she lost it for one moment. She was a spoilt, charming, demanding child, the joy of her middle-aged father's life.

Hugh treated her with tolerant kindness, amused and touched by the determination

9

with which the little girl, once he had recovered, would wait for him to come down the street, then run out from her house to drag him back inside. He never minded for he was fascinated by the doctor and his stories. They would sit all together in the drawing-room, the doctor holding forth, Hugh listening and questioning, Anne, her small face alive with excitement, crouched on a stool at her father's feet.

"That boy would make a very good doctor," Mrs. Torrance remarked one day.

"So he would," agreed her husband.

"Why don't you suggest it to him?"

"Why doesn't he suggest it to himself?" Torrance said.

"I don't think it has occurred to him," Mrs. Torrance said. "His mother tells me he is to read law like his brothers."

"Well." The doctor considered it. "I might have a word with him."

Hugh did not know of this conversation. He only knew that somehow during the next year the conviction that no other profession but medicine could ever satisfy him settled in his mind. He knew too how much he owed to the often impatient teaching and expostulation he received from the doctor over a long

10

period of time. And now the man from whom he had learned so much, who had fired his purpose with his own enthusiasm, was dead. The boy Torrance had encouraged to follow in his path was dead too. It was a very different man who was walking with Torrance's widow along the familiar street of Rivington village.

The doctor's house, a red-brick building some hundred years old, was barely fifty yards from the church, on the opposite side of the road. The front door opened directly on to the street. The entrance to the stables and the servants' quarters was down a narrow lane by the side of the house. Behind the house was a long, walled garden and beyond that, through a wooden gate in the wall, a vegetable garden, a small apple orchard and a paddock. Beyond that again were three fields which the doctor, having no use for them, had rented to a couple of local farmers, a small coppice, and two larger fields of rough grazing land which ended at the foot of a low hill. It was, in fact, a moderately sized property sustained by the moderate income which the doctor, without any means other than his practice, had maintained throughout his life.

The front door was opened by a young maidservant as Hugh and Mrs. Torrance approached. Black mourning bands had been stitched round the sleeves of her sober grey dress.

"Is everything ready, Betty?" Mrs. Torrance asked.

"Yes, ma'am. Cook got back from the church ten minutes ago. Everything's laid out in the dining-room."

"Come, Hugh," said Mrs. Torrance. "We will have a quiet glass of sherry in the drawing-room before the others arrive. We have time for a few moments talk."

"They were directly behind us," Hugh remarked.

"Well, then, Anne shall look after them. They are too kind to consider a short absence on my part as deliberate rudeness. Did you see Anne at the church, Hugh?"

"Very briefly. I have not spoken to her."

Mrs. Torrance sighed, a dry breath of a sigh that Hugh barely caught as she moved ahead of him into the darkened drawing-room. The blinds which customarily would have been raised at the time of the funeral had, at Mrs. Torrance's insistence, been left drawn for she could not bear the bright

12

sunshine in the house on such a day, and the maid had filled the empty grate of the fireplace with a huge fan of fluted black crêpe paper. After the heat and sunlight of the street, it was cold and cheerless and—a tribute, perhaps, Hugh reflected, to the careful efforts made—funereal. It was, in effect, no longer the room he remembered, the room he had spent so many evenings in; the room he had last been in with Anne. And for that at least he could be grateful. And yet it was only as he came into the room that he realised completely the fact of Torrance's death. The house that Hugh remembered had always been full of a sense of the doctor's exuberant presence. Now the life had gone from it. It was no more than an empty shell. And Mrs. Torrance, despite the courage of her pretence, was empty too. She drifted inside her clothes, a dried moth of a woman. When she spoke even her voice seemed drained of life.

"Anne is not speaking to me," she said. "Or only as little as she need."

"Why?" Hugh asked. "What has happened?"

"Oh—" She shrugged. "It is a long story. Anne will no doubt tell you about it. For various reasons she considers me disloyal to her father. You know how she worshipped him."

"You could never be disloyal to him."

"It is not as simple as that. A decision I have made recently could be said to be against his wishes, though he told me——"She broke off.

Hugh remained still as, with face averted, she struggled to control herself. From the hall came the hushed sound of voices. There was a soft knock on the drawing-room door and Hugh went quickly to open it, hoping it would be Anne; but it was the maid with a tray containing a decanter of sherry and two glasses. Hugh took it and shut the door behind her. He put the tray down on a table and poured out a glass. He handed it to Mrs. Torrance.

"Here," he said gently. "Drink a little of this."

She took a sip and then put the glass down again. "Thank you, Hugh, I am quite recovered." She looked up at him. "You mustn't think that Anne . . ."

He was becoming angry with Anne. "Whatever she feels, she should be with you now, giving you all her support."

"You know her," Mrs. Torrance said. "You know she can never hide her feelings."

"Then it is time she learned. Your husband, if I may say so without distressing you, gave Anne too much of her own way."

"Perhaps he did," she agreed. "But who can blame him. You of all people, Hugh, should know how hard it is to resist her."

She turned suddenly to him, grasping his hands. In an instant all her careful composure was lost and he was glimpsing the depths of her anxiety. "Oh Hugh, if only she had married you! Why did she refuse you? You were always the one who understood her, the one she listened to. She would be safe now. If only she had married you!"

Twenty minutes later Hugh left Mrs. Torrance and crossed the square hall to the dining-room. He had persuaded her to rest and intended only to find Anne and send her—order her, if need be—to her mother before leaving again for London.

He paused, his hand on the handle of the door. It was so quiet within the room he wondered whether everyone had already gone. He opened the door and went in.

Hugh had seen many deaths but it was long time since he had attended a reception for the mourners at a funeral and it occurred to him as he entered the dining-room that it must be one of the more awkward social occasions ever invented. Here again, as throughout the house, the blinds had been drawn down and in the half-light of the shadowed room the heavy pieces of furniture loomed up like islands. The massive mahogany table, its surface deadened by thick cloths of velvet and linen, bore its load of wines and cold meats and savoury pies with a restrained air of grim festivity. The whiteness of tablecloth and china gleamed dully, greenly, in a seaweed light. The guests who had gathered to pay their respects to the doctor and convey, as they had written in the sedate letters they had sent before them, their deepest condolences to his widow and daughter, stood about in solemn attitudes, all the natural warmth of their feelings suppressed into conventional gloom, holding their glasses of sherry and madeira and refusing, as if it might be construed as unseemly greed, more than a taste of the food the cook had spent such care preparing. Many of them were old acquaintances of Hugh's family and had known him since boyhood. The men greeted him gravely, the women inquired kindly after his parents. He found himself caught in a group recounting recollections of the doctor in low voices, with only now and again the narrator forgetting himself sufficiently to smile. He wondered that Anne could bear it.

He had seen her at once. She was standing by the window and as he finally disengaged himself and made his way towards her, he had the impression that she longed to fling up the blind and let the burning sunlight into the room. Her stillness did not deceive him. A repressed passion of grief or anger or regret racked that silent figure with an almost tangible vibration. The sombre black dress with its sweeping folds of skirt gave to her height an added majesty. Her profile was finely cut. In her her mother's features were reshaped and balanced to create beauty; straight, delicate nose, firm chin, a mouth that hinted at her deeper nature. Her dark hair, parted in the middle, was drawn back into a chignon. Her face as she turned to him—how pale it was! Her eyes, those lovely hazel eyes that changed their subtle colours with her mood, now almost green, now warmly brown, had the glassy blankness of the blind. Then he realised that they were indeed full of tears. At once the stiffness, the antagonism he had been building up inside himself to face the meeting, dissolved.

"Anne."

"Hugh . . ." She seemed not surprised, but confused by his presence, as if the necessity it forced on her to withdraw from her private world left her bewildered. She spoke quickly, almost at random. "So you came. Mother told me she had written to you, but I did not think you would come. Were you at the service? I did not see you. It was very hot, wasn't it?"

"Yes, it was."

"I was afraid Mother might faint."

He said nothing, but his expression mirrored his unspoken thought and Anne flushed. And at that, with an inward sigh so deep it was like the involuntary surrender of his whole being, he recognised that he still loved her.

Two years before, at the time his parents had left the village for good, he had asked Anne to marry him. He had asked her because he believed she loved him, because he believed she would accept him. He had been disillusioned to learn that she had never once considered it. Her manner was free and affectionate and gay with him because she had known him so long. But her feeling for him she did not think of as love. No, love was something else again, something wild and passionate and unexpected. How could Hugh imagine that she could marry him? Why, he was like a brother. And he was much too old. She was only eighteen after all and he was ten years older. How dull it would be to be married to him.

And she had been right, Hugh thought. She had been too young. She was, at twenty, still too young. But he still loved her.

She had recovered from her first uncertainty.

"You have not changed, Hugh," she said, more naturally. "You look the same."

He hesitated, unwilling to upset her by repeating what she must have heard so many times. "You know how sorry I am about your father, Anne——"

"Yes . . . Thank you." There was a silence which she broke by saying abruptly: "Have you decided?"

"Decided?"

"I know why my mother wrote to you. She

wants you to take over Father's practice. Are you going to do so?"

"I don't know." The suggestion, which Mrs. Torrance had first made in her letter to him informing him of the doctor's death, attracted Hugh, and yet he felt instinctively that he should refuse it. To come back here, to be within daily sight and sound of Anne was probably neither wise nor desirable. And yet it did appeal to him for many reasons unconnected in any way with Anne.

"Would you disapprove?" he asked.

She frowned. "Why should I?"

"I wondered if that might be one of the reasons you and your mother have quarrelled."

"Oh . . ." She glanced away, an expression he remembered well—stubborn, with-drawn—coming over her face. "What has she said to you?"

"Very little. She said you would probably tell me yourself. Anne, you should be with her now. She is near to collapse already, without this added strain. Why is there this coldness between you? What is the matter?"

She looked back at him, and he thought she might be about to answer him when they were interrupted.

"Miss Torrance, I regret I have to go. I should be grateful if you would make my apologies to your mother. I shall, of course, be in communication with her."

The speaker had a pleasant voice with the slightest trace of a Scottish accent. Hugh turned and found at his side the man from the churchyard. Anne had ignored him then and seemed ready to ignore him now, and Hugh studied him curiously, wondering why. He was an older man than Hugh, about forty-five, heavily built with brown hair already greying and a square-cut beard. The skin of his face was weatherbeaten, like a farmer or sailor, as if he had spent much time working out of doors, and there was a certain grim determined line to his mouth. His appearance was rougher than his manner, which seemed correct enough.

Unexpectedly, in view of her attitude, Anne introduced them. The stranger's name was Godfrey Bullivant. The two men shook hands.

"I caught sight of you at the church, Dr. Radlett," Bullivant remarked. "You arrived at the end of the service, I think."

"Yes, I was late. I came down by train from London."

"Ah, London." Bullivant glanced at Anne. "What a different journey now from in the old days, eh, Dr. Radlett? Or perhaps you don't remember the old coaching days? No, of course you don't. You were too young."

"We were never on an important route here at Rivington," Hugh remarked. He gave Anne a slight smile. "Everyone walked, I remember. They still do. But I wouldn't have thought the days of the coach were quite over yet. This is not the only place in England that is difficult to reach, off the main lines of the railways."

"Of course, it is still impossible to come here directly from London by train," Bullivant agreed. "Five years ago you couldn't have come as far as Warwick. I presume you came to Warwick, Dr. Radlett, from the junction with the Birmingham line at Coventry?"

Hugh raised an eyebrow, unable to see the point of these inquiries. "Yes, I came to Warwick, and from Warwick, Mr. Bullivant, since I see from your face you are about to ask, I got a lift on a carrier's cart. The last few miles I walked."

"That must have tired you out in this heat," Bullivant commented, unmoved.

"How much more convenient if the train had passed through Rivington itself. Don't you agree?"

"Very convenient," Hugh said. "But I hardly see anyone wasting money building a line to Rivington, especially after the collapse in railway speculation last year."

"Not particularly to Rivington," Bullivant agreed. "But a line, say from Warwick to Worcester would run very close."

"You seem very interested in railways, Mr. Bullivant," Hugh said. He looked at Anne questioningly, as a vague possibility occurred to him. She nodded.

"Yes. That is the reason for the quarrel, Hugh."

"The railways?" He stared at her in amazement. "Mr. Bullivant——"

"Don't let us keep you from your appointment, Mr. Bullivant." With the same coldness she had maintained throughout Anne dismissed him. "I will give your message to my mother." Bullivant appeared quite impervious to her disapproval. He bowed, nodded to Hugh—"Dr. Radlett"— and made his way out of the room.

"Anne, what is this all about?" Hugh demanded. "Who is that man?"

"It is very simple," she said. "Mr. Bullivant is the director of a railway company. They want to build a railway which would cut across our property—the two large bottom fields beyond the wood. Father refused to sell them the fields and so at first did some of the others whose land was involved, but many wanted the line and the company offered so much money that the rest eventually gave way. Father kept on refusing. He hated the idea, he refused to countenance even the thought of it." Her voice was hard and impersonal, as if she was speaking about someone else. "Then there was some trouble. You remember, last year, everyone was losing money on the railways. Companies were going bankrupt. We heard nothing more and we thought they had given up the idea; even, perhaps, wound up the company. . . . You see, I know all the terms of business. I have lived so long with this. But three months ago they appeared again. The line had been surveyed the previous year, you see, and the Act of Parliament approving it passed, so they had decided to go ahead. It would not be too expensive to build and would be, as Mr. Bullivant would say, commercially profitable. That was why he was asking you about your journey from London. It was meant as one more proof to me that such a line is needed." She leaned back against the frame of the window as if exhausted. "Father was very ill by then, in constant pain, but they pestered him. I believe they had been so sure he would sell the land that they had made their plans on that assumption and were finding it would cost too much money to alter them. After all, it was such a small obstacle, two fields only. Mr. Bullivant kept calling. I told him to stay away and then he wrote letters instead. In the end, Father told Mother, he told her . . ." Her voice faltered. "He was concerned about us. He said she could sell the land if she wished because we should need the money when he was dead. And she agreed!" She gazed up at Hugh, her eyes dark with anger. "She knows how Father felt. She knows it is a betrayal. And Bullivant comes still, even to-day of all days, trying to win my acquiescence, heaven knows why." She moved restlessly. "Oh, it is so hot. Do you find it hot in here, Hugh? I want to breathe, I feel stifled."

"Come outside."

"No, I can hardly leave. With Mother not well I must stay here with our guests. I must be polite." She looked round the long room. "Perhaps they will go soon. How long do people stay on such occasions?"

"I don't know," Hugh said. "I have little experience of them."

"Is it not ghoulish? How he would have hated it, Hugh! All the dark and gloom and quiet." She shuddered.

"Anne——"

"No." She touched his wrist. "No, I am all right, Hugh." She smiled suddenly at him, a pale echo of the brilliant smile he knew so well. "I hope you will come back. I shall not quarrel with Mother on that point. I should like to have a friend here."

Ten years before Hugh was born, the only railways in existence were short tracks worked by horses or by stationary engines. From colliery to canal, from quarry to works, the horses walked beside the road pulling the wagons along the rails as they pulled the barges through the canal waters; while the steam engine invented so long ago, yet still immobile, drew loads via pulleys up gradients steeper than a horse could walk.

By the time Hugh was thirty, by now, by

this year of upheaval 1848, the revolution was nearly complete. The engine had been given wheels. It was on the track and moving and the time had come to open up the world. It seemed a long time to the early builders from idea to achievement; from survey and persuasion and prospectus and committee, from company forming and share selling and the approval of Parliament; from the letting of contracts and the gathering of men and the first cut made in the earth, to the finished road and the opening ceremony with champagne in tents beside the line. But it was all completed in the space of a man's childhood and youth, the first vital framework of a system.

The great main lines were there, slashed across the country, over embankments, across viaducts, through tunnels, across swamps and quicksands, taking a man from London, north, west, east, south, at speed, for little money, in a comfort far above the stage coach; taking him for no other reason than his pleasure, if he wished, to see what his country was like.

Building the lines had caused deaths and disasters, had made fortunes and broken reputations. Men had been buried in earth falls and suffocated in tunnels, crushed by rocks and killed in brawls. The armies of navvies who built the railroads moved from site to site, their shanty towns springing up wherever they settled, feared and avoided by the local people, condemned by the clergy, drunken and vigorous and skilled and careless, proud as peacocks in their moleskin trousers, running wild every month when the pay came and penniless again next day. The engineers who used them learned as they worked, creating on the ground, day by day and obstacle by obstacle, becoming masters of a new profession. They tore the countryside apart and made a revolution and some knew it and many did not; but everyone soon learned that railways meant money.

After the first astounding successes, the doubts faded fast. The soundness of railway investment became accepted, a commonplace of commercial life, and the fever to be in on it, to take part in a financial bonanza grew to a mania that for a while touched every part of society. Its presence was obvious in every newspaper opened and behind every whispered story of sudden fortune. Old ladies and hopeful businessmen were each as ready to dig for this particular gold and each as credulous. For a few flourishing years it was merely necessary to put out a prospectus, float a company and whether the railway announced was possible, or needed, or ever intended to exist, people would clamour for the shares.

The collapse had had to come and it had come a year ago. Once begun the lack of confidence spread rapidly like a virulent disease. The boom ended with shouting meetings of shareholders, with the merging of lines, the withdrawal of capital and the painful hangover of sobering reality.

When Dr. Torrance, that hard-headed and practical physician, learned during those months on the edge of crisis, of the scheme to build yet another railway, this time close to home, Hugh was not surprised that he had had doubts. It was, moreover, in Torrance's character to detest the railway. He was a man of the old days and the old ways. He would profoundly distrust an innovation so radical and call fools those who preached about progress.

"Have that circus at the bottom of my own garden!" Hugh could hear him saying, "Drunken navvies and noise and the ruin of the landscape. By God, let them try!"

Well, they were going to try and it looked

as if they were going to succeed and Anne was unhappy and Hugh did not entirely trust Godfrey Bullivant or like, any more than Anne, the thought that old Torrance would have felt betrayed.

He stood on the threshold of the doctor's house, thinking about the dead man. He had said good-bye to Anne and now he said in his mind a farewell to her father. The mourning household behind him, its duty to convention completed, was, as the guests slipped away, turning in upon itself with the self-absorption of grief. No outsider, even one as close as Hugh had once been, had any place there now. Hugh closed the door behind him and it shut with a sound soft yet final. When he came back, if he came back, it would be to a different world from the boyhood that he linked with Torrance.

He began to walk up the village street. Save for a wandering hen scratching petulantly at the dusty road, it was deserted. He paused, and glanced back in the other direction, but there was no sign of the man he was looking for.

Hugh had left not long after Bullivant, and that was in a way deliberate. There had been in the back of his mind some idea of perhaps catching up with the man and questioning him about his company and the railway they proposed to build. Some idea of protecting Anne. This inevitable, foolish reaction, this involuntary involvement was one of the reasons it might be unwise to come back. He doubted if he could control the compulsion that was a matter of instinct with him, to interfere, to attempt to direct everything to do with Anne. She would resent it and she would be right to do so, for he had no claim on her, far less than two years ago when he had still been behaving with the sublime assumption that she was to be his wife.

Perhaps, however, in this one matter she might welcome his protection. He had felt her loneliness and she had asked for his friendship. His friendship. He wondered if she knew what she asked.

Anyway. . . . He shrugged. In the matter of Bullivant, it was obvious he had missed him. He had not seemed to be the sort of man to be travelling on foot, and Hugh did not even know in which direction he was heading. In any case, London was the place to make inquiries, not Rivington. He walked on, slowly, taking his time, past the church and out of the village along the Warwick road.

31

It was now the hottest part of the afternoon. The lane curved ahead of him, following the gentle incline of the land, ambling its way between broad hedges and beneath the spread of ancient trees. Oak and ash, chestnut and beech and elm; it was a landscape rich with trees, full of coppices and small woods and clumps guarding the corners of the fields and offering cool shadows on the hottest days. Hugh remembered, when he helped with the harvest as a boy, the relief of stretching out at the midday break under the trees at the field's edge, sweaty and hot and every muscle aching, eating bread and cheese and cider, and lying back drowsily watching the pattern of sunlight through the leaves overhead.

A nostalgia for this countryside and the days he had wandered so freely and carelessly about it began to lull him with a pleasant melancholy. Everything was burning with a brilliant green that almost hurt the eyes. After London, after the stench of the wards, this lushness, this quiet, this sweet, summer-scented air was like a balm. His steps slowed. When he came to a gate in the hedge leading to a field sown with young wheat, he stopped and leaned against it, his arms hooked over the top, his eyes half-shut against the light.

The sound of wheels on the road aroused him. He turned as the open carriage passed him and his movement caught the eye of the occupant. She called out to her driver, leaning forward in her seat to poke him in the back with her parasol.

"Joseph! Pull up, pull up!"

There appeared to be an abnormal amount of noise and upheaval, of shouting and raising of dust before this simple manœuvre was accomplished. It was transformed, as anything the Countess Sophia touched was transformed, Hugh thought with amusement, into a performance. He went forward smiling as she opened the carriage door for him.

"My dear Hugh, is it you? What are you doing here, lounging over a gate like a rustic lover? I thought you were in London?"

"I am," Hugh said. "I came down for Dr. Torrance's funeral."

"Of course. I should have expected it. I would have looked for you. Poor man, what weather for a funeral! It is quite unfeeling. I could not bear it. I stayed for half the service in the church but that was quite enough. Staring into graves is too serious an occupation for such a frivolous day. Where are you going? I shall take you there. Come along, get in, get in. I want to hear all your news. We cannot talk in the road."

Hugh obeyed her. She was an old friend, and besides, she was not a woman who brooked opposition. The Countess Sophia Esterkeros would have been intolerable if she were not so feminine. She was a Hungarian by birth, volatile, egocentric, gay, selfish, interfering and charming. She was in her late fifties and was thought to be in her late forties. Esterkeros was not in fact her real name since she had been married to an Englishman for nearly twenty years. Widowed young in Hungary, she was living in Paris when she met George Wharton. He was twenty years older than she and a widower himself. They married within a month and she became Mrs. Wharton. But the exotic creature whom plain Mr. George brought back to his Warwickshire house, of whom Hugh's first memory was of the delicious scent she wore, was altogether too flamboyant to be subdued to a plain Mrs. To the county, and Mr. Wharton's astonished children, the Countess remained the Countess. They developed a certain pride of possession concerning her and liked to point her out to their visitors. The young men fell determinedly in love with her. The young girls were either terrified of her or begging for her advice.

She was basically a warm-hearted, sensible woman and this was the side she showed to Hugh when, following her husband's death, his father was engaged in disentangling the Wharton estate. The Countess charmed Mr. Radlett as she did most serious middle-aged men. She dined with the family, she became their friend, but particularly the friend of young Hugh. She had a weakness for handsome men, she told him, especially when they were intelligent. He was delighted to see her again.

"You are as good-looking as ever, I see," the Countess remarked. "And more elegant. A little distrait, perhaps, but that suits you. A burden of sorrow adds a certain air to a man. Let me see—" she regarded him, smiling, her head tilted to one side "—I diagnose that you are still in love with Anne and that she is still refusing you. What a foolish girl she is!"

"Her father's funeral was hardly the moment for a proposal," Hugh commented.

"Of course." She patted his arm. "Don't listen to me. I am a vulgar woman. Tell me, do you know about the railroad?"

"I heard about it to-day. Anne is very much opposed to it."

"Yes, she has been foolish about that too."

"Is any of your property involved?" Hugh asked.

"Oh, they came to see me in the early days, but I sent them off with fleas in their ears. I do not see the necessity for people to go rattling from Warwick to Worcester and Worcester to Warwick and certainly not across my parkland. What is the point of it? Far better for them to remain where they are."

"But if you object to the railway," Hugh asked, "why do you call Anne a fool for doing so?"

"My dear Hugh, that is quite another matter. I am wealthy, Anne and her mother are not. The money they would be paid for their two fields would be a godsend to them. Anne has no dowry at all."

"Do you know the man who is negotiating this business, Godfrey Bullivant?" Hugh said.

"I have met him, yes."

"I am wondering if there is more to this than there seems," Hugh said. "Apparently he was determined to obtain their property.

Anne told me he was constantly at the house, and I met him there myself to-day."

The Countess, somewhat unexpectedly, began to laugh. "My dear boy, Mr. Bullivant's constant appearance at the doctor's house has nothing to do with the railway. He comes to see Anne. He is in hot pursuit. It is obvious."

"In pursuit of Anne?"

She nodded vigorously. "That is it. He is a rival suitor for your sweetheart, Hugh."

"Then she doesn't realise it," Hugh replied.

"Well, as I say, your Anne is a little bit of a fool." The Countess smiled, then looked contrite. "No, I must not be so unfeeling. I must contain my jealousy of the woman who takes your affections from me, Hugh. No, I will be serious. I am very sorry for her and her mother. It is a terrible thing to lose a husband and a father. And he was a very good man. Tell me, Hugh, do you know the cause of his death?"

"He starved to death," Hugh replied.

"What do you mean?"

"He had a growth in his stomach. Over a period of time it enlarged until it effectively prevented the passage of food. When it reached that stage he starved to death."

"What a dreadful business." The Countess had dropped her flirtatious manner. She regarded Hugh with shrewd eyes. "You seem very disturbed by it, by the manner of his death, I mean."

"Pay no attention to me, Countess. I apologise."

"No, no. . . . You are deeply troubled, I can see. I thought it was because of Anne, but now I realise it is more than that. Doesn't a doctor's life in London please you?"

"A doctor's life in London, as far as I am concerned," Hugh said, "is one of continual horror. No—" He immediately rejected his own words. "It is self-indulgence to say that. It's not horror, it's frustration, anger, helplessness. We reach a certain point and then we are blocked. It is no longer vital for a surgeon to be able to amputate a limb in a matter of seconds. He can take minutes, hours if he wishes. He can excise a tumour, help a woman in labour, probe for a bullet without pain—at long last without pain. But they still die. Because of chloroform we're going to attempt more and we don't know enough yet to do so. I operated on a boy last month, knocked down by a carriage outside the hospital. I was very pleased with my successful operation, but he still died two weeks later from an infection of his injuries. And for a man like Torrance there is nothing we can do, nothing. We don't know enough."

"It is very sad," the Countess said, "but it is not your responsibility, Hugh. You should not take these things upon yourself."

"Oh, I do not. I am not so arrogant." It was a calmer reply but it still carried that edge of bitterness.

If Anne Torrance had been asked to describe Hugh, the Countess thought, she would not have mentioned this quality of passionate concern because she did not know it existed. She might speak of his self-sufficiency, but never of his self-control. His customary calmness of manner, his quiet voice, the enlivening humour that was never far away, were all misleading. The control he exercised was a discipline his training had developed. It was a necessary virtue for a doctor but it was not inborn in Hugh. He had fought for it. It had made him a man in whom people were ready to place their confidence. They sensed a strength there upon which they could lean. Anne mistook it for stolidity. Too self-centred, in the Countess's opinion, to pay more than superficial attention to the character of this man who loved her, she had therefore never seen below the surface he presented to the world. But then Hugh had probably never talked freely to her as he had done to the Countess. The difference in age between Hugh and Anne and Hugh and the Countess had had an effect on his behaviour to the two women. He was not without blame for Anne's lack of response to him. He spoke to the Countess as he should have been prepared to speak to the girl, but perhaps that was hardly to be expected. The Countess did not underestimate the compliment to herself, though the implications behind the confidence with which Hugh talked to her might have been a painful blow to the vanity of a less realistic person.

He asked her now if Dr. Torrance had still been her physician when he died.

"Yes," she replied, "I suppose he was. I have had no occasion to need the attentions of a doctor for a very long time. Why do you ask?"

He did not answer for some moments, looking down at his hands, frowning slightly. The Countess watched him in silence, as ready to wait as she was to chatter. She observed the faint lines of strain round his mouth, the first flecks of grey in the dark hair that he wore unfashionably short. She thought he looked very tired.

They had come to a bend in the lane and as the carriage rounded it they moved out from the shelter of the protective trees into the full dazzling glare of the sun. The Countess tipped her parasol to shade her face, but Hugh relaxed into the heat as into the embrace of a friend.

"I want to come back," he said. "I want to put London behind me for a while. I have had too much death, too much pain, too much poverty and filth and despair, too much failure. I want to come where I can do little harm and perhaps some good."

"That is a very moderate request, I must say," the Countess said. "And are you to practise your despair and your failure on us in Rivington? Thank you very much, dear Hugh, but if that is the way of it I shall prefer to drive you straight back to Warwick and the London train."

He looked up quickly, with a sharp penetrating glance of his blue eyes. Then he shrugged and smiled and the tension eased from his face. "What an acid patient you would be, Countess. Would you be my patient, by the way, if I took over Torrance's practice or would you find it impossible to accept me as a doctor?"

"I thought you had become a surgeon," she replied.

"I'm a very poor surgeon. Have no faith in my knife at all. Two years ago, when I couldn't have Anne, I thought I'd have ambition instead. I paid a high premium to work with the best surgeon I could afford and I've learned a great deal, but principally that it's not my trade. Now I've reached a point where I must make a decision. I can either set up as a practising surgeon-physician myself, which I lack the money to do, or canvas for a hospital appointment or——"

"Or return here," the Countess finished.

"Yes."

"What does Anne say?"

"She doesn't object."

"Would you be buying the practice or inheriting it?"

"Buying it. They could not afford anything else."

"Can you afford it?" she asked bluntly.

"Mrs. Torrance has offered me an arrangement. Let us say that I should be renting it. I shall pay what I can and the rest when I have it. I see you're as direct as ever, Countess."

She laughed. "It is the only way to find out what one wishes to know. I think it is an excellent idea. I shall be delighted to have you back. I have missed you. And I shall send for you every time my head aches or I bruise my little finger. But whether the other ladies of the district will accept you so readily I do not know. A young, beautiful, unmarried doctor. They will be matchmaking from the start."

"I shall do my best to accommodate them."

"How delightful. Do you know I think we'll try it out at once. Joseph—" she leaned forward and prodded her driver in the back, a form of direction he acknowledged from long experience with a twitch of the shoulders— "Joseph, continue directly home to Waterford Park. I have a patient for you already," she explained to Hugh. "A young woman who is staying with me. My late husband's relatives seem to consider my house as a repository for difficult spinsters. Cousins and nieces and second cousins' nieces by remove descend on me regularly throughout the year for interminable visits. I think they expect me to find them all husbands and when I am unable to do so they go into a decline and have to be packed off home again."

"And is this one in decline?" Hugh asked.

"Oh, there is nothing much the matter with her. She is a pale, childish thing who never eats enough. I would say it is boredom that makes her ill, so a visit from you, Hugh, should enliven her."

"I have no medicine or instruments with me," Hugh remarked, but it was a protest made merely as a matter of form. To argue was too much trouble. And he had no reason for hastening back to London. He allowed himself to be carried off.

Waterford Park was a pleasant country house built at the end of the seventeenth century by George Wharton's ancestors. It had been built of red brick which had mellowed over the years to a warm rose, rich and satisfying, while its owners had mellowed with it into the rosy obscurity of a secure, prosperous, untroubled life. The civil wars were over for England when its foundations were laid and it was easy to let the quiet decades drift by in that green park-land without raising a head to listen to the faint, distant noise of change beyond the walls. A member of Parliament or two, an Indian nabob, an officer killed in some forgotten naval engagement, a churchman who should, of course, have been a bishop—the family ran true to form in each generation and grandfather might have been exchanged for grandson without any notable difference in attitude or achievement.

Such a long unbroken way of life gathers great strength, day placed upon day in a pyramid of years that by their own simple pressure, by the sheer weight of custom and tradition brought to bear on the inheritors, shape and influence whole lives. The Countess had been influenced. Twenty years at Waterford, twenty years of English country life had mellowed her also. It had given her a delightful repose. And she, in her turn, had placed her mark on the estate. She adored the house and it had become hers, feminine, light, graceful, a Petit Trianon of a house.

In the high-ceilinged main reception room, known as the Ivory room, and considered by the county to be incredibly austere, a portrait of the Countess gazed serenely down from a dominating position above the fireplace. George Wharton in his pride of possession had commissioned it in the first months of their marriage. Sophia had been painted seated at an open casement window. Beyond could be seen the trees of the park and a glimpse of the stream which ran through it. Sophia, dressed in a ball gown of pale ivory satin, was looking out of the picture as if she had just been spoken to and had turned her head to answer. The bright, heavy-lidded eyes which had always reminded Hugh's father of portraits of the Tudor Queen Elizabeth, bore an expression of amused inquiry. One of the long delicate hands, of which, also like Elizabeth, she was inordinately vain, lay in her lap, the other fingered a pendant at her neck, a magnificent emerald hung on a gold chain.

That painted emerald was the one flash of colour in the whole room. The pale silk which covered the walls, the ivory damask hangings at the windows, the embroidery—soft blues and greens and golds—of the chairs and stools, were all, by the position in which the painting had been placed, subordinate to it. It was the first thing to be noticed on entering the room and anyone visiting the house for the first time could be depended on to comment on it. Then the Countess would tell once again the history of the emerald, which legend said had in the fifteenth century been given to one of her ancestors as a reward for services by none other than Mátyás Corvinus, wearer of the Holy Crown of Hungary. The other legend, the Countess would add drily, which she thought was probably far more accurate, was that her ancestor stole the jewel during the upheaval following Mátyás's death. By all accounts, it was very old and very precious and when she died she would have liked it to be returned to Hungary, if only there had been true Hungarians ruling the country and not those foreign Hapsburgs.

Hugh used to tease her about her passion for her native country. "You are so very Magyar, Countess. Very fierce and warlike. The Turks wouldn't have stood a chance against you in the old days."

"Indeed they would not," the Countess said sharply. "And the Austrians would not now if I were still at home. Oppressors!"

"Isn't that the way the Slavs feel about the Magyars," he would bait her slyly.

She would shrug. "The Slavs. Rabble. We are the only real Hungarians. We Magyars were the founders of Hungary. The seven tribes under their elected king, elected, remember Hugh, they made the country, long before your Norman Conquest. The Slavs are nothing to do with it. No, Hugh, it is all very well for you to smile down your long English nose at me. You have forgotten what it is like in England to live subject to another country."

"But you've got your independent parliament, haven't you? Your Diet?"

"That means nothing. It has no power. We are ruled as if we are merely part of the Austrian empire. But you will see, Hugh. The tyranny of Vienna will not last for ever. You will see." And she would close her mouth firmly, and Hugh would change the subject and stop provoking her.

He thought about those conversations of five or six years ago as he entered the Ivory room with the Countess now. For this year, her prophecy was coming true. From the Atlantic to the Black Sea, Europe was exploding into revolution. Fanned by the burning passions of poets and visionaries, starved by famines and industrial depressions, dazed with dreams of universal brotherhood, of justice and liberty and all those illusory, magnificent concepts that seemed so certain of achievement once the

corrupt absolutist governments were destroyed, first France, then Prussia, then
Austria, the subject Italian states, Norway,
Denmark, Sweden took to the streets and the
barricades and won their democratic constitutions. They won them so easily, in matters
of days and weeks, handed over by terrified
and astonished monarchs, that it seemed as if
the old established Europe was crumbling in
the hand like a rotten apple.

Hungary had not been slow to follow that
first lead. In March, Louis Kossuth, the fiery
handsome young lawyer, demanded a free
constitution for his country and in April the
Hapsburg Ferdinand went to Pozsony and
approved the legislation which embodied it.

So the emerald, Hugh thought as he looked
up at the portrait, might well return to its
homeland after all.

That it was not so simple; that half the
revolutions would destroy themselves with
bitter internecine quarrelling or, in
nationalistic fervour, combine with old
imperial enemies to destroy their neighbours;
that France, the first republic, would again,
in a few years time, be proclaiming another
Bonaparte Emperor—was not foreseen. It
would have seemed as unlikly as that a

49

cancelled reform banquet in Paris that February would lead in three days to King Louis Philippe's ignominious departure by cab from the back door of the palace.

The fleeing king had come to England, as did the mistress of the King of Bavaria, and Prince Metternich of Austria, who had been at the beginning of the year the most powerful man in Europe. They all sought asylum in England, an England which in April waited with apprehension and disbelief for its own revolutionaries to strike. The Chartists, demanding universal suffrage, called a great meeting to present a petition to Parliament. The Duke of Wellington was ordered by a nervous government to organise the defence of London and the city was for a day in an uneasy state of siege. The Chartist leader, O'Connor, confused by a growing mental instability and alarmed by the show of force, compromised. The procession was called off, the crowds at the meeting, bewildered, unorganised, bored with speeches, grew aimless and depressed, and the rain came down and washed away the last enthusiasm.

"Were you in London on that day, Dr. Radlett?" The speaker was the young relative

Sophia had brought Hugh to Waterford Park to see. The Countess, having taken off her hat and ordered tea, had sent a maid to fetch the girl down from her room where she was no doubt, she told Hugh, reclining on the day bed with smelling salts and romantic novel.

"She is very dull," she remarked confidently. "You will see." Then she laughed and put her hand on his. "Poor Hugh, don't look so alarmed. I don't really expect you to examine her, you know. Of course, if it is obvious to you that she is dreadfully ill, you must say so. But you look more ill than she does. No, I am afraid I used her as an excuse to keep you with me a little longer. Aren't you glad I did? You look more cheerful already. In this house you are remembering happy times, not sad ones."

The girl came down with admirable promptness and was introduced. Her name was Wharton, too, Esther Wharton, but Hugh never quite grasped the relationship between her and the Countess, whether it was niece or first or second cousin or how she fitted into the family. Not that it mattered a great deal, but he did wonder as they sat and talked that she did not call the Countess by any family name such as Aunt Sophia or so on; nor did she call her Countess as so many friends and acquaintances did. No, she called her Mrs. Wharton, like a governess. She looked a little like a governess. She was indeed, as Sophia had said, pale and quiet. Her figure was slight, her face round, her hair a nondescript brown in colour. Her eyes were pale blue, without sparkle, and she kept them downcast, rarely looking directly at the person to whom she was speaking. She was like a shy little mouse, Hugh thought, except for one extraordinary fact. Though seemingly so shy, so modest, so quiet she was dressed in a vivid red gown. She appeared both to draw attention to herself and hide from it at the same time.

This odd trait grew more obvious to Hugh as the conversation proceeded. Miss Wharton would seem for minutes at a time to be taking no part in it at all, sitting quietly by with her hands in her lap, and then she would suddenly ask a direct question or make some observation that recalled her presence to the others, as if to remind them, in her modest way, not entirely to neglect her.

The Countess was indeed inclined to ignore her. She talked to Hugh about the revolution in Hungary, which had filled her with an exultant triumph. She gestured excitably with her hands as she spoke about Count Széchenyi and Kossuth and Count Batthyány and the April laws, growing more Hungarian with every moment, applauding her countrymen with a fierce pride. She was amused too that she could now bait Hugh, as he had used to do her.

"You see, we Magyars understand these affairs. That is the way to conduct such revolutions, with dash and fire and courage——"

"Like good cavalry officers," Hugh interposed.

"Better that, better that," the Countess proclaimed, "than the passivity of serfs. What have restraint and model behaviour to do with revolution? You English do not understand how to rebel. That farce of the Chartists, afraid of a few soldiers, meekly taking their petition to the House of Commons in a hired cab! Is that the way to overthrow a government?"

"We have already had our revolutions, you know, Countess," Hugh remarked mildly. "We were old hands at deposing kings in our youth. Now we're getting middle-aged we're much more circumspect."

"What nonsense! You've grown dull and frightened, that is all!"

They were well away together, enjoying themselves in one of their free-for-all debates in which each made more and more extreme statements until the wildness of their claims nullified their own arguments and induced a truce. Esther Wharton chose such a moment to interject her polite inquiry about Hugh's presence in London on the day of the Chartist meeting, bringing their general talk of politics and principles down to the particular and personal, focusing attention on herself and on Hugh; requiring an answer, however short, to her question.

"Yes, I was in London on that day, Miss Wharton," Hugh replied.

"What was it like?"

"As I remember, very wet."

"Hugh, you are impossible," said the Countess. "You treat everything as a joke. You know it is true that there might have been a republic at the end of that day if those men had had the courage of their convictions. The government was plainly frightened of them. But now the Chartists are finished."

"I am not so sure," Hugh said. "I've heard

rumours they plan something else, very soon. This month perhaps."

The conversation left Esther isolated again. But she seemed quite content as if she knew that she had done enough to intrigue Hugh, as if she was well aware that he would now glance occasionally away from the Countess towards her, puzzled and interested. As if she knew very well what she was doing.

"How long is Miss Wharton staying with you?" Hugh asked the Countess in a low voice as he left.

She shrugged. "Her visit has only just begun. I must admit I feel sorry for her. Her father is a depressed clergyman, depressed both as to money and temperament. Her mother is dead. She was brought up by an aunt, her father's sister, a strict and unlikeable woman. If Esther wishes to stay until the autumn——" She shrugged again good-naturedly.

"I see."

"Why?" She looked concerned. "Do you think she is really ill?"

"No, no." Hugh smiled. "She seems a very healthy young woman. Your diagnosis appears quite correct to me. She is bored."

They were standing by the open front door.

The carriage which the Countess had ordered round to drive Hugh to Warwick waited on the driveway outside, the horses nodding away the flies desultorily. The late afternoon sun struck directly across the tops of the trees into Hugh's eyes. He turned back to the Countess.

"How old is she?"

She paused before replying, considering him.

"She is older than she appears," she said at last.

"Twenty-two, twenty-three?"

The Countess smiled. "My dear Hugh, you know better than that. You are not her physician yet. If you needed to know, no doubt she would tell you. I certainly shan't."

"Ah," said Hugh. "As much older as that?"

The Countess laughed and patted his arm. "Go away. You are become too frank. Go and learn a little discretion before you become a country doctor. It will all be confinements, you know. Nothing else happens in the country!"

She did not remain at the door to wave to him once he had driven off. She had not kept her complexion by standing in the sun.

Hugh looked back once as the carriage crossed the ornamental bridge over the stream, taking in at a glance the balance of house and trees and space and light; the effulgent rich depth of light, golden and glowing, of the dying summer day.

He turned away in satisfaction and closed his eyes. He was finished with indecision. He was coming back.

2

IT took Hugh a month or so to clear up his affairs in London. During that time he was in constant correspondence with Mrs. Torrance. They discussed everything from the provision of drugs to the number of patients still attached to the practice. Most of them had, naturally, during Dr. Torrance's last illness, been obliged to seek the attentions of other doctors. But the nearest doctor was inconveniently far from Rivington and Mrs. Torrance considered the majority would be happy to return.

The last problem to be settled was one of accommodation. Hugh was to use the surgery and dispensary in the house and Mrs. Torrance wanted him to live there as well. Hugh disagreed but he had been so impressed by Mrs. Torrance's common sense in other matters that he eventually decided to follow her in this as well. His own feelings were so confused about whether this was the right or the wrong step to take in regard to Anne that he no longer trusted his judgment about it.

"People will know where to find you during the day and they will come to expect to find you there at all times," Mrs. Torrance wrote to him one August morning. "It may lead to all kinds of difficulties if you are living elsewhere. Do not be afraid that your privacy will be impinged upon. We do not use the long morning room behind the surgery and ante-room and we will make them into a suite of rooms for you that will be quite self-contained. You will be able to come and go through the entrance the patients use or by the garden door from the morning room without the knowledge of anyone else in the house. Though, Hugh, I admit I am being selfish in arguing so for it. It would be such a comfort to have you in the house. I miss the noise of a man about the place more than I can say. . . ."

The writing faltered and stopped. Mrs. Torrance put the pen down and sat in the silence of the drawing-room, the silence that had become her enemy. She turned in her chair and looked round the room. Everything so clean—the brass polished, the fireplace immaculate, the carpet swept, the windows gleaming—and all for what? To what purpose? Herself, Anne, the maids, the cook, revolving round and round in the same petty routine of living; as if any of it mattered, as if the careful repetitive preparation of meals, the endless pattern of the endless days had some useful end, other than that three women should look after two. The life of the household had been centred for so long on one person that now, with the reason for its existence gone, it was like a wheel broken from the axle, spinning on aimlessly, without direction. It did not matter for her but for Anne, it was dangerous. Mrs. Torrance acknowledged to herself that her hope was, when Hugh came, that Anne would unthinkingly become as involved in his life as she had in her father's. Then the right end might be achieved, even if by the wrong method. But she must avoid placing on Hugh a burden of pity——

She picked up the pen and crossed out the last three sentences of her letter with quick cross-hatching. She wrote a non-committal ending about the date of Hugh's arrival and signed it. She was sealing the letter when Anne entered the room.

"He is here again," she said without preamble.

Mrs. Torrance looked up. "Who is here?"

"Bullivant."

Mrs. Torrance regarded her daughter for a moment without replying. In some kind of gesture of defiance Anne had, since the funeral, refused to wear mourning. Whether it was intended as an attack on her mother herself, or on the conventions of death in general, Mrs. Torrance was not quite sure, but she was glad Anne had adopted that attitude. Her father would have hated to see her shrouded in black. To-day, in her thin summer dress of lavender and white cotton, trimmed with lavender ribbon, her dark hair tied loosely back, her pallor warmed by a flush of colour, Mrs. Torrance thought, with unmaternal detachment, that she looked very beautiful. She smiled at her daughter.

"Well, show Mr. Bullivant in, Anne."

"Mother——" Anne came farther into the room and put her hand out towards her mother as if to touch her. It was such a tender appeal, expressive in both its instinctiveness and its hesitancy of her inner conflict of feeling about her mother that Mrs. Torrance found it almost intolerably moving. She stood up, the skirts of her black dress rustling.

"What is it, my dear?"

Anne let her arm fall to her side. "You are

determined to go on with the sale of the land, in spite of everything?"

"The sale is already completed. The papers are signed. Mr. Bullivant brought them one day last week when you were out—No, Anne," she had seen the immediate change in Anne's expression, "it was not arranged so on purpose to keep it secret from you. It was merely by chance you were not here. He was sorry to miss you."

"Then why is he here again? To bring all the sacks of gold due to us?"

"If you ask him in we can find out." Mrs. Torrance spoke in the mildest of tones. "Don't leave him waiting in the hall, poor man."

Without another word, Anne turned and went to fetch Godfrey Bullivant. The railway director came into the room rather heavily, his bulk seeming to take up more than its share of space, overcrowding the room. He dwarfed Mrs. Torrance, but although so totally opposed in appearance there was a certain accord between them as they greeted each other; a certain respect such as might exist, Anne thought, between two business men.

She did not wait to hear the reason for

Bullivant's visit, slipping quietly away before either of them might attempt to stop her. She went through the hall and along the passage leading to the back of the house. Three doors faced her. She opened one of them and entered her father's consulting room. It was a square room lit by two windows and smelling of leather and polish. Tall glass-fronted bookcases crammed with leather-backed volumes jumbled together with a miscellany of papers and pamphlets stood against two of the walls. Behind the solid oak desk, Dr. Torrance's chair, its brown leather darkened in patches where his head and arms had rested, still bore the imprint of his presence.

Anne walked quickly past it and down a step into the dispensary—in area scarcely bigger than a large cupboard—which led off the consulting room. Its small space was totally lined with shelves and cabinets crowded with glass jars and bottles all meticulously labelled and arranged. There was little room for more than one person to move. Anne could almost see her father standing by the bench, making up some preparation, all the paraphernalia of his careful craft about him, measuring and mixing, the tail of his coat as he turned about in imminent danger of sweeping everything to the floor, and calling out: "Don't come in, don't disturb anything, you'll only make a mess." Then suddenly changing his mind and getting her to hold this or wash that, or write down the instructions on the white paper of the packet, and begging her to get it right or the whole Dobson family would be poisoned off as they always shared everything out between them including their medicines.

So much excitement there had always been, so much life——

On the bench was a package Anne had made ready earlier that morning. She picked it up and went out, through the other door of the consulting room this time, the one that led to the ante-room where the patients waited to see the doctor, and then by the outer door into the lane by the side of the house. She closed this outer door behind her and walked up to the village street.

At the church she crossed over and followed a narrow lane along the side of the churchyard. A row of cottages, their front gardens, in comparison with the ordered vegetable plots behind, a tangle of seeding flowers— hollyhocks and marigolds and poppies and small wild roses—stood in a neat line just beyond the church.

Anne knocked at the door of the end house. It was opened to her immediately.

"Oh, Miss Anne, I was about to come to you."

"Why, what is it, Mrs. Toms," Anne asked. "Is he bad again?"

The woman who greeted her was in a state of agitation, her round country face very red, her greying hair straggling untidily from the hastily pinned bun, fronds and ends hanging down on to the collar of her dress. She grasped Anne by the arm and impelled her over the threshold.

"Come in, come in. He wants to see you. He's been waiting for you. You won't mind seeing him, will you? He gets a comfort from it."

"Mrs. Toms," Anne protested, "if your husband is really ill——"

"He's up the stairs. He's been at me all morning to fetch you, but I said Miss Anne had enough to do without running after an old fellow like him. She came last week, I said, and she'll come again, don't you fret about that. I don't see why she bothers with you, that I don't, seeing as how you never

would do what her father said and she
said——"

"He really must see a doctor if he is ill
again, Mrs. Toms." Anne tried vainly to
stem the flow. "You know my father insisted
on that. If he had another attack."

"Oh, you know Toms. He wouldn't go to
anyone but your father. Thought the world of
your father . . ."

As she went bubbling and rattling on like a
tea kettle, talking over her shoulder as she
clumped her way up the steep staircase, Anne
realised that all the flurry of talk was merely
the garrulousness of relief. Mrs. Toms was
not desperately worried. She had been, but
whatever crisis she had suffered during the
night was over and she had seized on Anne in
a gushing release of the strain. Anne was
relieved herself and even more so when she
had seen Mr. Toms, for she had been experi-
encing a certain uneasy worry on his account
herself.

Arthur Toms was a simple man, a farm
labourer who had worked for the same farmer
all his life. He was a contented man who had
never questioned anything in his life. He
worked placidly and skilfully all the daylight
hours, drank his pint at the Fox and Grapes,

got drunk to smiling helplessness four times a year at the annual fairs, patiently endured his wife's berating tongue and next day went about his work again, absorbed in the same unvarying rhythm.

Then he began to be ill. At first the stirrings of trouble were slight enough to be ignored but one night he awoke sick as a dog and with pains that brought the sweat to his forehead and the terror of death to his eyes. Dr. Torrance was run for.

"It's not cholera, is it, Doctor?" Toms pleaded with him. "I've seen cholera. My Lord, don't let it be that. Oh, I do feel so bad."

Dr. Torrance examined him and reassured him that it was not cholera. The pains were abdominal, on the right hand side of the body. This factor, together with the fever, the sickness and the previous slight disturbances which Toms now admitted to, led the doctor to diagnose perityphlitis, an inflammation of the caecum, the blind gut at the entrance of the small intestine into the large intestine. He did not tell Tom that though it might not be as sudden as cholera, it was a condition that was often as fatal. In his experience a patient might survive one or two attacks, depending on their severity, but usually in the end the condition became acute and the inflamed gut burst, spilling its poison into the abdominal cavity, causing peritonitis and death. Only once, when an internal abscess had been formed which pushed its way to the abdominal wall and could be easily felt, had Torrance saved a patient at such a critical stage. He had lanced the abscess and the patient, a boy with a strong constitution, had survived. But that was merely one case; all the others he had known had died.

In the case of Arthur Toms, Torrance simply told him that he had got some poisoning in his guts and they'd have to clear it up as best they could. He prescribed poultices to be placed on the afflicted spot and gave him opium to ease the pain and, by checking the movement of the intestine, give it time to heal itself. He was very kind to the labourer, knowing all about the fear of death, carrying his own death as he already did within him.

Toms recovered from the attack and as he had been convinced on that night that he was dying, so he was equally convinced that it was the doctor who had worked the miracle and saved his life.

"Ah, you're too solid an old oak to be

blown down so easily," Dr. Torrance told him. "It was nothing to do with me."

However, as his own illness progressed and the necessity grew for him to abandon, as he thought of it, his patients, the doctor grew concerned about those of them whose illness was quiescent not cured, but whom, to keep their spirits up, he might have reassured too well. He called in to see Toms and told him there was a possibility the attack might recur, that some of the poison in his system, as he put it, might still be there. He instructed him to send for a doctor as soon as he felt the slightest suspicious sign.

"Oh, I will," said Toms. "I'll send across for you, Doctor, as soon as I feels it coming. I know you'll put me right."

"I'm ill myself, Arthur," Torrance said. "I'm not going to see any more patients."

Because he was on his feet, and though thin and grey, still joking and swearing as strongly as ever, Toms gave this statement little attention.

"I'll come to you, never fear," he repeated stubbornly.

"It's Dr. Williams at Two Crosses you must go to," Torrance insisted. "He has agreed to see you whenever you need him."

That it was as a favour to him and that he had undertaken to pay the fee, he did not say.

But Toms merely shook his head, in a blind irritating display of loyalty that could not be moved. So Dr. Torrance made what other arrangements he could for him. The only treatment then known for perityphlitis was by purgatives to remove the "obstructions" in the lighter cases and by opium in the more severe attacks. Once a month therefore, as a cautionary measure, Torrance made up a mild purgative which Anne usually took across to Toms. She called in every week at her father's request to see how he looked, if from fear he was hiding symptoms, and he taught her to prepare the drug to ease the man while Dr. Williams could be fetched, if an attack came suddenly in the night.

And now it seemed this had happened.

"Took terrible bad in the night he were," Mrs. Toms told her. "Woke me right up moaning and groaning and clutching at his stomach and carrying on. Fair frightened me, he did, with his moaning. I did all your father told me to do, all I could think of, and it got no better, and then it were nearly dawn, and the birds starting up and I was about to come across for you, Miss Anne, just as I was with my shawl over my nightgown, when it happened. . . ." She paused, her hand on the latch of the bedroom door and Anne, waiting relatively patiently on the top step of the stairs, realised that some comment was expected.

"What happened, Mrs. Toms?" she asked.

"He were sick that's what happened," Mrs. Toms announced. There was a faint triumph in her expression, as if Mr. Toms was to be greatly commended for it. "He were that sick, for half an hour or more, and then the pain all went."

"I am very glad to hear it," Anne said. "Is he quite recovered then?"

"He won't leave his bed till he's seen you, Miss Anne, that I do know. He's been at me all morning to fetch you and I was about to come over when you knocked on the door. I'm that glad you've come, he's been bothering me no end. He was worried about not having any of his medicine left, you see. It's been troubling him."

"I understand," Anne said.

After her father died, Anne had had no wish to continue her visits to Arthur Toms. But she did continue them, partly to begin with from habit and a vague sense of duty, and partly because it soon became clear that the Toms expected her to. Arthur Toms did more, in fact, than expect it; he grew to depend on it. As the visits went on, the bottle of medicine Anne brought with her from time to time became a talisman to him, a form of distant magic by whose means could still be extended to him, even now, the doctor's protection. And Anne, once the doctor's messenger only, gradually became in their minds and even in some slight way in her own mind, Dr. Torrance's substitute. The mantle of her father's authority fell on her shoulders and she could not deny that she received some pleasure and comfort from wearing it. To be so welcomed, to be regarded with such trust, her every word accepted with such unquestioning and flattering confidence, softened in some small measure the hard rock of her unhappiness—while, that is, Toms remained fit and healthy. The question of what might happen were he to be taken ill again, violently as before, had been one Anne had not wished to consider too deeply. They would fetch Dr. Williams, of course, she had told herself. That they would do no such thing, that they would wait and then send not for a doctor at all, but for her, was a possibility she had refused to envisage. She had not been able entirely to dismiss, however, a feeling that the way she was behaving was wrong and should be stopped. She had delayed preparing this last bottle of medicine for days until Toms himself had mentioned it to her with respectful hesitation and that same sublime conviction that she would not fail him.

He awaited her now, sitting up in the vast family bed that filled the upper room of the cottage, his long sheep's face neatly topped by a clean nightcap. Mrs. Toms might still bear the signs of that harrowing night, but her patient was impeccable. Once caught, Anne did not escape easily. Standing at the end of the bed, she endured a full quarter of an hour while Toms in his turn recounted the details of his illness. She was so relieved to find him pink and full of talk that she would have been willing to listen for an hour, especially as it was during this long recital that she realised that whatever had struck down poor Arthur Toms last night it was not a recurrence of the illness her father had diagnosed. The pain had been all in the middle of his stomach, "like it were stuffed full of burning coals"—and once he had been sick he was cured.

Mrs. Toms solved the problem to Anne's satisfaction as she at last said good-bye to her on the doorstep.

"Such a pity and all," she said. "All his nice supper wasted, and such a treat for him it was. My sister brought it over yesterday morning. Her boy had got it for her in Gloucester but she hadn't fancied it so she brought it for me and I gave it to Toms for a treat for it's not many times you get them round here, is it, so far from the sea?"

"What did you give him, Mrs. Toms?" Anne asked.

"A lovely big crab it was. Mind you, I don't care for shellfish much myself but Toms, he enjoyed it."

"Did it smell?" Anne asked curiously.

"Oh, yes, you know, the way they do. Shellfish always smell pretty strong, don't they?"

Anne left her and walked down the path to the gate. A crab, bought in Gloucester heaven knew how many days ago. No wonder poor Toms had been ill. No wonder he was better once rid of it. Anne laughed. It suddenly seemed all so ridiculous. The drama, the

74

threat of tragedy, and then the bathos of Toms in his clean cap, and the bad shellfish, and the endless details of his sickness. Was this what her father had had to listen to, year in and year out? Was this how Hugh spent his days?

Three doors down from the Toms lived a woman known as Granny Lane, a disagreeable, decayed-looking creature considered by the locals as a witch. Two hundred years before they would probably have drowned her. Now they took their warts, and their problems of love and their fears of ill-luck to her, and half-laughed at her and half-believed in her possession of strange powers. The fear that underlay that near belief was centuries old, bred in them, a distillation of old religions never known, never thought of, but that moved in the blood at certain times at night and at certain seasons of the year, creating an unease, an edginess, sometimes an almost hysterical gaiety, that they blamed upon the weather or a decline in the manners of the young. It echoed across the waiting ploughed earth at springtime, it made Toms drunk at harvest, it made the maids in the solid houses along the main street close the curtains tight against the winter darkness and light more candles than their mistresses wished to burn. It could rise up as quickly as the white mists of autumn rising softly from frosty fields, and when the fear grew thick as that, it was stronger than the tolerance or the laughter that kept it in check and it needed an object that its victims could recognise and mock at and so be comforted. A stranger was an easy enemy but few strangers came to Rivington, so they made a witch of Granny Lane and dispersed their fears about her shaggy head. They could dislike her for a dozen adequate reasons. Anne disliked her because her teeth were rotted and her clothes never clean. Her cottage always smelt and though it was the same size and identical in every way with the Toms cottage and all the others in the row it had always, since, as a child, her mother took her there on her charitable visits about the village, seemed different to Anne—smaller, darker, deeper.

She could have liked the woman better if she had been more conscious of the truth of what she was—a foolish, ignorant old woman, dependent on other fools or on charity for her living; if she had been humble, cast down, oppressed by her position in the village. But it was quite the contrary. Granny Lane was quite puffed up by her reputation. By now she believed in it as much as anyone and delighted in the power it gave her. She was surly, threatening to the children who harassed her, and dispensed her dubious wisdom with careless majesty to those who sought it and paid for it.

She had so frightened the little maid from the Torrances' house who had taken her two old gowns that Mrs. Torrance had kindly thought might be of use to her, that the girl had fled leaving a wicker basket behind. Anne had rebuked her for being such a silly child and had promised to retrieve the basket. She might just as well do so now, she thought as she came to the gate of the cottage, and be done with it.

She had meant to do no more than recover the basket and leave, but as she went up the path she saw through the open door an extraordinary sight: the vicar, Mr. Carrington, in his shirt sleeves, holding a spade, his hands covered in dirt and a smear of blood on his cheek. When he saw Anne he seemed disconcerted and quickly withdrew through the back door. As Anne came inside she heard the pump going in the yard.

"Done me a kindness." Granny Lane's throaty voice made Anne start. The old woman was seated in her customary chair by the fire. Her arms were folded tight about her body and she was rocking herself gently backwards and forwards, backwards and forwards, with slow monotony.

"Burying my cat," she said. "The old pigeons got him in the end. Pecked to pieces, he was. Vicar's burying him."

"I'm sorry," Anne said. She remembered the cat, a fat black Tom, always sunning himself on the window sill.

Granny Lane cackled suddenly. "Serve him right, old fool." She moved swiftly to a subject more interesting to her, watching Anne with sly avidity. "I saw you going past. Toms took bad, is he? Your medicine won't cure him. Let him come to me."

Anne said nothing. She had seen the wicker basket on the table where the maid had left it yesterday. She picked it up and found to her annoyance that the two gowns were still neatly packed inside it. She shrugged and put it down. She would leave it for now. It hardly mattered. But why didn't her mother realise how wasted her kindly gestures were on people like Granny Lane. They were not appreciated. The old woman wore her ancient clothes from choice. She would not change.

"Miss Torrance, my apologies." Mr. Carrington, maintaining his dignity with what was clearly a considerable effort, re-entered the room, his face and hands clean once more. He hovered about Anne for a moment and then, with an expression of extreme embarrassment plunged forward past her, so close as to brush her sleeve with his arm, and recovered his coat from the chair beyond. His reluctance to ask Anne to hand it to him had involved him, after all, in the greater social difficulty. He drew back, murmuring further apologies. Anne moved away, smiling.

"You have been engaged in a work of compassion, I understand," she said.

"Yes, yes . . ." His coat on, the vicar regained his confidence, as if the black cloth was indeed some kind of celestial armour. His voice deepened to its familiar rich note. "Very sad. This poor woman—the cat, companion of her old age . . ."

"She does not appear to mourn its loss greatly," Anne remarked.

"She is overwrought. I found the animal in the lane outside and when I broke the news to her, she grew quite distraught, laughing and saying that as I was a clergyman, so should I bury it. I felt I could do no more. And now, dear Miss Torrance, I must go. I must go!" he cried to Granny Lane, who was in no way afflicted with deafness but with whom the vicar employed the same manner with which he treated any elderly person as far beneath him in the social scale. It was indeed, considering his character, a very noble and religious act of him to bury Granny Lane's familiar and Anne respected him for it. She wished that she did not find the episode so grotesquely amusing. Her pity was for the cat; and although she realised the old woman had made a fool of the parson, yet the combination of the two of them in this fashion was so incongruous it was absurd.

That was the second absurd situation in which she had become involved that morning and their joint effect was to jolt Anne free, temporarily, from the restriction of her own emotions and to lighten her mood. It was an

80

alteration in her which Godfrey Bullivant immediately recognised.

He was waiting for her outside the house when she returned home and he made it quite clear that he was waiting for her, so that Anne could not this time walk past him with no more than a nod. She stopped in the street and made him come forward to her.

"You have finished your business with my mother?"

"I am sorry that you did not stay."

"Mr. Bullivant, you know my feelings in this matter. I have never hidden them from you."

He did not reply, regarding her with that heavy gaze she found so disturbing. He was not a man to be easily dismissed. He stood in front of her squarely, blocking her way.

When the business of the railway began, when her father was still alive, Anne had found it easy to dismiss Bullivant from her mind. Her father had been in her eyes so unreservedly the stronger, the more superior. Nothing could defeat him. But death had defeated him and Bullivant remained. Her world shaken to its foundations, she had clung to those factors with which she could still identify her father. He had not liked

Bullivant, he had not wished the railway to be built near Rivington. Those, therefore, were the tenets of her new creed. Bullivant was mistaken in thinking that the smile he had surprised in her eyes, the new freedom of her walk so perceptibly different from her tension at the funeral, held any message of hope for him. Until she accepted what had happened to her, it was impossible for her to change.

"Everything is signed, sealed and delivered, I understand," she said. "So I do not suppose we shall be seeing very much of you now, Mr. Bullivant."

"I shall still be about the village a good deal, Miss Torrance."

"Do you mean when the laying of the track, or whatever it is called, begins?"

"It has already begun," Bullivant said gravely. "That is what I came to tell you and your mother—as a matter of courtesy."

"Begun already? Where? Does one group of men begin at Worcester and another at Warwick and work towards each other until they meet?" She smiled unexpectedly at him, a smile Hugh Radlett would have recognised, devastating in its sudden brilliance. In this mood, she was prepared to bait the bear.

He answered her with all seriousness. "No,

we do not build a railway that way. We divide the line into sections and let the work out to contractors. They provide their own men. It goes on more quickly in that way."

"I see." Anne was cold again. The railway had seemed far away, even after her mother's decision and Bullivant's many visits. Now he was bringing it nearer, too close, creating the reality of it with his words. "You mean they will build here, at once?"

"They have begun already."

"I have seen nothing, no one."

"You see . . ." Even at this moment when his purpose was to be conciliatory his voice and appearance did not soften. "You will not be disturbed, Miss Torrance. It has been a false alarm, this fear of the railway. The men have already been in the neighbourhood for some time and there has been no trouble. You have heard nothing, you admit."

"But they will come closer. They are bound to."

"As they work, yes. But they keep together as a community. They lead their own life, Miss Torrance." There was a slight change in his expression, a dry humour. "They have no more wish to intrude on you than you on them. They are not here to make trouble, but to work. And they work very hard, as you will see."

"Where are they?"

"Beyond the hill. Do you wish me to show you?"

"No," Anne said sharply. "No." She moved forward then towards him and the house, her figure stiffened with the authority that anger gave her, so that Bullivant no longer opposed her passage, but stood immediately aside. She went past him into the house and shut the door.

Later it seemed to Anne as if Bullivant's visit that morning had been the signal for an agreed silence to be broken and rumour given free rein. Before his announcement to her she had heard nothing about railway navvies being in the district or any works being begun. After it the village was full of talk of nothing else.

The rumour came from a dozen sources— from the inns, the farmers, the carriers, the blacksmith, the village store, the market women—and were filtered through to Anne from the maids and from her mother's visitors. The men had been coming into the area for the past month it was now revealed. At first they had taken rooms in the villages nearest to the site of the first workings, but as more men arrived accommodation grew impossible to find and a shanty town of bits and pieces, huts made of odd timbers and tarpaulins and tents of canvas and cloth, was going up along the hill Bullivant had pointed out to Anne. No one knew how many more were coming but one navvy had told the landlord at an inn that in his last job there had been three thousand men taken on for a five-mile stretch of workings. "Three thousand!" The villagers of Rivington stared at each other incredulously.

But that was for a railway cut through hard and treacherous ground, with rocks and tunnels and mud and so on. The knowledgeable shook their heads and said that no such problems would arise in so easy a country as theirs. Barely a third of that figure would be needed, in their opinion.

But a third was a thousand men, Anne thought to herself. A thousand men descending like an invasion on the quiet villages. Already, Arthur Toms told her, a ganger employed by the sub-contracters for the section that would run past Rivington had been going round the farms to see if any of the labourers wanted to change their jobs and become railway men. They were offering twelve to fifteen shillings a week, according to the amount of muck the men could shift in a day. If they stayed on till they became proper navvies, with their endurance and skill, they could get sixteen, even eighteen shillings, even now, with times harder than they had been for years. To farm labourers getting seven shillings a week, it was a temptation.

"But it's not steady work," Anne protested. "They finish at one place and move on. There is not the security you have here."

Oh, I'm not thinking of myself," Toms said. "I'm too old for that, haven't got the strength any more, and I'm satisfied with what I got. But the young lads find it tempting. I'm telling you, Miss Anne, some of them'll be off before long. Only needs one to make the first move."

A week later Robert Wood from Holts farm had gone, and young Jack from up the lane.

"Have you seen the works?" his mother asked Anne.

Anne shook her head. "Oh, you should, Miss Torrance. It's a sight like you never seen. We were there the other day. They're building a mountain, right out of the earth. Oh, you should see it, Miss Torrance. Such a sight!"

It was becoming a trip for a holiday, going to see the workings.

But the wonders of engineering and the transformation of the landscape made less interesting gossip than the men responsible for it and new facts or myths about them emerged every day. They drank a gallon of beer each a day and more at night; they were of enormous strength and wore weird clothes and called each other by odd names like Pegleg or Dancing Jack. They were all pagans and never went to church. They were Chartists and held meetings at night plotting revolution. They had women in the camp, which was growing daily along the ridge of the hill so the camp fires could be seen at night from the doctor's house. The ladies who came to Mrs. Torrance for tea were simmering over with hints of unspeakable orgies.

"Has anyone seen these women?" Anne asked curiously.

They turned on her as if she had denied their existence. Yes, yes, they came into the villages to buy meat. They seemed to have plenty to spend. Very vulgar creatures. No one could understand half of what they said and half of them were drunk by afternoon.

Anne believed half of it, when she would have liked to believe it all. The stories were told with too much shining-eyed excitability to convince her.

"You know Mrs. So-and-so," a typical story would run, "six children and two grandchildren, a more respectable and trustworthy woman it would be hard to find, well Mrs. So-and-so was walking through Leasham, barely fifty yards outside the village she was and these three navvies came walking by, and what they said and what they did we cannot repeat and if Mr. This-and-that had not come riding by at that very instant we tremble to think what might have been the result."

"Mark my words," said one visiting lady, "that episode will be repeated in every village within reach."

"The vicar must do something," another said. "He must speak."

The other ladies nodded, their faces quite flushed at the prospect before them, respectable matrons all, and agreed that

Mr. Carrington should do something. The thought of poor Mr. Carrington defending the honour of his lady parishioners against the assault of brutal navvies was too much for Anne and she retired behind the teapot. It was becoming strange to her that she could find no one person who had seen anything remotely resembling a navvy in the village. Rivington seemed, so far, to be escaping any contact with the railwaymen. And sometimes she wondered if this was in any degree the doing of Mr. Bullivant, and again, without vanity, if it was connected with herself.

Amid all this excitement and stir Hugh Radlett arrived to take over Dr. Torrance's practice. This event, which would normally have been the cause of great interest and speculation for some weeks, passed almost unnoticed. He settled into the rooms Mrs. Torrance had prepared for him, he bought a riding horse which he preferred to use during the day to the doctor's old trap, he spent long hours in the dispensary, and long hours talking to Mrs. Torrance about the patients. He walked and rode about the country, visiting people and renewing old acquaintances. He went to see the Countess and stayed on for dinner. As a matter of deliberate and thought-out policy he left Anne alone and concentrated on the work which had brought him to Rivington. Before very long patients were once again coming to sit in the waiting room, and messages were being sent by the gentry asking the young doctor to call.

Anne found herself in an extraordinary state of mind about it all. She had been looking forward to Hugh's arrival. Her genuine affection for him gave her the happiest expectation of his companionship. She felt he would be on her side in the household, in which her relationship with her mother was still not entirely easy. She thought that she and Hugh would spend a great deal of time together, that he would ask her opinion and advice on matters pertaining to the practice. She had visualised pleasant evenings in the drawing-room, excursions, and parties to which they would go together. Unconsciously she had been looking forward to being the centre of his world, the focus of his admiration. She had come to feel that she had no real place or function left and had been expecting Hugh to restore her, not realising what little effort she had been prepared to make herself. She had been expecting to be sought after and had been prepared to tolerate dullness, seriousness, boredom, in the virtuous knowledge that every careless minute thus bestowed on Hugh remedied any other neglect.

Instead she found she saw Hugh perhaps once a day, at luncheon. He ate his breakfast early, in his own room, and during the day, if he was not out, he remained in his own part of the house, seeing patients, working, reading. He consulted her mother, not her, about anything he needed to know and indeed seemed to find far more to interest him in Mrs. Torrance's company than her own. As for dinner, his family and he himself were well known in the district and had always been popular and before very long, invitations were being extended to him from many houses. Anne went so far one day as to ask him if he was not dining out a little too much.

"Suppose you were needed, Hugh. By some patient."

"Do not worry, Anne," he replied. "As the practice grows I shall no doubt curtail my riotous social life, but at present it is a pretty safe thing. However, to put your mind at rest, I have engaged William Broom, your own groom, to look after my horse as well as your father's and to act as a night driver if the necessity arises. The maid will give him any urgent message and he will come and fetch me, with the bag I shall leave packed ready." He smiled. "I understand from your mother that this is precisely the procedure your father employed, so I do not think you have cause to be concerned."

Anne found the smile irritating. She found everything in her life irritating. She no longer felt free to wander in and out of the consulting rooms whenever she wished. It became alien ground to her and she resented it. She took to going for long walks through the autumn countryside, wrapped up in melancholy thoughts, full of restless disillusion. Her unhappiness seemed to be curdling inside her like sour milk, tainting every aspect of her life. The only relief she found was in the countryside and that now was threatened by the ominous army whose flickering camp lights could be seen from her bedroom, and whose work had now come so close that the murmur of it could sometimes be heard, carried across the plain on the still air.

It was on one of these walks, on a day of

wind and cloud, that Anne saw her enemy for the first time.

She had taken a path she had not been along since early summer, that led across fields to the foot of a long sprawling hill. At the top of this hill stood a small brick tower, built by one owner some fifty years before to mark the highest point of the ridge. As a child Anne had believed it to be very ancient, put there for defence, and had woven romantic fantasies about the battles which must have raged round it, looking over her shoulder for the ghosts of dead warriors. But as she grew taller, the tower grew less impressive. It lost its power to stimulate or frighten and no longer seemed to brood with sullen dominance over the view spread out below it.

It was a magnificent view. You could see for miles. The whole stretch of Rivington village lay visible, and all the farms around it. The village of Leasham was to the left, and the river and Tirham mill. To the right, facing Rivington, was the hill along which the navvies were encamped, and before Anne, at her feet, the chaos they had been creating.

Anne had not admitted to herself beforehand why she was taking that particular walk but in fact she had known the reason very well—otherwise why that strange mixture of apprehension and excitement, the breathlessness that had nothing to do with the steepness of the climb. It was to the tower that people had been coming to see the workings. "The best view of all," they had assured her. She had refused to go. To admit any curiosity was to become as one of the vulgar crowd, to whom the railway was an excitement and the navvies a welcome source of money and gossip; who cared nothing for the ruin of their peace and the ravaging of their countryside because they had cared nothing for what they had previously possessed and had put no value on it. But it was something more than curiosity which had driven her here at last. It was a realisation that she must, in the end, face what was happening. The railway would not go away simply because Anne Torrance refused to admit its existence.

Even so, the actuality was more shattering than she had anticipated. She gasped, clutched at the strings of her bonnet which the breeze was blowing loose. A mountain taken out of the earth, they had said, and it was true. Below her a great embankment was being built. In front of it were fields yet untouched, the stubble of the harvest still golden. Towards them the pile of earth, like a huge earthworm, heaving and writhing its way across the countryside, crawled forward to obliterate them. The edge of the embankment was the scene of the greatest activity, but all along the top Anne could see men and horses and wagons involved in an ordered and purposeful movement, like the perpetual movement inside a nest of ants.

She realised then, looking down upon them, that nothing would stop them. They never could have been stopped, even if her father had lived and had still refused to sell his two fields. They would have found another route and gone on again. They were irresistible, like a Juggernaut. Her little battle, her indignation and hatred had had no more power to offend or change than a paper dart tossed against the wind. Instinctively, she drew nearer to the tower, leaning up against the brick, as if it might yet be able to protect her.

"An extraordinary sight, is it not? Like something from another world."

A man had appeared from behind the tower and was standing watching her. He must have been there, hidden from her, all the time. Perhaps he had watched her climb the hill.

He was no one Anne had ever seen before, and she would have remembered him. He was tall and well-made and strikingly handsome. His colouring was unusual, his eyes being dark brown, not the brooding liquid brown of the Italian but the lively sharp eyes of the gypsy; in contrast his hair was fair, a mixture of all shades from pale yellow to light brown, as if it had been unevenly bleached by a strong sun. His clothes were expensive and elegant, though there was something indefinably foreign about them, a certain extravagance of cut which no English tailor would have permitted. And his voice was foreign too, the perfect English too perfect with every syllable given equal weight. He came forward closer to Anne, smiling with considerable charm.

"I am so sorry. I startled you. You did not realise that I was here?"

"No," Anne said.

"I have been here some time, admiring the works of those mechanical geniuses over there—" He waved his hand towards the scene below. "Though I am not exactly sure what they are doing."

"They are building a railway," Anne said drily.

He turned his head quickly, giving her an amused and appreciative glance. "That I do understand, but why are they building it in this way, up to the skies?"

"I don't know," Anne said. "I believe it is because the finished railway track must be as level as possible from beginning to end. The gradient must not alter too abruptly or the engine cannot pull the train." At the expression on the stranger's face, she suddenly burst out laughing. "But surely you know more about this than I. Men always know about such things as engineering."

"I know about horses and pictures and beautiful women, but nothing so clever as railways. They are still a rarity in my country."

"Your country?"

"In Hungary."

"Hungary!" She looked at him with some amazement. "You are very far from home."

"Yes." He paused. "Yes, that is true. I am a long way from my home." He paused again, and then asked, gesturing once more towards the railway, "Do you often come here to watch these—insects?"

"No." Anne turned from the edge of the hill. "This is the first time I have seen the workings." She began to move away, down the path that led away from the view. The stranger walked with her.

"I thought from your face as I watched you that you did not approve of what you saw," he said.

"No, I do not like it," Anne said. "It is ugly and destructive and I do not think that here, at any rate, it is necessary. But I see also that it is too ruthless and powerful to be prevented."

"Nothing is too powerful," he said. "There is nothing so strong that it cannot be overthrown."

She glanced up at him. "You say that very seriously. As if you mean it."

"Certainly I mean it! I have told you I am Hungarian. You have heard what is happening in my country, in all Europe?"

"Why, yes," Anne said. She was a little taken aback by the sudden effusion of passion into the stranger's voice. "There is revolution."

"Revolution, indeed. Revolution—" He murmured the word like a man invoking his God. "Tyranny is being overthrown, justice is being exacted, revolution is setting all Europe on fire. For years we have waited, and now . . ." He paused, seeming to search for words in the air as if his thoughts moved too fast for them to form. "The discontent, the unrest has been growing like—like a long trail of powder waiting for the fuse. Now a spark has been set to it and the flash of that glorious explosion is lighting up the world."

"You speak with great feeling," Anne said. "You must be very proud of your countrymen."

"We are a proud people. Hungarians have always been independent, you know. We have remained intact as a nation no matter who held the power. Now we hold it ourselves—temporarily, at least."

"You think it will not last?"

"They—the enemy—do not give up so easily. We have won a breathing space and we must use it. Kossuth, you have heard of Kossuth? I am a friend of his. Kossuth has sent me, among others, to discover what support I can find for our cause in England. You see, we believe in the English as the great supporters of freedom. You have tamed your monarchy. Your queen, for instance, could not imprison you, indefinitely, without just cause?"

"I do not believe so." Anne was becoming bewildered and her voice betrayed it.

He smiled suddenly, and as if it was something that could be altered at will, at the snap of a finger, his mood was changed. His tone lost its intensity; his manner, no longer that of an evangelist preaching a new religion, became light, amiable, conversational. "I am boring you. Forgive me. I was practising on you and I was carried away by my own speechmaking."

"Practising on me?"

"I have to try and arouse people's interest in our cause and I have little experience in such matters."

Anne could not think what to make of him. She was both confused and dazzled by the stranger; by the lightning leaps from impassioned rhetoric to a kind of self-deprecating gaiety; by his appearance, his foreignness. She said, "Well, you may certainly say that you have aroused my interest."

"And you will forgive me my impertinence in speaking to you?" he asked.

She smiled at him. "I will forgive you."

As they talked, they had been following the

twisting pathway down the hill. Anne was so absorbed by her companion that she did not watch with enough care where she was treading. She stumbled and would have fallen if the stranger had not put his arm under her elbow to steady her. She recovered her balance.

"Thank you," she said.

"You have not injured your ankle?"

"No. I am quite unhurt."

For a moment he remained with his hand on her arm. Then he withdrew it. He gave a slight, almost formal bow, and said: "Perhaps after this long conversation we have shared, you will permit me to introduce myself. My name is Laszlo Bathory."

"I am Anne Torrance," said Anne. "I live not far from here——"

"But I know where you live! I know you!" A delighted smile had broken across the Hungarian's face. "The Countess Sophia has spoken of you. You live at Rivington. We passed by your house only the other day."

"You know the Countess?" Anne asked. When she thought about it it was only natural that he should. She had forgotten the Countess was also Hungarian.

"I was given an introduction to her,"

Bathory said, "and she has been kind enough to extend to me the hospitality of her house."

"So you will have a corner of your homeland to return to each night from your expeditions."

"Miss Torrance, I think you are laughing a little at my fervour for freedom."

"No, indeed not, I assure you."

He raised a hand. "You are right to object to my flinging my patriotic emotions at a complete stranger, however sympathetic."

"I would object only if they were not sincere," Anne said. "If you were indeed merely rehearsing a speech."

He smiled again. They had reached the foot of the hill by now and no difficulties faced them but the easy walk through the fields to the village. But Bathory halted.

"I regret that I cannot give myself the pleasure of escorting you to your door," he said. "I have an appointment at Treadwell Manor."

"But you are going the wrong way," Anne said. "Treadwell Manor is in the opposite direction."

He nodded. "That is why I must leave you; I am afraid I already am a trifle late. Miss Torrance—" He bowed and kissed her hand.

"Very honoured to have made your acquaintance. I shall see you again."

"Good-bye, Mr. Bathory."

He had been taking a short cut over the hill, Anne realised, when he had met her by the tower. He must have been told that by climbing the hill and taking a track down the other side, his journey would be a mile less than if he followed the lane to Treadwell that skirted the hill. But instead of continuing he had returned down the hill with her and now must begin again. It was a very flattering action. She turned to look at him once more and as she did so, at that very moment, Bathory also paused and looked back in Anne's direction. He waved his hat in a salute to her and she found herself smiling. She went on her way back to the village, still smiling.

If Anne and Laszlo Bathory had remained on the summit of the hill overlooking the embankment a few minutes longer, they would have witnessed an abrupt alteration in the pattern of movement beneath them. They would have heard shouts, the scrape and scream of metal on metal, seen the cloud of dust arising, the moment of stillness and then the frenzied renewal of activity that meant accident. The first death had just occurred in the building of Godfrey Bullivant's railway.

Hugh Radlett learned of it from a boy sent pelting across country to fetch him.

"How many are hurt?" he asked, gathering up his bag.

"One broke arm, one dead, one near dead," the boy said succinctly.

"What happened?"

"Wagon went off the rail," the boy said. "Knocked them over the edge, buried two. Stove the dead 'un's chest in."

By the time Hugh reached the site they had brought the dead man and the injured ones down in one of the wagons. To carry the earth needed to make the embankment from the cutting to the site, a tramway had been constructed along the top of the workings. The heavy wagons loaded with soil were brought to within fifty yards of the edge. There they were uncoupled and each harnessed in turn to one of the horses. The horse, urged on to a gallop by its handler, drew the wagon at full tilt towards the verge of the embankment. At the right, the very last moment, the halter was slipped, horse and man sprang clear and the wagon, crashing against the solid wooden bar at the end of the tramway, tipped out its load of earth. On this occasion, the wagon once released had become derailed, careering off the rail at an angle, too fast and unexpected for three of the men to jump clear. The wagon went over the edge and the men went with it.

A group of ten to twenty navvies watched while Hugh examined the injured. The man whose left arm was broken was sitting on a lump of rock stoically smoking a pipe. He waved Hugh away.

"I'm right enough. You want to look at that poor devil first. He'll not last long else."

The dead man lay on the ground covered by coats. After confirming that he was dead and that there was nothing to be done for him, Hugh left him and went to kneel beside the third victim. He was unconscious, filthy from the earth that had so nearly entombed him, his face grey, his clothes torn and bloody. There was a cut on his head as deep as if he'd been hit with an axe. Hugh explored it gently with his fingers.

"He's broken his head, hasn't he?" one of the men said. "Edge of the wagon caught him. You could hear the crack across three counties. Like a nut cracking."

"He'll be all right," Hugh said. "His skull's not fractured." He looked up and smiled. "I'd like to see what he did to the wagon."

The men grinned. They were a tough-looking lot. They looked as if the beer and beef they were rumoured to get through each day was no more than an adequate measure for their needs. And Hugh could see that they were unlike other workmen in their air of casual independence. There was one man, smaller than the others, with a face like a peevish grocer, who had ever since Hugh arrived been issuing sharp-voiced orders to the men to get back to work. Though he was, Hugh was told, the sub-contractor for this five-mile stretch of the railway and so the navvies' direct employer, they took not the slightest notice of his demands, ignoring him as if he had not spoken, all their attention on Hugh and their workmate.

When they saw Hugh begin to clean and dress the wound, they began to disperse, as if satisfied, and started to drift back to the work site. The train of earth wagons began to move and several of the navvies ran off to jump aboard and get a lift along the tramway. One of those left, a burly fellow of about forty, a blue rag tied round his neck, shouted after them then turned, shrugging his shoulders, to Hugh.

"If you can't stop 'em taking damned stupid risks like that five minutes after a mate's been killed, when can you? They're forbidden to ride the wagons but they pay no heed. Doesn't seem to strike 'em another wagon could come off. It's always the other man's going to get it, never them."

"What caused the accident?" Hugh asked.

"Rain caused subsidence, *I'd* say." He stressed the fact that this was his opinion, glancing across at the contractor. "Mr. Simpson there no doubt will blame the men; he'll say the rail wasn't properly laid. And as I'm the ganger, no doubt of it, the blame will end up at my door. But he'd better not make this an excuse for docking money, that's all *I* say."

Hugh made no comment on this. Finished for the moment with his concussed patient, he was making a temporary splint for the broken arm. The injured man continued to smoke his pipe, studying everything Hugh did to him with a calm, impersonal interest.

Now he removed the pipe from his mouth and jabbing it in the air towards Simpson, the contractor, said: "Haste, that's what's up with this job. Too much bloody hurry. This won't be the last time you'll be called up here, Doctor."

"We must get your friend to hospital," Hugh said. "And you too."

"Oh, no you don't," the navvy said. "Once they get you in hospital, you never get out alive. We're none of us going there."

Hugh, from experience, was inclined to sympathise with him. He said merely: "He needs nursing. And with that wound he can't work for a while yet. Nor can you. Who's going to see to you?"

"What's there to see to? A bump on the head and a broken bone. We'll manage. I've got sick money put away, I should tell you. I had a feeling about this railroad. Had an unlucky feeling about it from the start. I've been a navvy a long time. It's not the first accident I've been in. I've got a few bob put by. I'll pay you."

"I shan't be sending you a bill for this," Hugh said.

The navvy looked at him, frowning, whether from pain or suspicion or surprise it would be hard to tell. He was about thirty-five or six, Hugh guessed, though he looked older. He had a square, weatherbeaten face, every line of it marked out, as his hands were, by ingrained dirt. He had lost his hat in the accident and his thick ginger hair was matted about his forehead. He pulled at his straggle of beard with his free hand.

"Who's paying then? You won't get it from him." He nodded at the ganger. "Though they say he's the one sent for you. Simpson would never have troubled. Mr. Simpson doesn't approve of accidents. Work stopped means money lost to him."

Hugh tied a knot in the sling he had fastened round the splinted arm.

"What's your name?" he asked.

"They call me Ben—or Ben Redhead, on account of the colour of my hair."

"And that's all your name?"

"We don't bother with other names in our trade."

Hugh stood up. "Well, Ben Redhead, where do you lodge?"

"Up there, up in the camp. I've got a bunk in Meg's shanty up on the hill."

"And your friend?" Hugh asked. "Is he living in the encampment too?"

"Aye. And in the same hut."

"Right." Hugh closed his bag. "Let's be on our way."

The navvy looked puzzled. "What d'you mean?"

"How does your arm feel?"

"Why, it feels easy, it feels grand. I could swing a pick with it."

"Then you can walk and lead the way to the camp. We must get this man to his bed."

"Who's 'we'? Do you mean you're coming up to the camp, Doctor?"

"Yes," Hugh said.

"Why?" Ben asked bluntly.

"To keep an eye on my patient," Hugh said. "Don't look so shocked, man. It's not you I'm concerned about, it's your friend."

"Oh, I'm not shocked, Doctor," the navvy said. "I'm not surprised, either." He shook his head in a resigned manner. "I see my mistake. I should never have said I'd money put by."

In spite of himself, Hugh smiled. "I'm not after your money. To tell you the truth I'm merely curious to see how you all live up there."

He left Ben still gravely shaking his head and went back to the ganger to organise the carriage of the injured man to the camp. A stretcher was improvised and two navvies conscripted to carry it. As Hugh watched them strapping the man safely to it, Simpson, the contractor, came up to speak to him.

"I can't expect to get any more work out of them, eh, Doctor?"

"It depends how long you take to build your railway," Hugh said.

Simpson grunted. "Damned nuisance. I can't afford these accidents. They hold everything up. I expect they were drunk. If these men didn't drink so much, they wouldn't get hurt." He saw Hugh's expression and added aggressively: "They're not my responsibility, you know."

"Well, he is," Hugh remarked. He indicated the dead man.

"But, surely, Doctor . . ."

"You didn't send for me, Mr. Simpson, I understand," Hugh said. "And whoever did, called me to treat the living. You'll have to look after your dead workman yourself. But I'll do you one service. I'll report on his death at the inquest."

"Now, look here, Doctor," Simpson said. "You've not been in the district long, I'm told, and you may not know much about the

111

situation here, about this railway. It's behind time already. There's been delay and opposition and God knows what. Now I've got a contract and I'm going to fulfil it. I don't want trouble with the authorities or with anyone else, and I don't want any more delays. Now I don't know what that man you were talking to has been telling you, but that was a plain, straightforward accident. Nothing more."

"I thought you said they had been drinking," Hugh said. "The authorities don't like that, I understand, Mr. Simpson. They blame the contractors for allowing it. Especially when it results in a death."

He was not sure why he had taken such an instant dislike to Simpson or why he was bothering to bait him in this way; except, perhaps, that he had met his kind so often in his years in London, on Poor Law Boards, on hospital committees, on magistrates' benches, in various positions of authority over others whom, by reason of poverty or illness or misfortune, they held to be inferior to themselves and therefore without need of consideration or compassion. It might have been, too, that from the first brief sight of the railway, the contrast between the men who were building it and the men responsible for it, seemed too great. Hugh did not think at first glance, that Simpson had the ability or control or experience for the work he had undertaken. He rather agreed with Ben Redhead that it would not be the only time a doctor would be called here.

He had turned away but Simpson followed him, putting his hand on his arm to draw his attention.

"I didn't like what you said then, Doctor, about the drinking. I hope you're not intending to repeat that at the inquest."

"I know my duty, Mr. Simpson," Hugh said. "I shall give my evidence according to the facts and my conscience." His tone, full of a lofty dignity, quite foxed Simpson. He stepped back, letting his hand fall. Hugh nodded to the two navvies and the small procession of the stretcher party, led by Ben Redhead and brought up by Hugh, set out for the encampment.

3

HUGH returned from the encampment on the hill tired and rather depressed. No patients waited to see him, no messages had been left on his desk. He dropped his bag on to the floor and sat down in the leather chair that had belonged to Dr. Torrance, putting his feet up on the edge of the desk. He leaned back his head and closed his eyes.

"Hugh? Are you there?"

The sound of Anne's voice pulled him from the edge of sleep. He opened his eyes. Turning his head, he saw Anne standing in the doorway that led from the consulting room to the other part of the house. The soft glow of the lamplight in the corridor behind her threw a faint halo about her figure. She was wearing a dress of some dark shimmering material that left her white shoulders partly bare. Her hair gleamed richly and he could see the earrings of jet that hung from her ears, but her face was shadowed, its expression hidden from him. Coming from a drifting, fading consciousness to an awareness of her presence, almost as an extension of a dream, she seemed to Hugh, as he looked at her in silence, strangely beautiful, strangely mysterious.

It was the unexpected moments such as these, Hugh thought, that betrayed him. He was as vulnerable as ever. To him, it would have been the right, the necessary, the inevitable action to go to Anne now and take her in his arms and kiss her out of all resistance to him. He did not care at such moments whether she loved him or not. He simply wanted her.

"Were you looking for me, Anne?" he asked quietly.

"Yes, yes, I was." She came forward into the room, into the clearer light. "You are not dining out to-night, are you, Hugh?"

"No, I am not."

"What a relief! Mr. Carrington is coming. I do not think I could bear an evening of our Vicar without some support. Another man, to keep reassuring myself that the Vicar is not the masculine rule." She laughed; a low, charming gurgle in the throat.

Hugh swung his feet down from the desk. "I'm gratified to know that you consider me masculine enough to counterbalance a clergyman."

"Oh, Hugh . . ." She smiled down at him, standing just beyond the desk. Her eyes looked enormous—and alive, Hugh realised; that slightly blank, far-away expression had gone. She was suddenly as he remembered her two years ago, only in some elusive way more mature, more of a woman, and the more intriguing and puzzling because of it.

"What have you been up to?" he asked. "You look decidedly mischievous."

"I went out for a walk," she said. "It was a good day for a walk." She paused. "Hugh, I know you often got to see the Countess. Are you going again soon?"

"I may be."

"To-morrow—?" She explained hurriedly: "I have promised to repay a call on her for some time. I merely thought, if you were going, I could go with you. For the company——"

Hugh studied her. Then, abruptly, he stood up. "Why not? We'll go and visit her to-morrow afternoon. She has guests there but I doubt if she will mind."

"Guests?" Anne said vaguely.

"A young relative called Esther Wharton——"

"Oh, is she still there?" Anne smiled. "Such a dull person."

"Well, you should not find the other guest dull," Hugh remarked.

"What do you mean?"

"You will see." Hugh smiled. "Yes, I think he might be as pleasing to you as he is to the Countess. He has that certain flamboyance you like, Anne. He is a Hungarian. Naturally, being a compatriot of the Countess's she will not hear a word against him."

"And do you speak words against him, Hugh?"

He shrugged. "I don't like actors."

"But he is not——" Anne broke off.

Hugh turned. "Yes——?"

"I mean, surely the Countess is not entertaining an actor at Waterford Park?" she went on quickly. "That does not sound very probable."

"He is not an actor by profession," Hugh said. "I'm not sure what his profession is, if any. I meant he had an actor's face; capable of expressing a great many different moods and so well that it is impossible to tell which is reflecting his true thoughts." He paused. "Your face is sometimes like that. You hide a great deal, do you not, Anne?"

"I wonder why you should say that," Anne said. "You have always told me I had an open face."

"Not any more," Hugh remarked. "There is a change."

"A pleasant change, I hope, Hugh."

"I hope so too," he replied.

It was not the answer she expected. But she did not deny to herself that he was right. A pointless deception such as concealing her meeting with Laszlo Bathory from Hugh, would not have occurred to her two years ago. If Hugh had known, he might have been encouraged. You do not deceive those in whom you have no interest.

Mrs. Torrance was sorry for Mr. Carrington, and that, in Anne's view, was a grave mistake. It led to his being at dinner with them at least once a fortnight. He was a bachelor, so that it was difficult for him to entertain; he had only come to the parish eighteen months ago and he was still regarded as being on trial by the villagers, who watched him warily for any signs of the Romish tendencies they felt his celibate state warned of. Mrs. Torrance saw him as a lonely man, isolated by his pretensions, and put up with them herself out of kindness.

Mr. Carrington, however, was not in the least sorry for himself. He considered himself cultivated, of distinguished appearance and manner, belonging rightfully to the highest society and an obvious catch for any lady he deigned to notice. One day, when he met some suitable person of his own social level and fulfilling all the many necessary qualifications for the position, he intended to marry. He was forty-two years old, and was, as a result of an epidemic which had recently carried off a mother and elder sister he had not greatly cared for, quite free of hampering relatives.

His one virtue was the courage his prejudices gave him. He never hesitated to speak out for what he thought was right and against what he thought was wrong, and since he did most of this speaking out from the pulpit he had so far met with little opposition. Indeed, any attempt at contradiction always alarmed him. It was so palpably wrong. That was why Hugh Radlett disturbed him.

Although Hugh, out of deference to Mrs. Torrance, rarely said one provocative word when he met Henry Carrington in her house, he could not control his expression and his silence, and the vicar had gradually absorbed the accurate impression that Dr. Radlett disagreed with him on every possible topic of importance. Now each time they met he felt impelled to correct this unsatisfactory state of affairs, worrying away at Hugh's quiet restraint with an increasing persistence that now and then, as on this occasion, grew to open attack.

It had been an unusual evening from the start. Anne Torrance, whom he delighted to impress and who was, he thought, looking exceptionally well, seemed in an odd irrepressible mood. She smiled at everything he said but it seemed to him that often her smile was more directed across the table at Hugh Radlett than at himself; and once or twice she even smiled when the remark he had made had been of the utmost gravity. Though he liked her commendation, he would have preferred it to be more suitably expressed.

"It is strange," he said, continuing a dissertation on parish affairs, his deep-toned voice a trifle edged, "strange and sad that the spiritual guidance the people might expect to look for from the natural leaders of our local society should be so lacking."

"Why, Mr. Carrington," Mrs. Torrance said mildly, "I think the church is well-supported here. It has always seemed so."

"Ah, yes!" He swung round to her. "You, my dear lady, are the noble exception. I see evidence of your charity wherever I go. But there are others."

"Hugh," Anne said, "Mr. Carrington has noticed that you do not go to church."

Hugh smiled at her and continued peeling an apple.

"You consider that a joke, I see, Dr. Radlett," Carrington said. "But Miss Torrance has brought up a point that, I confess, has been exercising my mind for some time. You are not often at Divine Service."

"Not often," Hugh agreed. The peel spiralled from his knife in perfect, unbroken coils. "From your orchard?" he asked Mrs. Torrance.

"Yes. I am quite pleased with the crop this year."

Hugh bit into the apple. He nodded. "Delicious."

"Dr. Radlett," Carrington expostulated. "If you please, I was addressing you on a matter of some importance."

"Too important for a dinner-table, surely," Hugh remarked.

"Ah!" Carrington pounced eagerly. "There is your error, Dr. Radlett. Religion cannot be kept to the church. It must be brought out into the market place. Faith should be publicly demonstrated, publicly preached."

"You are a great preacher, I know, Mr. Carrington," Hugh said. "Very fervent for the Lord."

"Dr. Radlett, if it is your purpose to mock——"

"Not at all. I admire your oratory very much. Indeed I admire it so much I feel that it should have a wider audience."

"A wider audience?"

"Yes, Mr. Carrington, I know of an audience of hundreds, many hundreds, a mass of lost souls waiting for the Word. They are waiting for you, Mr. Carrington"—he took another bite of his apple—"up there."

Mr. Carrington was confused. He felt it

was Hugh's intention to be offensive, but on the other hand, he found it difficult to resent praise of his own powers when it was, as it so obviously was, justified.

"I am not sure of your meaning," he said. "Who are these souls? Where are they to be found?"

"In the encampment," Hugh said.

Anne, who had been following their exchange with growing amusement, looked up, the smile fading from her eyes. "The navvies' encampment?"

"The railway workers?" Carrington asked in horror.

"Exactly," Hugh said. "There they are, up in their camp, as isolated as a siege force in hostile country. I have been there, I have seen how they live. I would say they are a thoroughly godless lot, even worse than I. If you believe, as you say, Mr. Carrington, that your Christianity should be publicly demonstrated and all-embracing, then it is your duty to go and preach to them."

The vicar, utterly dumbfounded by this sudden counter-attack, was momentarily silenced. Anne leaned forward towards Hugh. "You have been to the encampment? When? Why?"

The accusation of betrayal was implicit in the coldness of her voice. Hugh met it with an equal seriousness.

"I went there to-day, Anne, because I was summoned. A man was killed and two others injured."

"In a drunken brawl, I presume," Carrington interposed.

"No." Hugh spoke only to Anne. "During the course of their work. A wagon was derailed. It swept them over the edge of the embankment."

"How dreadful. . . . Did they fall all the way? It seemed such a height."

"You've seen it," Hugh said.

"Yes . . . yes," she admitted. "I saw it while I was out walking." Hugh held her glance and there was an expression in his eyes she could not interpret. She looked away.

"There will be an inquest, I suppose," Mrs. Torrance said.

"Yes, and a funeral." He turned to the vicar. "Have they approached you yet, Mr. Carrington?"

"Approached me?"

"Yes. They were saying in the camp they wished to give their friend a reverent burial. I told them you would be glad to conduct the service."

"Then you told them wrong," Carrington said angrily. "Really, Dr. Radlett, you take too much upon yourself."

"I am sorry if I was mistaken in you," Hugh said.

"These men are lower than common labourers. They have no respect for law or order, or any kind of morality. My duty is to my flock. My church is not going to be used for the convenience of those riff-raff!"

Mrs. Torrance saw that the time had come to intervene. By rising from the table and suggesting that they follow her to the drawing-room, she effectively ended the dispute.

Hugh soon excused himself, saying that he had work to do, and Mr. Carrington had had his feathers so ruffled that he could not settle down as he usually did to a further hour's exercise of his beautiful voice. He left early.

When he had gone, Anne, seeing a light still shining in the consulting room, took Hugh in some brandy as a nightcap. He was in the dispensary, making up some medicine.

"Has he gone?" he asked.

"Yes." She put the glass down on the table. "Hugh, what is it like up there?"

"In the encampment? As squalid as you might imagine, Anne. As you must wish."

"What do you mean—as I must wish?"

He stopped what he was doing. His gaze was very direct. "You keep your bitterness on the boil, don't you, Anne? When I told you of the dead man, I sensed that you felt like exclaiming: 'Now there is one less of them.' But your good manners made you say: 'How dreadful.' "

"Hugh, that is monstrous! It was not so."

"I hope not. Keep your hatred for the inanimate things, Anne, for the rails, the engines, the earthworks. Don't extend it to people. It is destructive."

"You read me moral lessons now. You will expect me to smile on Mr. Bullivant next."

"By all means smile on Mr. Bullivant. Though not, of course, too ardently. I don't wish my rival to be too well encouraged."

Anne smiled, and the nervous tension he had been aware of in her relaxed. "You can always make me laugh."

"Well, that is an advantage. They say the ugliest man can win a woman by making her laugh."

Anne moved nearer, fingering the bottles on the table. "You speak of rivals, of winning a woman. Does that mean, Hugh, that you are still . . . still——" She hesitated.

"Still a suitor for your hand, you mean, my dear Anne. Not at all. I say these things merely to amuse you." He put a hand under her chin and before she realised his intention kissed her on the lips.

"There," he said calmly, "that was not a lover's kiss, was it?"

"Hugh, I——"

"It was not, for example," he said, drawing her towards him, "like this. . . ."

When he let her go, at last, from that long, intense embrace, there was for some seconds, silence between them.

"Now that was a great mistake," Hugh said at length, looking down at her. "Now I have made you feel triumphant again. I think you had better go, Anne."

"Hugh——"

"Go to bed." He took her arm and propelled her across the consulting room. "Good night."

She paused on the threshold of the room and he could see that she was smiling. With a soft rustle of skirts, she went out, closing the door gently behind her.

"Damn," Hugh said. "Damn, damn." He went back to the dispensary, picked up the glass of brandy she had brought him and downed it in one gulp. Then he went on with his work.

They did not go to Waterford Park next day as Anne had planned, nor for about a week after. Hugh was called away to a patient on the first afternoon and after that one thing or another made it inconvenient for him to go. But Anne was not over-concerned for a day or so later she met by chance the man who had been the sole reason for her proposed visit to the Countess.

Walking home from the next village, on a day of clear, frosty weather, she met Laszlo Bathory riding one of the Countess's horses. He dismounted and walked part of the way with her, talking with fluency and charm about the countryside and speaking nostalgically of the great plains and forests of his homeland.

"Are you having much success with your mission?" Anne asked him.

He shrugged. "Things move so slowly. People do not understand the urgency of the situation. They take a week of time and then another week, and then I can see they will ponder it another month or so, and then go hunting."

Anne smiled. "But the Countess is not reluctant to help, I am sure."

"Oh, the Countess! She is a true Hungarian."

"Do you hear often from Hungary? From your home?"

"I have heard, but letters take a long time to arrive. When I go to London next week, I hope to learn more recent news——" He broke off, looking ahead along the lane. "Who is that old crone? Is she your local witch? She looks exactly like an old woman on my father's estate who used to terrify me when I was a little boy. I believed from the servants that she could turn into a bat at night and would come and attack me if I upset her."

Anne looked at the bent figure shuffling along, searching beneath the trees for firewood.

"You are quite right," she said gaily. "That is Granny Lane. She has such terrible powers even the Vicar comes under her spell." And she told Laszlo about the cat and the joke the old woman had played on Mr. Carrington by getting him to bury it.

Laszlo laughed at the story and Anne thought, looking up at him, how pleasant it was to be with this man, how worldly and polished he appeared, how amusing and feminine she felt in his presence. When they parted, he left her with what seemed the greatest reluctance and asked when he might have the pleasure of a longer period of time in her company. Anne told him of her intention to call upon the Countess.

"I shall make it my business to be at Waterford Park when you do," he said.

"But you may be in London," Anne said. "Did you not say so?"

"It is only for a few days. I shall postpone my journey until I have seen you, you may be sure of that, my dear Miss Torrance." His glance, the pressure of his hand as he said good-bye, held meanings far beyond the polite conventionalities; as if this was a deliberate, romantic rendezvous they were arranging, the culmination of many more meetings than two chance encounters in the open air.

If it had not been for this air of intrigue with which Laszlo Bathory had already surrounded their acquaintanceship, Anne might perhaps have told Hugh of this second meeting. But she did not. She kept it as a secret. And the same romantic, impulsive part of her which had led to that deception was delighted when, finally taken by Hugh on the delayed visit to Waterford Park, at last formally introduced to Laszlo by the Countess, the Hungarian acknowledged the introduction without by any word or gesture revealing that he had ever set eyes on her before. Their mutual acceptance of this behaviour made the tenuous, tentative link between them stronger. A conspiracy existed.

The Countess, in her usual manner, made of Anne's informal afternoon call a positive occasion. She swept Hugh and Anne from the small drawing-room into which they had first been shown, and into the main salon, with its ivory walls and its dominating portrait of herself. Bells were rung, orders given and a tea was brought in as lavish as a banquet. The Countess seated herself in benevolent authority behind the silver tea service, with the butler in close attendance and two maids, looking in their starched aprons and flutter-

131

ing caps like anxious butterflies, hovering devotedly about her.

The Countess was, in fact, so stimulated by the presence in her house of her fellow-countryman, so involved with the struggle which he symbolised, that her vivacity and brilliance seemed to Anne more overwhelming than ever. Sophia always alarmed her a little. That magnetism, which had nothing to do with age, always threatened to overshadow her own attractions. To-day, however, with Hugh so recently revealed by that betraying kiss to be, in spite of himself, as much her captive as ever, and with the excitement of her subtly growing relationship with Laszlo Bathory, Anne herself was in a sparkling mood. Hugh, watching her with the sensitivity of a lover, had little difficulty in putting two and two together.

"Your fiancée is very beautiful, Dr. Radlett," a soft voice observed. Esther Wharton had come, with her customary quietness, to sit beside him. She was, in a dress that echoed the green of the painted emerald in the Countess's portrait, a point of vivid colour amid the cool tones of the room.

"Miss Torrance is beautiful, I agree," Hugh said. "But she is not my fiancée."

"Oh—" She bowed her head. "I am sorry. From the way Mrs. Wharton often speaks of you both . . ." Her voice trailed away, in apparent distress at her *faux pas*.

"Well, we all know how the Countess speaks," Hugh said kindly. "She is inclined to be over enthusiastic at times. She thinks it would be an excellent arrangement if Miss Torrance and I were to marry, that is all. It would neaten up the countryside."

Esther looked up and smiled and the assurance of the smile surprised him. She had a habit of surprising him each time he saw her. She was always there whenever he called at Waterford Park and always so unobtrusive, so quiet, so negative, and yet she had this facility of making her presence felt. As for example now, when she got up offering to fetch him another cup of tea and paused as she asked him, standing at an angle to him that was no doubt accidental but which gave him every opportunity of seeing her figure to the best advantage. It was a very neat figure, Hugh admitted, and the cut of the dress flattered her; but the colour of the dress was too sharp for her. The green drained her complexion. He wondered as he watched her walk away from him how deliberate it all was:

133

the bright colours of her clothes, the face so often downcast—might it not be intended to make a man forget or overlook that she was plain and notice only that she was a woman?

"Hugh! You are too far away over there. Come and sit beside me." The Countess beckoned him. Hugh rose obediently and joined her.

"Mr. Bathory is trying to persuade me to wear the King's emerald," she said. "But I have told him it is a jewel that needs an occasion."

"Then create an occasion," Laszlo cried. He turned to Hugh. "Have you seen the emerald, Dr. Radlett?"

"No, as a matter of fact, I have never seen it," Hugh said.

"I have," Anne said. "When I was a child, Countess. You showed it to my father."

"So I did. I remember. I do not bring it out very often, Mr. Bathory. It is too precious. It is a heritage, you must remember, not a trinket."

"Then wear it in celebration of the restoration of that heritage. In hopes of a free Hungary."

"It would be appropriate, indeed. But you overlook one thing. When that portrait over there was painted, I was a young woman. Now I am an ageing one. Only the emerald remains the same." She spread her hands out towards them in a graceful gesture. "My dear young men, how could you expose me to such a contrast, to such cruelty."

"You seek flattery in the most obvious ways, Countess," Hugh said. "And I refuse to pander to you."

She turned to Laszlo. "Well, Mr. Bathory," she demanded. "Will you flatter me?"

"There is no need," Laszlo said. "As you well know, madam."

The Countess looked from one to the other with evident enjoyment. "Very deftly spoken. Now I think there has been enough coyness. Anne, come and tell me how your mother is."

Laszlo, dismissed, wandered over to the portrait and stood looking up at it. After a moment, he turned as if to ask a question, but the Countess and Anne were deep in conversation. Esther Wharton went to speak to him instead and Hugh was interested to hear that they talked in German. Miss Wharton, he was realising, was a woman of many parts.

As he drove Anne home in the trap through the early evening, Hugh asked her if she knew that Esther Wharton could speak German. Anne was uninterested. No, she had not known that, but she supposed that Miss Wharton as the daughter of a clergyman had had a good education.

"Of course, I knew that Mr. Bathory would speak German," she went on with a much greater show of enthusiasm. "That is the second language for most educated Hungarians. The right to have their own language, Magyar, as the official language of the country, has been one of the things the patriots have constantly fought for. He has been telling me about it. He speaks French too, you know, as well as English. His accent is excellent, isn't it?"

"A very talented fellow," Hugh remarked.

"Hugh, you are so acid these days. You must take care. You are becoming a misanthrope."

Hugh smiled. "Is that one of the English words Mr. Bathory pronounces so excellently? Well, if I hate mankind, then I have certainly chosen the wrong profession."

"Perhaps it is your profession that has made you so intolerant." Anne's words, spoken so casually, had an edge of truth in them that touched Hugh. He made no reply and remained silent for so long that Anne began to regret upsetting him. She did not like Hugh taciturn.

"What happened to that man," she said, to make conversation, "the one killed in the accident?"

"He was buried," Hugh said.

"Not by Mr. Carrington!"

"No, by a less nice clergyman."

"Will you have to give evidence at the inquest?"

"I have already done so," Hugh replied. "Three days ago."

"Oh . . ." She paused. "I did not know. Why did you not tell me?"

"You did not ask." He glanced at her. "You know, Anne, although at most times you show no interest whatever in my work, at others you show too much."

"What do you mean?"

"I'd be obliged if you'd stop taking useless medicine to Arthur Toms."

Anne was taken completely by surprise. She felt herself blushing as if he had caught her out in some guilty activity. She looked away from him.

"What do you mean?" she repeated.

"You have been going into my dispensary

137

when I am out, making up some potion, what, I'm not sure, though I can probably guess, and taking it to Toms. It must stop."

It was the phrase "*my* dispensary" that made her angry.

"I was following Father's instructions," she said coldly.

"Well, now you can follow mine."

"Arthur Toms expects the medicine. It keeps him well."

"Your father recommended a course of treatment for a certain condition at a certain time. He would never have intended that you should go on and on blindly in this way. If the man is ill, he needs——"

"Oh, he is not ill," Anne said. "Not now. He has been recovered for a long time. But he imagines he is ill. The medicine comforts him."

"I shall be the judge whether he is ill or not," Hugh said. "Leave him to me."

"He won't come to you," she said stubbornly. "He will not trust anyone but me."

"He will learn to, if he is encouraged. If you are not working against me."

She stared at him, startled.

"Well, that is what it means, doesn't it," he

said quietly. "I am the doctor here now, Anne. Not you, or your father."

She was silent. Her face was grief-stricken. And she had been so carefree this afternoon, Hugh thought, flirting with her Hungarian. Jealousy had made him speak as he did, as sharply as he had. All he had achieved had been to remind her of the loss of her father. He put a hand on her wrist.

"Why don't you go away from Rivington for a while? You have not left the village since your father died. Stay a month with some relative. With my family, perhaps. It would be good for you, for your health."

She did not respond to his touch. She drew her hand away.

"I do not want to go away," she said.

The desolate mood that had come upon Anne remained with her all evening. It was not lightened by the knowledge that Laszlo Bathory was leaving for London the next day. He had told her he would be away for a week or ten days, perhaps longer. They had arranged no future meeting.

To divert herself, Anne began to plan a way in which she could see the Hungarian again.

Perhaps she could ask her mother to invite the Countess and her guests to dine with them. But that would mean that wretched Esther Wharton would come, and though Anne was sorry for her, being so poor in looks as well as property and with few prospects but that of a governess ahead of her, she found her social presence difficult. She was so lacking in any kind of charm or interest; a heavy weight upon the company.

If, however, she thought, it could be arranged for the party from Waterford Park to come on the same evening as Mr. Carrington, then those two tedious people could be turned upon each other. Pacing restlessly up and down her bedroom she decided to speak to her mother about it the very next day.

She paused at the window, gazing out. It was a clear night and the moon had already risen, washing the countryside with a pale, luminous light. It was a blue light, unreal and faintly sinister, that transformed the familiar fields and orchards into unknown country. A lost and lonely landscape, full of secrets and shadows that by a trick of the eye appeared to move, or perhaps did move, stirred by a breeze or an animal slipping past, or a bird fluttering in its sleep with the approach of danger. Everything seemed to rustle with a furtive life, murderously intent; stoat and weasel, fox and owl, hunter and hunted sliding along the hedgerows, waiting and watching, trembling and crying, sharp, broken-off cries full of despair and death, threatened and afraid.

At the far end of the orchard a shadow detached itself from the trees and moved forward. It became lost for a moment in a general darkness and then Anne thought she saw it again, nearer—much nearer.

From her bedroom window Anne could see the whole length of the garden, the vegetable garden that was separated from it by a brick wall and the orchard beyond. Now, straining to see, wondering whether the uncertain light and her imagination were deceiving her, she waited. She thought she saw something, a mass thicker and darker than the surrounding blackness, close to the wall. It merged with the wall. There was a click, a faint creaking and then the click again. Anne knew then that she was not mistaken. Someone, a man or a woman, had opened the wooden gate in the wall.

She thought from the height and because

she wanted it to be so, that it was a man and that man Laszlo Bathory. It would have been an impulsive, romantic thing for him to have done, to come seeking a glimpse of her, or to leave a message for her before he went away. She should have been afraid, she realised later, because of the nearness of the encampment and the stories that circulated in the villages about the railway navvies; but she did not, at first at any rate, feel afraid, only tense and taut as if her whole being was concentrated in her eyes, watching, waiting.

It was a man. He moved away from the shelter of the wall, walked a few feet across the lawn and stopped. He stood quite still looking up at the house. He stood there for what seemed to Anne an endless eternity of time but was in reality no more than a few minutes. Then he turned away and went towards the side wall that separated the garden from the narrow lane that ran beside it. There was a door into the lane from the garden and he opened that as if familiar with it. A little way along the lane a lantern was hung to give illumination to the stable entrance and by that clear light Anne saw his face. It was Bullivant.

A shock like a cold hand placed upon her

neck jerked Anne away from the window. Bullivant walking in her garden. Bullivant watching her house. What was he doing? What did he want? The uneasiness that the man's presence had always aroused in her was replaced in an instant by fear. Reaching out, she seized the curtains with both hands and swept them together, shutting out the night. But she did not go down to tell her mother or Hugh about the intruder. She knew from the beginning that this was something that concerned only herself.

4

BY the last months of 1848 the glorious revolutions which had begun so hopefully in the spring all over Europe were dead or dying. Where the reformers had not dissipated their chances of success in futile squabbling, their failure to seize control of the armies destroyed them. They were crushed by force. And where the Radetzkys and the Windischgrätzs did not reach with their firing squads, the cholera came to sap away the life blood of the insurrections. Of the few revolutions that survived, Hungary was the strongest.

It had many enemies. Not only the Austrian Court but those several nationalities that co-existed within the Hungarian kingdom; the non-Magyars, the Serbs and Rumanians and Croats who resented the arrogance of the Magyar elite as bitterly as the Magyars resented the too heavy hand of Vienna.

Their leader and the ally of the Austrians was Count Jellacić, Ban of Croatia. He quarrelled with the new Hungarian government, refused to recognise it, raised rebellion against it among the Slavs. Throughout the spring and summer, while Batthyány of Hungary meticulously maintained his loyalty to the Emperor within the limits of the free constitution, the Austrians gave secret encouragement to Jellacić.

In September, with the other uprisings within their territories under control, the Austrians felt strong enough to come out into the open. With their full approval and support Jellacić led his army against the Hungarians.

The treachery of the Emperor shocked all Hungary. The moderates, the Széchenyis and Batthyánys, felt the betrayal the most bitterly. Every action they had taken in the past months and years, everything they had struggled for, had been in their eyes within the limits of their ancient rights; rights that had been denied or suppressed for three hundred years but that nevertheless remained legitimate and constitutional. They had been reformers, not revolutionaries. Kossuth was the true revolutionary. He wanted the radical reorganisation of the whole of Hungarian society. He wanted the people freed of economic burdens, educated, politically equal with their masters. He wanted an independent democratic state and he was prepared to fight for it in any way he could.

Such a man was needed now. The narrow limitations of his fanaticism were to prove his weakness, but at that moment his single-minded determination was his country's strength. He was resolute where others were disheartened. At the prospect of open war Széchenyi temporarily lost his reason, attempting suicide. Batthyány resigned as head of the government. Kossuth, given authority to organise defence, became the virtual ruler of the country. He had no army to fight with, no weapons, no officers. But he had his power of words, his passion, his reputation as a man who had suffered and been imprisoned for his country. The people rallied behind him. They became their own army. Young Hungarian officers took off their Austrian uniforms and became the colonels and generals of the national force. With their long-repressed nationalism bursting out as free and fierce as it ever did against the Turks, the Honved, the citizens' army, and the dashing cavalry officers Europe had considered no more than graceful horsemen combined to drive the enemy from their homeland.

At that most desperate moment, with Jellacić advancing from the south, the Austrians' Italian army attacking from the west, and with the Austrian-fomented rebellions of the Slav minorities sabotaging the defences from within, the Viennese gave Kossuth a breathing-space and an opportunity. Revolution broke out once more in Vienna. Kossuth ordered his hastily mustered, inexperienced army across the Austrian border to help them. He did not succeed. The rising was suppressed, and on 30th October the Hungarians were halted by Jellacić in the first serious battle of the war.

Laszlo Bathory brought the month-old news back to Warwickshire from London. Anne found it all difficult to follow. The complexities of Hungarian nationalism, the subtleties of class, so infinitely more detailed in its rigidities than anything in England, the profound sense of historical privilege, the intricacies of the Triune Kingdom and the demands of the Slavs, the charges and counter-charges of perfidy and betrayal, all seemed so remote and incomprehensible. But she did not need to understand when she had

Laszlo before her, for he embodied to her all the exotic glamour of that far-off clash of arms.

The day he returned to Rivington he came to see her. She had not hoped for anything so positive and that single action did more than anything else to convince her that she was inevitably falling in love with him. It seemed as if their relationship was progressing not by what was said but by what was left unsaid between them. It appeared to her that there was already a proprietary air towards her beneath his formality.

She discovered that she liked simply to look at him. She admired very much the aristocratic features, while the boyish fall of fair hair about the forehead touched maternal feelings in her. His eyes, brown, watchful and sharp, were at variance with the rest of his features. To fit the cast of his face, his eyes should have been melancholy and dreamy. And they were not; they were not in the least like that. The contrast, the unexpectedness, created its own excitement for her.

Sitting in her father's chair, the one that was automatically given to male visitors, he brought to their small drawing-room an aura of cosmopolitan sophistication with the elaborate elegance of his clothes, the smooth courtesies of his manner to her mother, his lively evocation of events and people so foreign, so romantically involved in the dangerous turmoil of revolution.

When he rose to leave after a visit of a punctiliously judged length, Anne announced that she would walk a little way with him, to take the air. He gave no sign then if he was surprised or pleased, but outside when she took his arm to cross safely a patch of ice on the rutted lane, he put his right hand over hers and held it there.

"What will you do now?" she asked. "Will you stay here?"

"There is cholera in London," he remarked. "It would be foolish to go back."

Anne would have preferred to hear that it was her attraction rather than the fear of cholera that made him stay, but she was glad of the fact if not the reason.

"The Countess has had an excellent idea," Laszlo said. "She intends to invite groups of your local gentry to come to Waterford Park and I shall speak to them. I shall ask for their help."

"What kind of help is it that you want them to give you?" she asked.

He said simply: "Money."

"Not the support of action or speeches in Parliament?"

He shrugged, and Anne felt she knew, for the space of a second, exactly what he was thinking. She said in surprise: "You believe the revolution will fail!"

"No . . ."

"Yes. . . . What is it? What else did you learn in London?"

He disengaged himself and walked away from her. She stood where she was, watching him. There had been snow during the night and a layer of it still lay, limply white, over the fields. Laszlo turned and looked back at her. He flung his arms wide in an extravagant gesture as if appealing to the cold English skies for aid.

"How can they succeed?" he cried. "They are ringed by enemies. The Italian states cannot help them. The French have collapsed. The Germans will not fight. The Turks are waiting, and the Russians. England will do nothing. The States of America will do nothing. The longer we have to fight the less chance of success we have. Even if

Jellacić is beaten back, how can we stand against the Austrian armies? We have only our courage to fight with. The world will watch us die, without lifting a finger to save us."

"No, no, if you tell the world, if you speak to the people as you have done to me . . ."

"Petty bourgeois, minor landowners. How can they understand what is at stake? They cannot understand Hungary. They will not care. They have no breadth of vision."

Though he spoke of failure and despair, there was none in his voice. There was a magnificent contempt, an arrogance in his stance, in the pose of his head. Looking at him, the tall figure in its dark clothes, standing out so starkly against the winter scene, Anne was reminded suddenly and unwillingly of Hugh's words: "I don't like actors."

True to her word the Countess Sophia organised a meeting at Waterford Park shortly afterwards to discover what aid the neighbourhood was prepared to render to the threatened government of Hungary. Hugh went to it in a mood of detached curiosity, to

151

please Sophia and to keep an eye on Anne. The Countess had arranged the largest room in the house, the main dining-room, in the manner of a lecture hall, setting benches, with a scattering of straight-backed chairs, in orderly close-packed lines down the centre of the room. Her sense of occasion told her that anything other than this austerity would be inappropriate. The audience, sitting in a moderate but not unbearable degree of discomfort, could imagine that they too were sharing in the rigours of a war of liberty. Unconsciously Sophia had sought to attain the atmosphere of a revolutionary cell meeting amid the dangers of a hostile régime. What she actually achieved on that late December afternoon, with the thick curtains drawn against the freezing dampness of dusk, and the lamps casting most light on the dais built for the speaker, was the atmosphere of a theatre.

There was not much entertainment in the country during the winter months; any diversion was welcome, and the nearness of Christmas endowed this particular gathering with a positive air of festivity. Everyone came whom Sophia had invited and many more whom she had not. The fact that there were more women present than men was not surprising. Women were known to be more charitable and sensitive to suffering foreigners than their husbands, and besides, the chance to see the mysterious young man the Countess had had staying with her for the past weeks was more than anyone could resist. As the novelty of the navvies' presence in their midst had begun to wear off, the stranger had taken their place as the main subject for local gossip.

The room filled rapidly. Each seat, each space of hard bench was taken. The murmuring voices, the turning heads, the rustle of skirts, the waves and giggles, grew in number and volume. Anticipation generated its own excitement.

Most of the audience had no idea where exactly in Europe Hungary was and a general vague vision of Hussars galloping endlessly across great plains was the most they could summon up when they heard its people mentioned. But that, of course, Hugh realised, was entirely to Bathory's advantage. As soon as he appeared he won sympathy. He was what they had expected. A better-looking more romantic young man could never have galloped across any plain.

After the Countess's introduction, which she performed with grace and a touch of regality, Bathory spoke. He was impressive, Hugh admitted. He stood well and he had the ability to dominate an audience. He was not afraid to look at it directly and spoke firmly as if assured of his response. He was soberly dressed in dark clothes which suited the gravity of his purpose.

He began by outlining in simple terms the background to the insurrection—a straightforward question, as he told it, of black and white, of tyranny and injustice against brave hearts and noble minds. It was possible to feel the audience warming to him with every phrase he spoke.

Hugh glanced at Anne sitting beside him in the middle of the hall. She was gazing at the young Hungarian with an expression of absorbed attention, like an acolyte. Every word he uttered commanded her complete concentration, but Hugh doubted very much if it was revolutionary ardour that held her in thrall. Two rows in front he saw the bright red dress and neat head of Esther Wharton. He wondered what her expression might be.

An event of great importance had occurred within the last month, Laszlo was saying.

Something he had learned of only two days ago. Another act of treachery by the Austrian court. The Emperor Ferdinand had abdicated, bestowing the joint crowns of Austria and Hungary on his nephew, Francis Joseph.

"It was Ferdinand who accepted the April laws," Laszlo said. "It was he who gave his sanction to the new constitution, becoming as King of Hungary legally bound by it and all its reforms. Now he has abdicated, and by that act created a situation in which the Austrians will claim they may legally destroy our sworn constitution. Francis Joseph, they will say, did not ratify it. Francis Joseph has not agreed to it. The new monarch has not sanctioned it and therefore he is not bound to it. He is free, they will say, of any legal obligation to uphold it. It is yet one more example of the cynical ruthlessness with which the Hapsburgs treat the laws and the rights of men. It is yet one more example of faithlessness, yet one more oath broken, yet one more betrayal!"

There was a ripple through the audience, a hiss of indrawn breaths, a sigh of indignation. They swayed on the uncomfortable benches, leaning forward as if drawn towards the dais by the magnetism of the speaker. It was better

155

than they had expected. It was drama. It was enthralling.

Laszlo lowered his voice. "We do not know at this moment how the struggle is going. But we know that the full might of the Austrian armies has been turned against us. There is fighting now, at this very moment, in the towns and villages of my homeland. The enemy is marching towards the capital. Buda may already have fallen. Kossuth may even have been captured, arrested, shot. But even if that were so, we should go on fighting. We would die rather than surrender. Help us, my friends. Help us to gain our liberties as you once fought to gain yours. You who understand what freedom means, help your comrades. Put the weapons in our hands, give strength to our endeavours. Help us!"

Throughout this final peroration, begun so quietly in a low reasonable tone that made his listeners strain to hear him, Laszlo's voice had been rising; rising to a rhythm like the beat of music, like the slow persistent beat of drums. As he spoke the last words his voice soared to a shout. He flung his arms wide in that same despairing, appealing gesture he had made to Anne, standing in an empty country lane, and his voice rang out like a

156

summon to arms. The audience rose to its feet, clapping and cheering, roused to a pitch of high enthusiasm. Liberty, after all, was an old call, a popular call. The English responded to it instinctively. They felt that they were the authorities on liberty. The young man had been right to come to them. Where else could he go? Where else had so many battles been fought and won in that cause? It was a triumph.

The meeting ended in the atmosphere of a party. The people crowded round Laszlo, the men no less than the women, so that he was lost to Anne's sight, only a glimpse of that fair hair visible when he turned his head. The Countess came down from the dais, her eyes brilliant with emotion.

"Well, Hugh," she said. "What did you think of that?"

"A splendid performance," Hugh said. "Perhaps next week he could play Henry V for us."

"Hugh!" Anne cried. "How can you be so . . . so childish, so shallow!" She turned to Sophia, both women for once united against Hugh. "He was magnificent, Countess. Such force, such power, such sincerity."

Sophia nodded. "Passion like that is not

often come upon in English politics. That is what disconcerts our cold English Hugh. He is too reserved to appreciate it. I am proud of Laszlo Bathory. He is a true Hungarian."

Hugh was not put out. "He should collect a great deal of money from that eager crowd of well-wishers."

"I hope so," Anne said. "And for a cause even you, Hugh, cannot deny well deserves it. I shall go and congratulate him myself."

She swept away with an indignant susurration of silk skirts, a tall, beautiful girl whose every movement expressed a vivid, joyous life. It was as if Laszlo's oratory had been the fire she needed to melt once and for all the numbing misery of the last months. Fire was the word that came to Hugh's mind as he watched her. A flame, a burning flame. He spoke his thoughts aloud.

"He has set her alight."

"He has set us all alight," the Countess replied. "Except you, my dear Hugh."

"You relieve my mind, Countess. Then you don't think that—that—" he indicated Anne—"is more than the response of any of this audience?"

Sophia turned to follow, as Hugh was doing, Anne's progress through the room.

"That is difficult to say. You might call her response, as I could wish it to be, an awakened passion for our cause; you might call it, as you fear it is, an obvious infatuation with a handsome young man. But I think, my poor Hugh, that Anne will call it love."

Anne was not analysing her emotions. The involvement she felt with Laszlo, the pride she took in his success which was as personal as if it had been her own, were factors she accepted without thought. She made her way along the rows, apologising, nodding to acquaintances, smiling at strangers, borne up by her excitement. She edged impatiently past a group of chattering women and came face to face with Godfrey Bullivant.

For one extraordinary second Anne thought that she was going to faint. She had not met or spoken to Bullivant since the night she had seen him trespassing in their garden and at this unexpected encounter all the shock and sense of threat she had experienced at that time came back to her in a wave of fear. She stood still, the noise around her swelling and fading in her ears like the wash of the sea. She put a hand to her throat, staring at him as if mesmerised.

He bowed. "Good evening, Miss Torrance."

His voice was quite normal, his manner perfectly ordinary. With an effort of will Anne recovered her self-control. There was no reason to be afraid.

"Good evening, Mr. Bullivant," she said. "You have come to support the Hungarian cause?"

He shrugged. "I was in the district."

Normally, on meeting Bullivant, Anne would have spoken the few phrases politeness necessitated and then left him. But now she went on talking because she wanted to reassure herself that she had no reason for her uneasiness. She wanted to ask abruptly: "What were you doing in my garden at night, staring at my window?" but feared what might develop if she made the conversation so personal. She might embarrass and defeat him, but on the other hand he might have some simple, reasonable explanation that would make her appear foolish, and what would be worse, inquisitive, as if she had been deliberately spying on him.

"I will not ask you how the building of your railway is going," she said. "For I can see that for myself now."

"They are not troubling you," he said. "The men . . . ?" There was for an unguarded moment, soon gone, a fleeting expression in his eyes that disturbed her.

"I have never seen any of your workmen in Rivington," she said. "Not one."

"There," he said triumphantly. "Do you see?"

"What do you mean, Mr. Bullivant?"

"I have ordered your village to be out of bounds to the men. They are not to go there. I have forbidden it."

This definitive statement, so bluntly put, brought back all Anne's aversion to him. It implied an intimate interest she would not tolerate from him.

"There is no need for you to do any such thing," she said sharply. "Do not interfere with us, Mr. Bullivant. Do not make orders for this and that. Leave us alone."

His face flushed a dark red. For a man of such a taciturn, imperturbable manner it was the greatest sign of emotion he had ever shown her. He spoke with sudden intensity, his voice low. "Am I not doing that?" he said. And for the first time since she had known him, he used her name. "Am I not leaving you alone, Anne? Whatever it costs me?"

He gave her a long look, almost of hatred,

then turning, pushed his way roughly out of the room.

A few minutes later, Hugh, noticing Anne standing alone in a now empty corner of the room, went over to her. She looked up at him, her eyes dark. "Take me home, Hugh."

"What, have you finished already with the conquering hero?"

"Hugh, please——" To his surprise he saw that she was trembling. "I feel a little faint. Perhaps it is the heat in here."

He was immediately solicitous. His arm tightly around her, he guided her outside. On the way home she did not speak. She rested her head against Hugh's shoulder. She felt comforted by it and by his silence. Comforted and safe, as she used to feel with her father.

When the excitement had died down and the people had left, the Countess called Laszlo into the Ivory drawing-room where she sat with Esther Wharton.

"I have something to show you."

A heavy, elaborately carved wooden box was set on the table before her. She raised the lid of this box, beckoning to Laszlo to come forward. On a bed of ancient yellowing white velvet lay embedded the most magnificent emerald he had ever seen.

It was also the largest emerald he had ever seen; pear-shaped, cut *en cabochon* in a smooth dome. It was set as a pendant on a roughly-worked chain of yellow gold.

"The King's emerald!"

"I thought it would be fitting on such an occasion to show it to you," Sophia said. She removed it from the case, handling it reverently. "Look at the transparency, the colour. Flawless." Her long fingers caressed the stone. She held it up delicately by the chain so that it swung gently, turning about. Laszlo could not take his gaze from it.

"What depth," he said. "What richness."

"The legend has it that it came from the Egyptian mines, the same mines from which Cleopatra obtained her emeralds; and I think that is probably true. The emeralds from the Russian mines that I have seen have a yellower tone than this."

They were speaking almost in whispers, as if in the presence of something awe-inspiring.

"Can you not imagine," Sophia continued, "what it has seen? The court at the time of our greatness, more luxurious, more culti-vated, more crowded with artists and craftsmen and thinkers and scientists than that of Lorenzo the Magnificent himself. *Un altra Italia* Buda was called then, full of Italian sculptors, architects, painters, Italian goldsmiths and jewellers—perhaps an Italian jeweller cut this stone—and at the centre of it all, the supreme Renaissance man, the soaring eagle, the last true Hungarian king, the last Hunyadi. This stone, this very emerald may have hung round the neck of Mátyás Corvinus himself. And now, nearly four hundred years later, it lies here in our hands."

"It must be very valuable," Esther Wharton remarked in her small, flat voice.

"Valuable? Ha!" The Countess snorted with contempt. "It is priceless. It would be of exceptional worth as a stone alone, for a flawless emerald of this size is very rare indeed. But how can you value its meaning for us, for us Hungarians? No, you cannot put a price on that, can you, Mr. Bathory?"

Laszlo glanced away across the room to where the painted Sophia watched them, fingering her painted emerald. "The portrait does not do it justice."

Sophia raised her shoulders eloquently. "How could it?"

"I had not realised it was so fine a stone. I had expected it to be, perhaps, more barbaric, a cruder piece altogether."

"No, this was cut and polished by a master. The simplicity is that of art, not ignorance. That is what makes me inclined to believe in the more disreputable version of the way in which my family acquired it. I think it unlikely that the king would give this stone away, no matter what service my ancestor might have rendered him. But after his death, in the confusion of the elections, who knows?"

"If the opportunity arose, it would certainly be difficult to resist the temptation to 'acquire' it," Laszlo agreed.

The Countess smiled. "I shall give my ancient relative the benefit of the doubt and call it patriotism that impelled him to protect it, as I am now doing. It has always been well-cared for, that is beyond doubt. And I continue that tradition. I allow no one to touch it, no one but myself to clean it. I allow few people to see it."

"I am the more honoured," Laszlo said.

Sophia smiled and touched him affectionately on the arm. "You are Hungarian! Here, you shall hold it."

She put the emerald into his hands. He held it in his palm, looking down at it. Esther Wharton, for the first time revealing any sign of curiosity, got up from her seat and came to stand close beside him so that she too could examine it.

"Will you ever wear it again, Mrs. Wharton?" she asked.

"I do not know. I may, perhaps. I may . . ." Laszlo handed the pendant back to her and she replaced it carefully in its box. "Perhaps I shall wear it in Buda, eh, Mr. Bathory? When the battle is finally won, shall you and I take it back to Hungary together?"

"Would you like me to put it away for you, Mrs. Wharton," Esther said. "I should be glad to do so, to save you the trouble."

"I am not so old or infirm that I cannot take a small box up a flight of stairs," Sophia retorted snappishly. "Thank you, Esther, for your kind thought but as I have said, I allow no one, no one at all, to look after this precious jewel but myself. I regard myself as its guardian." She nodded to Laszlo. "I shall not be long and then we shall dine."

When she had left the room, Esther resumed her seat and picking up shuttle and bobbin continued the work she had been

166

doing. Laszlo also sat down. He leaned back, one arm carelessly resting along the back of the sofa.

"You had a very great success to-night at the meeting, Mr. Bathory," Esther said.

He inclined his head in acknowledgement.

"Miss Torrance was quite overwhelmed, I believe," she went on. "She had to leave, I understand."

"She felt faint, the Countess tells me," Laszlo said. "She is delicate."

"So many pretty women are," Esther remarked. "It is fortunate, is it not, that the plainer ones of my sex appear to possess so much stronger constitutions, for I have noticed that they do not readily find such immediate assistance as Miss Torrance obtained this evening."

Laszlo's fingers drummed a light tattoo on the top of the sofa. He was restless, paying little attention.

"Of course, it is far-sighted to take a doctor for a husband," Esther continued, "for then you are never without that instant help."

"You intend to marry a doctor, Miss Wharton?"

"No, not I. Miss Torrance. She is betrothed to Dr. Radlett."

Laszlo looked at her more directly. "Miss Torrance is engaged to marry him?"

"It has not been publicly announced but it is quite understood."

"No, I think you are mistaken. She is not betrothed to anyone."

"I assure you . . ."

"There is no indication of that in her behaviour." His interruption was brusque.

"You are so insistent, Mr. Bathory, that I realise I must be mistaken, for I am no authority on her behaviour. But I did see Dr. Radlett with his arm around her shoulders and I would not have thought Miss Torrance would allow such familiarity lightly. Of course, her disposition may be more openly inclined to show affection to her male friends than most. That may be another trait of pretty women."

"In my experience," Laszlo remarked, "it is truer of plainer women."

Esther did not reply to this. There was a silence of some moments. Laszlo was watching her now. She had never ceased her work during the whole of their interchange, her profile remaining bent to her task.

"You are very industrious, Miss Wharton. What is it you are doing?"

"It is called tatting."

"What an odd name. What is it?"

She turned her head and looked at him, and then with the manner of a magician producing wonders from the air, she slowly held up, with a slightly mocking smile on her face, the long strip of netted thread.

"Voilà!" she said.

He smiled back at her. "And what do you do with that?"

"It is for decoration. I have already netted a purse and shall use this to trim it."

"And then you will keep all your treasures in it."

She put the tatting down. "I have no treasures, Mr. Bathory. No jewels, no emeralds. . . ."

There was another pause. She glanced at him quickly and then away again, and then sat still, looking down at her hands folded meekly in her lap. Laszlo stood up and walked across to the fireplace. "The Countess takes a long time to put away her emerald."

"You heard her say what care she takes of it. She must be putting it in a very special place of safety."

"Do you know where that place is, Miss Wharton?"

Silence. His question hung in the air. "No," she said at last.

"You see, having seen it . . ." He began to speak rapidly, his accent, his foreign stresses on words, becoming noticeable. "I had heard of the emerald belonging to the Countess's family, but until I have seen it just now, I did not understand its importance. It is of immense value, immense historical and national value. I think without doubt it belonged to the king. It should be with the other treasures, with the royal regalia, St. Stephen's crown and the other great pieces. It should not be left here in an English country house where anyone can steal it. I have no doubt my presence here has been noted. There will be Austrian spies everywhere. They will not hesitate to take it."

"You alarm me . . . but how will they find the emerald?"

"They will break in and search. Could you not ask her?"

"Could you not ask her yourself, Mr. Bathory?"

"I do not wish to frighten her. Miss Wharton, I have taken you into my confidence, rashly, perhaps . . ."

"No, I do not think you will find you have

been rash. I appreciate your confidence. I understand it. I shall try and discover where the emerald is kept. . . . For the Hungarian cause, Mr. Bathory." She smiled again. Laszlo suddenly laughed. He came and sat down again, nearer to Esther this time, and lounging more carelessly than before, in a relaxed way he never sat when the Countess was in the room.

Esther took up her tatting again. He watched her, a slight smile on his face.

"I am fascinated by the speed with which you do that," he remarked after a while. "You have such small hands."

She turned her body in its red dress very slightly in the chair. "It is practice," she said.

The weather was holding up the railway. An iron frost, then brief falls of early snow, were followed by mild days of steady, penetrating rain that turned the earth to liquid mud, loosening foundations, causing greater hazards.

There had been too much delay in beginning the project. It should have been begun in the spring of the year, not mid-summer.

But difficulties in organising finance and clearing property rights such as those held by the Torrance family had made it inevitable.

Simpson, the sub-contractor for the stretch of railroad past Rivington, saw his chances of large profits fading; saw, indeed, the threat of ruin. If he failed to complete his contract on time, he would be finished. He had too little margin to survive. He was not a real gambler. It had been no gamble when he borrowed money and became a sub-contractor for another railway two years ago. An easy fortune had been his mark. It had happened to others, why not to him? There had been no depression then. There had seemed no end to the demand for railroads. Now he saw it all slipping away from him, slipping through his hands like melting snow. This had happened to others too. There was a navvy working on that very site who had once been a middle-man with his own equipment, wagons and so on for hire. Simpson could not bear to look at him. He imagined a knowing, satisfied look of malicious prophecy on the man's face.

When they could not work, the men hung about the camp drinking and getting deeper into debt. They found when the wages were paid out that most of their money already belonged to the tallyman. There were arguments between foreman and contractor about the hours worked and the pay due. There was a succession of minor accidents and one or two more serious which brought Hugh to the scene. He found an edgy, tense situation. It was not a happy working. The navvies were well aware that the booming days were over, that fewer and fewer railways were going to be built. They resented Simpson hiring local labourers at cheap wages. They said they could not work with them, they were too inexperienced and lacked stamina. Fights became common. Godfrey Bullivant, after his latest visit of inspection, took a room at a nearby inn, the Wharton Arms, and made that and not Birmingham, his headquarters.

At Christmas there had been a general exodus from Rivington. Hugh, to Anne's surprise, announced he was going to Lincolnshire to see his parents. He arranged for his practice to be looked after, kissed Anne in a cool fashion on the cheek and left. He was away for two weeks.

Esther Wharton departed by the same train. She had received a plaintive demand from her clergyman father that she should return for the holiday to her rightful place and duty as a daughter. Her aunt required her assistance in household matters and he required her presence in church. Her absence at such a time would be commented on. She obeyed, her thin-lipped mouth one straight line of resentment, but endeavoured to make sure of her position at Waterford Park by informing Sophia of the exact train by which she intended to return.

It seemed for a moment that she might have strained the Countess's hospitable nature too far. Sophia hesitated before she replied, looking the other woman up and down, observing the blue travelling dress and the bonnet, vividly trimmed with yellow, the white face, the pale eyes; her gaze fell on the hands in neatly patched gloves twisting and turning the handle of a travelling bag.

"Does it amuse you so much to be here, Esther?" she asked.

Esther said nothing. She waited. Sophia gave a slight sigh. She waved her hand permissively.

"Very well, I shall see that you are met at the station. Give my Christmas wishes to your father, if he remembers me."

"After all," she remarked to Laszlo, "she is

no more trouble than a cat about the house. And the life they lead in that derelict vicarage is not suitable for any young woman, however insignificant. They become preserved in their spinsterhood like wax-works!"

"You are very generous to Miss Wharton, Countess."

She laughed. "She is my charity for this year and will absolve me of many sins, I am sure. However, I am glad she is gone. My two stepdaughters and their families are descending on me for a week and Esther Wharton, I feel, would not fit well into the tumult of family life. We shall have, let me see, fourteen children here. Esther would have been trampled underfoot!"

Whether or not Laszlo took this statement as a warning to himself, he did not say, but when Anne called with presents at Waterford Park on Boxing Day, he had left.

"I did not question him too closely," Sophia said. "There is a certain secrecy essential to his work, you understand, Anne. You have seen him since the meeting, yes? And he said nothing of his plans? It means nothing, my dear. He says nothing to me. You must accept it. But he will be back. Oh, yes, he will be back. He is to make Waterford

Park the centre of all his activities from now on, so long as he remains in England."

The reminder that he must leave one day not only Warwickshire, but England, chilled Anne. "How long will that be?"

"I do not know, my dear."

"What is the news from Hungary?"

The Countess sighed. "Not good, not good. But let us not be dispirited. Let me see these beautiful presents you have brought us. How kind you are, Anne, the children will be enchanted. Let us go to them."

Anne was glad to be absorbed in the mêlée of a family Christmas. She and her mother had been invited out but had chosen to eat their dinner alone. The memories of their last Christmas were too acute—as Hugh had understood. They did not speak of it, but Anne, happier in her feeling for Laszlo and therefore kinder, seeing on occasion her mother sitting hand to cheek, staring into the fire, would come and sit with her and make a joke and tell her some news of the village, or simply touch her shoulder in silence.

She was tempted, strongly, to tell her mother her fears about Godfrey Bullivant. But she was held back each time by some strange sense of guilt as if she and Bullivant were linked by an incriminating secret. She knew she had not encouraged him in any way, yet the intensity of his feelings, whose true nature she had only recognised that night in the garden, and the concentration of his powerful personality upon her which had left her so shaken after their encounter at the meeting, forced on her an unwanted sense of responsibility. By telling no one, she could refuse to acknowledge it. She dismissed Bullivant and those two disturbing incidents resolutely from her mind, but his presence in the area, now almost permanent as he stayed to oversee the work on this stretch of railway through its worst difficulties, was a constant shadow on her life, oppressing her like the approach of a distant storm.

Its effect was to make her cling the more closely to her feelings for Laszlo. She nursed her own emotions, fanning them into a stronger blaze, with every meeting; and afterwards, when she was alone, going over and over every word, every glance, every nuance, trying to decide what they meant, what they might mean, wondering when he would speak openly to her of what she had become convinced lay understood in their silences. His enigmatic behaviour, his sudden departures and unexpected returns, stimulated her love of intrigue. Their whole relationship was a complex puzzle she delighted in trying to solve.

Anne had no mental or physical work exhausting enough to absorb her energies. Hugh's restraint and his growing professional involvement with his practice detached her from him, and since his rebuke about Arthur Toms she had, in an unconscious attempt at retaliation for the injury to her self-esteem, ceased to take the slightest interest in his work. As for the house, her mother and the servants ran that with smooth efficiency. Anne had little to do to vary the placid routine of village life, but feed and nourish her love and her fears.

Early in March, Mrs. Torrance invited the party from Waterford House to dinner. It was a full complement; the Countess, Esther Wharton in yellow silk brighter than any daffodil, and Bathory, Laszlo was unusually tense, tautly strung, his brown eyes bright, his whole manner almost feverish. Anne was beginning to understand the Magyar temperament. The news from Hungary, she decided, must either be disastrous or wonderful. She could only wait to find out which.

The fall of Buda in January had reduced Laszlo to suicidal gloom. The Countess had greater resilience. She knew her countrymen, it seemed, better than he did although she had been away from them so long. Her faith was justified. Before long the news came that Kossuth had removed the government to Debrecen and was carrying on the fight.

But now when Laszlo was afire with nervous energy, Anne's spirits were low. The encroaching railway was at last within sight of the house. On the very morning of the dinner party she had narrowly avoided a meeting with Bullivant in the centre of Rivington. He was there for professional reasons. Work was taking place on the land neighbouring on the Torrances' property; in another week or so the whole enormous circus now churning and toiling its way over the flat meadows would have engulfed those two bitterly defended fields.

It was not the noise of the railway construction that distressed Anne. When the men were working well there was not a great deal of noise. Nor was there much disfigurement of the landscape seen from the house. The great embankment did not come as far as this. Built to a gradually decreasing height, the downward slope carefully judged by the engineers, the line carried by it in a gently declining gradient was now on the level and would run so for the next few miles. It was the inevitability of it that depressed her. The visible defeat of her father's wishes.

When she saw Bullivant he was turning the corner into the lane by the church. Anne, walking back along the lane from the next village, was level with the row of cottages. There was another man with Bullivant; they were engrossed, discussing some matter. Anne took her chance and slipped into the porch of the Toms cottage, only to find as the door was opened to her knock by Mrs. Toms, a visitor there as disconcerting as the railway director. Granny Lane, so often dismissed by Mrs. Toms as an interfering troublemaker, was ensconced triumphantly in the best chair. The embarrassment this produced between Mrs. Toms and Anne was visibly enjoyed by the old witch woman. Anne left as soon as she could. It was clear that since her desertion, as she knew Arthur Toms would term the cessation of her visits, Granny Lane had taken over the rôle as provider of the magic medicine he so depended on.

There had recently been trouble over

Granny Lane's interference. Hugh had been waging war against her ever since a desperate farm girl had died following a draught bought from the witch to rid her of her child. It had been impossible for Anne not to know of this case. It had been yet another cause of dissension between the vicar and Hugh, besides being a major scandal in the village.

Granny Lane had denied giving the girl anything. Carrington, more than a little inclined to see the girl's death as a just reward for her sin, gave her his support. Hugh's remark that not only was he lacking in charity, but what was infinitely worse, common sense, was reported faithfully to the vicar and did nothing to improve the relationship between them.

Anne decided that she must tell Hugh what she had seen, but other matters put it out of her head and she only remembered it as she was dressing for dinner. She would speak to him before she completely forgot. She disliked Granny Lane as wholeheartedly as he did. She went downstairs and along the corridor leading to his rooms. As she did so the carriage from Waterford House arrived. Laszlo caught sight of her from the hall and while the Countess and Esther were being greeted by Mrs. Torrance and led away to remove their wraps, he joined her in the shadowy corridor, seizing her hands in his, his face alight with excitement.

"My dear Miss Torrance," he said. "My dear Anne. It is a whole week since I have seen you. You look beautiful, beautiful. . . ."

He raised her fingers to his lips and was kissing them as Hugh came out of his room. Anne could read his opinion quite clearly in his face. To tell him that she had been on her way to speak to him about Toms would seem to him, especially in view of their past clash over the man, a feeble excuse quickly thought up to explain being caught in this furtive fashion in a back corridor with the Hungarian. Anne had no intention of excusing or explaining any of her actions to Hugh. Since there was nothing whatever she could say that would not make appearances seem worse, she took the initiative and walked quickly down the corridor to the drawing-room, the two men following behind.

The effect that that piece of gallantry had had on Hugh was soon obvious. His manner at the dinner table was of an elaborate courtesy that Anne thoroughly distrusted. His tongue grew more genially offensive as the meal progressed. His target remained the Hungarian.

Victories, substantial victories, it seemed, were the cause of Laszlo's exalted state of mind. The young general Görgey had driven the Austrians out of Upper Hungary; the Austrian cavalry had been defeated at Szolnok. Not waiting for the winter to end, the Hungarians had been attacking on every front.

"We have four armies now," Laszlo cried. "One hundred and twenty thousand men."

"Don't you long to be one of them?" Hugh remarked. "What could they not achieve with you in their ranks, Mr. Bathory."

"When I was a child," the Countess said, "I remember being told of the Magyar warriors who rode to battle with their own gypsy musicians at their side. Played to war! What a magnificent idea. I wonder if they still do so."

"Perhaps Mr. Bathory would sing them into war," said Hugh. "He has an exceptional voice, and in constant practice."

"Mrs. Wharton is going to hold a reception for the Hungarian cause," Esther Wharton stated.

"What a pleasant idea, Countess," Anne's

mother said quietly. "The house is so suitable. It looks its very best, I have always thought, on such occasions."

"That is so. It is a house which responds."

"She is to wear the emerald," Esther said.

"The meeting we held at the end of the year was so successful," Sophia explained, "I decided something on a larger scale would be an excellent way of encouraging further interest. And with the news coming from Hungary so good, I believe the time is ripe for it. A month ago—no. But now there is real hope. That is why I shall wear the emerald."

"A great many people will be interested to see it," Mrs. Torrance said.

"Are there to be speeches this time?" Hugh asked.

"No, my dear Hugh, simply a reception."

"What a pity! With the talent you have at your disposal. Surely Mr. Bathory will be present."

"I intend to be," Laszlo said, glancing at Anne.

"Of course, since it was your idea . . ." Hugh continued. "I am right to think it was your suggestion, am I not?"

Laszlo said nothing. Anne spoke quickly to change the subject. "I wish Mr. Bathory could suggest how to deflect the railway away from us."

"How far has it reached?" Sophia asked. "We hear nothing at Waterford but gossip from the cook about the gross habits of the workmen."

"It has reached us," Anne said. "From my bedroom I can see the site clearly. They will soon be upon our two fields."

"Two fields," Laszlo smiled at her with an amused fondness. "When all Hungary——" He finished with a shrug.

"Yes," Hugh remarked, "but the two fields happen to be at the bottom of Anne's garden whereas Hungary——" He too shrugged. Esther unexpectedly laughed.

"What do you mean?" Laszlo said. "Are you saying the railway is more important than Hungary?"

"More important to Anne certainly," Hugh said. Anne began to protest. Hugh ignored her.

"When are you going back to Hungary?" he asked Laszlo. "Your countrymen are fighting with enormous courage against terrible odds. They could do with an able-bodied young man like you to fight with them. Speeches are all very well, but they don't turn back armies."

Anne turned to her mother in appeal. Hugh had at last managed to go too far. Laszlo half-rose to his feet. "What are you saying, Dr. Radlett? Please be certain what you are saying. Are you calling me a coward? Are you calling me, a Bathory, a coward!"

"I think this is nonsense which should be stopped," the Countess said.

"I entirely agree," Mrs. Torrance said. "I must apologise, Mr. Bathory, that you, as our guest . . ."

"Don't apologise for me," Hugh said. He was smiling and looked, Anne thought in bewilderment, calmly pleased with himself. "I apologise, Mr. Bathory. Unreservedly. I see you are not a coward."

Laszlo sat down. "Speeches may not win battles, Dr. Radlett, but they can buy arms."

"Indeed, you are right. I understand now the reason that keeps you here. Devotion—to one cause or another."

It occurred suddenly to Anne that the whole of Hugh's conversation had been on two levels. He had been concerned with something more than his surface rudeness, provoking Laszlo for other reasons than the

186

jealousy to which she had attributed his attack. Then what did he mean by "Devotion—to one cause or another"? Did he mean devotion to her?

Laszlo too appeared to have become aware of another purpose in Hugh's behaviour. He had subsided into quietness, his eyes watchful. In the silence that ensued the knocking on the house door sounded twice as loud.

Anne had been conscious for some while past of a vague noise in the background, a confused medley of shouts and laughter coming from somewhere out in the street. It had grown louder, closer, momentarily ceased. Now as the dinner party sat startled by the knocking, it began again.

"What is that?" Mrs. Torrance exclaimed.

"It is not the front door," Hugh said. "It must be the surgery." He pushed back his chair and was half-way to the door when the little maid rushed in. "Oh, madam, sir! A whole crowd of men, sir, calling out for you. Navvies!" She spoke the name as she might say "Lions!"

"All right, Betty, I'm coming. An accident," he said to the others. "They will have come for help." He left the room.

"That does not sound to me like the noise of men coming to fetch medical aid," the Countess remarked drily. "They sound very drunk to me."

They were very drunk, Hugh discovered. Eight of them, lounging and swaying around the outer door, one still hammering at it, others shouting and calling his name. All at the dangerous stage between conviviality and aggression.

"Well," Hugh said. "What's all this about?"

"Doctor." One lurched up to him and put a leathery hand on his arm. "Remember me—Ben? Old Ben Redhead? You put my arm right when it were broke. Look, look at this." He flexed his arm. His fist up against Hugh's cheek. "Iron, that," he said triumphantly. "Kill a man with that. Iron, iron. You done that, Doctor. He done that!" He swung round to his mates. They cheered. "Best doctor in the country. Mended Jack. Where's Jack. Here, Jack!" Jack was thrust forward, stumbling against Hugh's chest.

"I'm glad you are all so fit," Hugh said. "What are you, all my old patients?"

"All patients. Celebrate. Payday. Come on, buy you drink. Buy you drink, Doctor."

They pulled at him, drawing him away from the door. He stepped back.

"I'll get my coat. Wait," he said. He closed the door and went back to the dining-room.

"What is it, an accident?" Mrs. Torrance asked.

"No, fortunately. Just some of the men. I shall have to go with them for a while. There's nothing to worry about."

"Go where?" Anne asked.

"Oh, nowhere in particular. I'll get them away from the house."

"Are they hostile?" the Countess asked, as if referring to a tribe of natives.

Hugh smiled. "No. They wish to buy me something to drink to celebrate my great virtues as a doctor."

"You are going drinking with them?" Laszlo asked.

"Yes, and quickly too before they break the door down."

Laszlo leaped to his feet. "I'll come with you!"

"There's no need."

"No. I shall enjoy it. We used to go drinking with the workers in my student days in Vienna. It is amusing. I shall come with you!"

"As you wish," Hugh said. There was a great roar from outside. "Come, if you are coming." He nodded to Mrs. Torrance. "There is no cause for concern. But I should lock the door behind us, just in case."

"It is like being besieged," Esther commented. Her pale eyes had quite a sparkle.

There was another roar from the navvies as Hugh and Laszlo appeared and then the noise gradually faded away. The four women looked at each other.

"Bullivant," Anne said.

"What do you mean, Anne?" her mother asked.

"He told me he had put the village out of bounds to the men."

"Why should he do that?" Esther asked.

"Out of consideration for the people who live here, I presume."

"Well, they do not appear to be paying a great deal of attention to his commands," Sophia observed.

"They have done, until to-night," Anne said. She was coldly certain that Bullivant had withdrawn his order deliberately, as a demonstration of his power. He must have seen her to-day, turning to hide from him. It would have been sufficient to anger him.

"It will be a great nuisance for you, my dear Mrs. Torrance," Sophia said, "if you are to have intoxicated workmen rampaging up and down your quiet streets. I should complain immediately."

"No . . .!"

The Countess turned to look at Anne. "Why not?"

"Let us wait and see," Anne said. An appeal to him was what Godfrey Bullivant would be waiting for. "It may be an isolated instance. Because of the help Hugh has given them."

Nobody mentioned Laszlo's desertion of them. Anne tried to persuade herself that he had gone in case Hugh became involved in trouble, but she could not forget the genuine delight there had been on his face at the prospect of a night's drinking. She would not have thought that would have attracted him in preference to an evening in her company.

They moved to the drawing-room. "How very comfortable this house is," Sophia said, settling herself on the sofa. "And how charming to be by ourselves. Let us have a sensible gossip."

By ten-thirty the men had not returned. "We shall not see them now until the morning," Sophia announced matter-of-factly. "Come along, Esther, we shall leave our young friend to find his own way back to Waterford."

Anne sat a little longer with her mother. The room was warm, the only sounds the occasional shift and fall of ash in the fire, and the ticking of the hall clock.

"I am sure that was a new dress Esther Wharton was wearing," she remarked. "I thought she was poor."

"Probably the Countess gave her the material," Mrs. Torrance said. "It did not suit her very well, poor girl." She glanced at her daughter. "I think you should go to bed."

"I had thought to wait to let Hugh in."

"Neither of us shall wait to let Hugh in. He may be some hours yet."

"Poor Hugh," Anne said. "Carried off by his own patients. He will probably be in need of his own medicine to-morrow."

"Really, Anne. . . ." Her mother smiled. Anne smiled back. She began to laugh. Her mother joined in, both giving themselves up to the reaction from the extraordinary evening. But compared with her mother's plain enjoyment, there was an edge of nervousness, the slightest touch of hysteria to

Anne's laughter. She did not know indeed whether to laugh or to cry. When she went to bed she did cry, long painful sobs that exhausted her until she fell into a heavy and dreamless sleep.

5

THERE was no work done on the railway the next day. Only half a dozen men turned up. The maid coming back across the fields from the farm with the morning's milk saw them sitting on the ground, smoking pipes, their shovels and picks in a heap beside them. They waved their hats and whistled at her as she went by and one of them called out, asking for a drink of the milk.

"I'll give you fair exchange. I'll give you some of my milk," he shouted, holding up a jug of beer. They all laughed and the man who had called out stood up as if he might come after her, frightening her so much that she ran all the rest of the way home, spilling half the milk, and told the cook she wasn't going that way again, even if she had to go a whole mile round to avoid it. An hour later even those six had gone and Simpson alone was to be seen, pacing along the muddy track of the future permanent way, furious and fuming.

"Betty," Anne asked in a whisper, catching her outside the dining-room. "Is Dr. Radlett in?"

"Yes, miss, I took him his breakfast as usual an hour ago and he was there then."

"How is he?"

"Why, just as usual."

Anne went down the corridor and knocked on the surgery door. Without waiting for a reply she opened it. Hugh was sitting at the desk, writing. He looked up questioningly.

"What happened last night?" Anne asked.

"Mr. Bathory went home quite safely if slightly unsteadily at about two o'clock," Hugh replied.

"I didn't mean . . ."

"Didn't you?"

"Why were you so rude to him?" she said.

"I don't like him, I don't trust him. Is that enough to be going on with?"

"But, why . . .?"

"Anne, I am busy."

"Oh!" She turned away angrily.

He relented. He gave a sigh and as she turned, he stood up and grasped her hand. He said nothing, but looked at her very carefully, very gravely. She noticed how blue his eyes were, and realised with something of a start that it was a long time since she had looked at Hugh as one looked at a stranger, seeing his face afresh. She was so used to him as part of her family life, a reassuring figure in her background. Or he had been. Since he had come back to Rivington he had been different—awkward, unmanageable, elusive.

"Were they difficult to control?" she said. "The navvies, I mean."

"No." He let go her hand. "They were off the leash, that is all, newly paid. They only get paid once a month and it has become a ritual occasion for them. All work stops, the celebration and the recovery goes on for days. But they are quite harmless, you know, Anne. Not devils, or anything like that. And they are not moronic savages. They know a lot of things I don't know."

"Oh. . . ." She smiled disbelievingly. "What things do they know?"

"Fascinating things such as the specifications of all the engines at present running on the London to Birmingham line and what is wrong with them. And up what steepness of gradient which locomotive can haul what number of wagons before it starts running backwards, and who was killed by under-cutting a bank of earth and burying himself last year and who blew his arm off dynamiting on what workings last month and where they'll be tramping when this job is done. . . ." He touched her cheek with his finger, tracing the curve down to the chin. "Mr. Bathory thought they were excellent fellows and told them so many times. He sang with them too. In fine voice, as usual."

"So there was no fighting." Anne was relieved.

"Not with us. There were some less restrained rowdies at the Fox and Grapes."

"I wish they would finish and go," Anne said vehemently. "I hope that affair last night does not mean they are going to come into the village all the time from now on."

"Perhaps you had better stay indoors if you are so fearful."

"You think I take this too seriously, don't you, Hugh?"

"To be honest, yes, but I understand why."

"No, you do not," Anne said. "You do not, Hugh."

The navvies did not come battering at any more doors during the next weeks but they were more in evidence than they had ever been. They began to use the narrow lanes between the houses as shortcuts to the workings, they brought their carts through the streets and bought chicken and beef and eggs from the farmers. The hucksters and pedlars and ale-sellers and packmen who had followed them up the line, planted their stalls by the roadside and hawked their wares up and down, up and down, creating the atmosphere of a seasonal fair and throwing up an aura of confusion and cheapjackery. Anne began to realise that it could be true that nearly two thousand men were engaged on the site of this railway; there seemed to be hundreds on the Rivington section alone. To see them at work on a fine morning was an impressive sight, the chain of men extended along the line, each moving with purpose and knowledge, with few words spoken, the only sounds the pick on rock and metal on metal and wagons creaking along the roughly laid temporary way. A kind of rhythm emerged, the disparate figures settled into a pattern, order was imposed on chaos. The bed of the permanent way was levelled, the first ballast of broken rocks put down, the sleepers and heavy cast-iron chairs that held the rails in place laid down, the lengths of rail stacked in piles beside the site were lifted and swung and put into position, and the railroad moved on another few feet through the countryside. The gangs spread out across the fields, blocking up the little streams, building culverts, cutting away hedges; slow but implacable; very slow but always advancing, leaving their silver trail behind them like a snail.

The village people, inhabitants of an occupied country, reacted in different ways to the invading army. Most, after a few weeks of suspicion accepted them. They made life more interesting, more profitable, altogether more exciting. They brought possibilities with them, possibilities of change, of money, of contact with a wider world. Rivington could never be the same now they had been here. The villagers and the villagers' lives were being altered by them, and the children who chased after the swaggering figures strolling down the streets to the beer house in their fine round hats and their heavy boots, the working trousers tied round the calf with string and stained with the earth the farmers had held as their own and none others' these long centuries past, those children were to travel along the new rails to Warwick and beyond, even to London perhaps, or still farther, where their grandparents had never gone fifteen miles from Rivington in the whole course of their lives.

The village boys tagged after the navvies like terrier dogs. They spent days watching them. The women, when they found they were not chased or assaulted in their own gardens as rumour had cried they would be, grew less reserved. One or two even gave the navvies lodging in their village houses, much to the horror and disapproval of Mr. Carrington.

It was disconcerting to Anne to find her one ally against the railwaymen was the vicar. It was not the support she would have chosen. But even Toms, for instance, had come round. "If I drink with a man at the Fox and Grapes one night," he said, "I don't turn my head away when I see him next day in the street. I gives him a civil nod, same as I would any other."

Bullivant was often to be seen. His constant presence alarmed Simpson whose worry about his failure to fulfil the contract on time had led him to the extravagance of taking on more men. He thought Bullivant, a silent, brooding figure, a general contemplating a ragged army, was watching him with an ulterior motive, looking for a reason to cancel the contract, perhaps, and dismiss him from his precariously achieved position of authority.

Anne had not discovered if withdrawal of Rivington's immunity had been a deliberate policy on Bullivant's part. She believed he had kept the men away from the village on purpose, as he had told her, and that he no longer cared to exercise any control over where they went or what they did, but she could see how impossible it was for the railway to run so close to any village without in some way disrupting its life.

Her mother's continued tolerance did slightly surprise her. Anne had thought that, face to face with the results, she would regret what she had done. But on the contrary, Mrs. Torrance stopped to speak to the men walking past her garden wall and in wet weather she made no objection when they sheltered under her orchard trees, or ate their hunks of bread and meat sitting on her boundary wall. One very wet day with the track of the railroad turned into a river of mud, she went so far as to invite both Bullivant and Simpson up to the house.

Anne, trapped in the drawing-room by

their arrival, took refuge in a kind of mocking disdain. Both men were uneasy; Simpson full of social anxieties, Bullivant aware, it seemed to Anne, that a situation such as this gave her the advantage over him. She held the power now. What could he say in company in her mother's house? He had gone too far at their last meeting, revealing too much, to think she could now be deceived by his reverting to his former manner. When Mrs. Torrance left them to arrange for some refreshment, Anne taunted him in an oblique way by addressing provoking remarks of deliberate stupidity to Mr. Simpson.

"I am very much afraid of the conclusion of the railroad," she began.

"Why is that, Miss Torrance?"

"They say when the railway is finished, the sparks from the engines will set the fields on fire and the crops for miles around will be destroyed. What are the farmers to do then, Mr. Simpson?"

"You have been misinformed, Miss Torrance. There is no danger——"

"And the cows will stop giving milk. They say they are so terrified by the rushing trains that they quite dry up."

"No, no, you need have no fear——"

"But our chickens have stopped laying already, Mr. Simpson. How do you intend to recompense us for that?"

Simpson stared in dismay at the beautiful girl sitting upright in her chair, questioning him in this imperious and impossible way. He looked round to Bullivant for help, but his employer was silent, his bearded face sombre, his eyes watching Anne with an unreadable expression.

Anne's glance flickered to him. A shadow of a smile crossed her face. "You are very quiet to-day, Mr. Bullivant. You were always so talkative before about the railway and its virtues. And you spend so much time here. One would think it your sole interest."

"It is my sole interest, Miss Torrance," he replied gravely. "If I were to say to you that my life depended upon the building of this railway, I should be telling you no less than the truth."

"Indeed." The seriousness of his tone disconcerted her. She became even more careless in what she said, probing words tossed at him lightly, determined to win her victory over him, over her fear of him, by making him the first to turn away. "Does your life really run along such rigid parallel lines, Mr. Bullivant?

Have you no diversions at all? No sidetracks? No passions but railways?"

Bullivant stood up. "It has stopped raining, Simpson. There is no need to trouble Miss Torrance any more. Let us get back to our work."

"But you must wait for the refreshments my mother is preparing," Anne protested. "She would be very hurt if you did not. And poor Mr. Simpson is only just beginning to steam dry. I insist you stay." She smiled dazzlingly at Simpson. "You will stay, won't you?"

Simpson, half-risen from his chair at Bullivant's command, struck dumb by Anne's attention, hovering between them in an agony of uncertainty, was saved by the re-entrance of Mrs. Torrance, accompanied by the maid bearing a large tray. Now he knew what to do. Here were doors to be held open, tables brought forward, cups and plates to be passed. There was no question now of their going. They stayed for a full half-hour, the conversation which he had previously found such an obstacle, swept along by Anne's ripple of words. Her smiles were of such gaiety and charm, her manner showed what seemed such an absorbing interest in his opinions that by the time they left Simpson believed he had made quite a conquest.

The reception which the Countess was giving had grown from week to week in scope and grandeur. It had developed from an appeal for aid into the celebration of a cause. The emerald of Mátyás Hunyadi demanded it. It would not allow itself to be used merely to be shown off for the curiosity of a group of bourgeois English. It took charge. It turned them instead into its courtiers, imposed its own authority on them. And the news which had reached Waterford Park on the day before the reception added to the intensity of emotion that Anne and Hugh found there that night. The battle of Vat had been fought. Arthur Görgey had defeated the combined armies of Austria and Croatia. Hungary was free.

Sophia no longer remembered, Hugh saw at once, that she had expected anything of her guests but that they should rejoice with her. She overlooked the lack of culture and taste and quality among many of them that she would have remarked so closely and made the object of her malicious wit on other occasions. She ennobled them all that night. The house was charged with an electric excitement that was captivating and infectious. There had been originally no intention to have music, but now an orchestra played incessantly. There had been no intention of dancing, but Laszlo took Anne in his arms, swirling and sweeping her round to the music and calling to the others to join them, join them! Then the long room was filled with a swaying, laughing, moving crowd. The women's modest jewels caught the light as they turned, gaining fire and sparkle. Their faces were flushed with enjoyment and the delighted satisfaction that they had followed their instincts and put on their best gowns to come to Waterford that evening.

As the Torrances and Hugh had crossed the bridge over the stream in the park and had their first sight of Waterford, the house had seemed to be already dancing, its windows bright with the flickering lights of many lamps; and the murmur of voices and laughter had welcomed them across the lawns.

They were all there, all the immediate circle of people who touched upon Anne's life. Mr. Simpson had not been invited but

Godfrey Bullivant was there in a well-cut suit of evening clothes which only emphasised his bulk; beside Sophia's graceful femininity he looked massive. He greeted the party from Rivington with a nod and soon left them, talking when Anne saw him next to two local men of business. He was smoking a cheroot and drinking from a full glass of spirits. The glass in his hand was equally full every time Anne noticed him that night. He seemed to be avoiding her, for which she was grateful. She decided she had succeeded in vanquishing him. She thought he would not trouble her again and it was like a burden lifted from her.

Esther Wharton, while never giving sufficient appearance of movement to be said to hover, was nevertheless on the fringe of every group the Countess spoke to as she moved among her guests. Hugh wondered why when this was an occasion on which she could surely spread her wings; unless it was that the people whom Sophia sought out and who came first to her were those most prominent in the neighbourhood by reason of birth or wealth. Esther wished to be noticed, but only by those she considered important—perhaps that was it.

Hugh waited his opportunity to speak to Sophia alone. She looked magnificent. She flattered the emerald, hung on its gold chain about her throat, as much as its beauty embellished her. She wore no other jewellery and had chosen to wear a gown of great simplicity and purity of line.

Hugh kissed her hand. "I have never seen you look so beautiful, Countess." He spoke with perfect truth.

She smiled. "That is because I am feeling all the triumph of a conqueror. This is a wonderful night. It is strange. We never escape our origins, do we, Hugh? To-night"—she gestured round the room—"I am reminded of country balls when I was a young girl in Hungary, the same atmosphere of——" She hesitated.

"Of bucolic revelry?"

She laughed. "Always the *mot juste*. What do you think of the emerald?"

"I have never seen a jewel to match it. I feel I should stand guard over you in case Bullivant or some other were to snatch it from your neck and flee the country."

"Oh, I have no fears. This is an extremely law-abiding district, would you not say so? Besides I think the size of the jewel would frighten them. They would be afraid to touch it—or me. I am formidable enough, surely to protect it." She glanced at him. "Why did you mention Bullivant's name?"

"I don't know," Hugh said. "Perhaps he has a hungry look I had not consciously noticed before. Now I think of it, Mr. Carrington would have been a better choice. He has a penchant for elaborate vestments and costly silver church pieces——"

"Ssh, he is behind you——"

The vicar, so carefully polished in clothes and manner that he positively shone, seized Sophia's hand and began in a deep tone a dissertation on her virtues, her condescension to her inferiors, the generous opening of her house to so many and so on and so forth.

Hugh withdrew, with an equally polished celerity, only to find himself nearly colliding with Esther Wharton.

"Miss Wharton, I beg your pardon." His hand was upon her elbow, steadying her. "I am not usually so clumsy." Like a cat under one's feet, he thought. Wherever one turned she was there, so quiet, so—the word flashed into his mind—so sly.

"Please do not apologise, Dr. Radlett. It was I who was at fault." Her gaze went beyond him and instinctively he turned to follow where she was looking and to see Laszlo and Anne, gay and breathless from dancing, coming across the room to them. The anger he felt at the sight of them astonished him. He had thought jealousy was merely pain. Now he knew it could be rage.

"I saw you retreating from Mr. Carrington," Anne said. "For shame—leaving the battle-field!"

"It was Mr. Carrington left the battlefield when he encountered the railway workers, eh, Doctor?" Laszlo cried. He turned expansively to Anne who watched him, Hugh saw, with such eyes—

"The men told us this that night, you remember, when they came for Dr. Radlett and I went with him. Apparently your vicar decided it was time to bring the ungodly fellows to holy order and went up to the camp to preach to them. He created such a riot, they said, that four of the women pushed him bodily back down the hill telling him he had better learn to save his skin before he tried to save any more souls! Can you not imagine him, tumbling down the hill in full flight!"

"I think it courageous of him to go," Hugh said.

"Come now, do you defend him? I thought you despised the man."

"I don't despise all his actions."

Anne laughed. "Oh, Hugh, don't be pompous."

"You think him a brave man, eh," Laszlo said. "Well, we know you have strange views of bravery and cowardice, Dr. Radlett."

"I think I should like to dance," Hugh remarked. "Perhaps you would honour me, Miss Wharton?"

"Running away again?" Laszlo said. He was smiling, his brown eyes sharp and amused, his stance very relaxed. Hugh held out his arm to Esther; as she took it, as they turned to go, she said something in German to the Hungarian, spoken so casually and quietly that Hugh might have missed it. But he did not miss it and he wondered why she should say to Laszlo about him: "Do not antagonise him."

The evening was not going well for Hugh. There was no pleasure for him in holding the slight, light figure of Esther Wharton in his arms; no pleasure for him in dancing with the eager country girls whom politeness made it impossible for him to ignore, or in the conversation with the mothers whom the evening had excited into flirtatious forays of which the handsome young doctor was an obvious target. He caught glimpses of Anne throughout the evening, always with the Hungarian. Catch a sight of that distinctive blond head and there Anne would be.

Why had he come back to Rivington, he wondered. Why had he put himself deliberately into this vulnerable position? He could live with Anne's indifference, but he did not believe he could endure for very much longer her radiant adoration of another man. He felt, accepting another glass of the Countess's champagne, very much inclined to indulge in a prolonged bout of drunken self-pity. It seemed the only alternative to knocking Bathory down and carrying Anne away, like Lochinvar, across his saddle-bow.

"Dr. Radlett. If you please, Dr. Radlett." The butler had appeared unobtrusively at his side. "Your groom is here with a message, sir."

"William Broom?"

"Yes, Doctor. He is waiting in the hall."

As they made their way out of the room, Hugh looked round for Anne; but at this moment, when he wished to speak to her for an unemotional reason, she was nowhere to be seen.

William Broom looked worried and slightly guilty, a combination which Hugh knew from experience meant that something serious had happened.

"Who is it?" he asked.

"It's Arthur Toms, sir."

"I'll come at once."

He turned, but the butler had already interpreted his wishes. "I'll fetch your coat, Dr. Radlett."

"My bag?" Hugh asked Broom.

"In the trap, sir."

"Good." Waiting for his coat, he walked back to the door of the room. Anne was still not in sight, but Mrs. Torrance saw him and came out to see what was the matter.

"It's Arthur Toms, madam," Broom explained. "They say he's very bad."

"The same trouble as before?" she asked.

"Yes, madam. But worse than before."

"My husband thought it likely the perityphlitis would recur," Mrs. Torrance said to Hugh.

He nodded. "I am glad they have had the sense to send for me. Ah, here's my coat.

Perhaps you would tell Anne where I am gone. If," he added ironically, "she should ask."

"The butler can tell Anne. I shall come with you," Mrs. Torrance announced. "No, no, Hugh, I may be useful. I attended upon my husband when he cut a boy with an abscess in his side caused by this very complaint. You may require some assistance. I have my shawl. Come along."

Hugh did not dissuade her. To do so would be to waste time. What details Broom knew, he could tell them on the way.

The bedroom at the Toms cottage smelt of vomit, sweat and fear. The old man lay grey-faced and motionless on the bed where he had been born and where, Hugh realised as soon as he examined him, he would, unless a miracle occurred, very shortly die. He drew the cover back over the reddened, rigid abdomen and turned to Mrs. Toms.

"How long has he been ill?"

She stared at him, her round face blankly stupid. It was a look Hugh had seen many times before and it aroused in him a familiar mixture of sensations, frustration, anger, compassion. He spoke very gently, with great patience.

"It is obvious to me that your husband has been suffering for some time, Mrs. Toms. When did his pains and fever begin? Yesterday? The day before?"

She whispered her replies. "About three days ago, sir."

"Why did you not call me?"

She glanced at the figure on the bed and shook her head in a helpless, defeated way. "He wouldn't have it, sir. He didn't trust any doctor but Dr. Torrance, you see, and when he were gone . . . Then he thought—" She hesitated. "You see, he had a turn about a month ago and she cured him."

"She?"

"Granny Lane."

"I see." Hugh paused. "It was not a very effectual cure, was it, Mrs. Toms? She has been doctoring him again, I presume, these past few days. Has she been giving him the same medicines as she did before?"

"Yes, sir."

"Strong purges and emetics?"

"I don't know what they were, sir, but they didn't make him any better. Oh, he were in terrible pain, sir. And he could keep nothing down. It seemed to weaken him so much. I—I were frightened."

"Where is Granny Lane?"

"She went, sir. She said she done all she could. She said there were no more to be done."

"So you sent for me as the last resort." The sense of failure sickened Hugh. In this enlightened age, for a doctor to come second to the local white witch in the treatment of the sick seemed to him to be quite as much the fault of the doctor as of the ignorance of simple people such as the Toms. He should have been more observant, more insistent, more of a bully. More of a Torrance, in fact. The thought of the pregnant farm girl's unnecessary death at Granny Lane's hands was still bitter.

He left the bedroom and went downstairs to the kitchen where Mrs. Torrance was waiting.

"I am going to cut him," he said.

"Then it is like the case my husband saved?" she said. "You are going to lance the abscess?"

"It is more complicated than that," Hugh said. "I cannot wait for an abscess to appear on the external abdominal wall. As you may know from Dr. Torrance it is by no means a common development for it to form so conveniently. I don't think it will happen in this case. The inflammation is already far advanced. When I examined him, I could feel a hard lump deep in the man's abdomen. I intend to cut down to it and try and release the suppurating matter safely. If nothing is done, it will burst of its own accord and the man will die of peritonitis."

"You mean to cut right into him? Isn't that too dangerous, Hugh? Surely——"

"It has been done at least once before. Henry Hancock, a surgeon at Charing Cross Hospital, did it last year. He saved a young woman at the point of death. I know of his report. He advocates cutting down to the inflamed tissues and lancing the abscess even if it means section into a deep area." He looked at her. "It is the man's only chance. Treating him with opium would have little effect now. If I had been called sooner——" He shrugged. "But he has been subjected to such an assault on the affected organs by the woman Lane's poisonous rubbish that the illness has been accelerated beyond the point of sedative treatment."

He looked round the room. "I shall have to operate here. On the kitchen table. I must go across to the surgery to fetch a few necessary things. Perhaps you would stay with Mrs. Toms."

"Of course. And you must tell me what I may do to help you during the operation."

"Thank you. I shall need you." His manner was matter-of-fact and workmanlike.

While Hugh was gone, Mrs. Torrance cleared the kitchen table of the loaf of bread, the knife and the odd plates left on it. She removed the cloth and arranged the chairs to make a space round it. On Hugh's return, he and Broom carried the ill man down the steep staircase and placed him upon the table.

It was very hot in the small, crowded kitchen and Hugh took off his coat. Mrs. Torrance had found two large aprons and insisted that he put one on to protect his evening clothes. She wore the other. Hugh rolled up his shirt sleeves and before doing anything else, washed his hands and arms in the kitchen sink, a habit he had inherited from working with Dr. Torrance, who had possessed, unexpected in so exuberant and personally untidy a man, a passion for cleanliness and order in his professional work.

Dressings and bandages and bowls were put ready. Hugh's instruments were laid out and from his bag he produced the precious bottle of chloroform. To Mrs. Torrance and Broom, who had never witnessed anaesthesia, its effect was miraculous. Hugh took a piece of cloth and folded it into a cone. He carefully dripped a precise amount of chloroform on to this cloth and placed it with the open end of the cone over Tom's nose and mouth. Within a few minutes the man was unconscious.

Hugh half-smiled as he saw Broom staring in amazement at the prone figure of the patient. "William, perhaps you had better go outside with Mrs. Toms. This is likely to be a messy affair."

"I don't mind the sight of blood, Dr. Radlett. It's screams and groans I can't stand."

"Very well. If you think your hands will be steady enough you can hold the lamp for me. I want a clear view, no shadow."

"Like this, Doctor?"

"Yes, that's very good."

They were ready. Hugh stood for a moment considering his patient. Looking up, his eyes met the gaze of Mrs. Torrance. He said nothing but his lips tightened slightly. Then he took up his knife and made the first incision.

At Waterford, Anne and Laszlo were walking in the garden. She had complained of being hot. "The champagne is intoxicating me!" So they had gone through the shadowed, empty library and out of its long windows on to the path that surrounded the house.

The cool air was delicious, and so were the scents of the garden at night; the flowers grey, their colour lost, all lost but a fragile perfume, the trees like monuments, solid and black, the lawn a mysterious plain that stretched beyond sight. It was a night of trailing clouds; a night not moonlit, but not totally dark, even away from the glow of light the house spread round itself. Laszlo's face was visible to Anne but its clarity was blurred, and his voice, as if muted by the example of the night, was low and secret like the murmurs of intrigue.

A dreamlike languor enveloped Anne. The wine sang in her head, her body moved lightly, remembering the dance. She had had all evening a strange sense of unreality, as if this night was to stand alone in the ordinary pattern of her life. It was a culmination, she felt, a beginning or an end, and she thought it strange that events in a distant country she had known nothing of a year before, should influence her life and have the power to make her sad or happy.

"You are very quiet, Anne," Laszlo said suddenly.

"I was thinking," she said, "that there is nothing to keep you in England now. Your country has won its battle. You have no need to go on raising money for arms."

"It is not only arms we need money for."

"Do you mean that you will be staying?"

"Would you be sorry to see me go?"

She did not answer for a moment. She walked on ahead, then turned again to face him in a swift, graceful movement that made her pale skirt swirl round her like a wave of water.

"Would you stay for my sake?" she challenged him. "For my sake only?"

It had been like this, all these months, like a game between them, much implied, little said. The hand held and kissed with more than formality at greeting or parting, the compliments, the courtesies—Now she was breaking free of the game and she was asking him to break from it and this, she realised, was what this night had done to her.

"Why else have I been returning here each

time," Laszlo said. "It was to see you. I had no other reason. To see you."

When she said nothing to this, he smiled and said: "Give me your hand," with all the authority of a man whom women had never rejected.

Anne took the step towards him, and he took her hand and kissed it, and kissed her and it was with the relief of love admitted and the ending of a formal game that she slid her arms round his neck and kissed his smiling mouth.

"Anne," he whispered. "My beautiful Anne——"

Why should she remember at that moment the actor and hear Hugh's voice making its sardonic remarks? Why should she question the murmuring of her name so caressingly—"Anne, Anne——" like a deliberate evocation of passion? How could she judge the sincerity of love when she had never loved before. And she loved him; his arms tightening about her, his mouth on her mouth, how could she doubt it?

"It is cold," he said. "You will be cold. Come inside."

It was part of the dream as he drew her back into the dark library, darker than the night outside; darkness that was warm and welcome.

How sweet, sweet, sweet it was—to love, to give, to yield. Dizzy with wine, with love, with happiness after a year of grieving, she ceased to think. The softness of cushions melted into the softness of his arms, the low tones of his voice were soft, sensuous music. When the light struck her eyes it was like a physical blow.

Someone had opened the door of the library. From the lamps in the corridor behind, a shaft of yellow light fell like a sword blade upon them. There was a sound, an exclamation. The door was pulled to. It did not close entirely and light seeped into the room. Laszlo said something in German. He got up and Anne heard him making his way to the fireplace. He found the candlestick on the tall mantelpiece and struck a light. With the lighted candle in his hand, he turned and looked at her.

"I should have locked the door," he said.

Anne sat still, her hand to her face. The light had broken the dream, it had awoken her.

"Who was it?" she asked.

"I don't know."

"A man or a woman?"

"A man, I think."

Anne felt a churning in her stomach. Not Hugh. She did not want it to have been Hugh.

She stood up. "I must go back."

"Anne——"

"No. We must go back. People will wonder what has become of us."

"Do you care what people will think?"

She looked at him and saw that he was smiling. "I can see the spell is broken," he said. "Should I apologise for loving you, or for being prevented from loving you?"

"I should apologise," Anne said, "for having drunk too much wine."

"But it was not the wine," he said.

"No." Suddenly and unexpectedly she smiled at him. "It was your great Hungarian victory, and the Countess's emerald, and the dancing, and the night air——"

He laughed. "Then forgive me and I shall forgive you and all is well." He held out his hand. "Let us go and eat, Anne. This is the answer to all our problems. We must go and eat a great deal of meat."

At the corner of the passage outside, Godfrey Bullivant called to Esther Wharton who was approaching the door of the library. "Do not go in there!"

She stopped and was looking towards him in a puzzled fashion as the door opened and Anne and Laszlo came out. For a moment, no one spoke. Then Laszlo remarked: "If you are going into the library, Miss Wharton, you will find this candle of use to you. None of the lamps is lit."

Esther looked slowly from Laszlo to Anne. Her lower lip was sucked in as if she nibbled at it with her teeth.

"No, I was on my way elsewhere," she said, and walked quickly on.

"Here," Laszlo said, going forward and thrusting the candlestick at Bullivant so abruptly that he was forced to take it. "I believe you had intended to study a book or two. Now you have solitude to do so." He returned to Anne and with his hand on her arm, guided her away. Drawn to look back, in spite of herself, a moment later, Anne saw the candlestick, its light extinguished, lying on the floor. Of Bullivant, there was no sign.

Broom stared in fascination at the sight revealed by Hugh's knife. Layer upon layer.

It was like a butcher's shop, like the cutting of a carcase, except that the flesh of this animal was alive. The blood looked dark and ominous in the lamp light; life's blood. It seemed strange and wrong for poor old Toms to lie so still and quiet without a protest while the doctor slit and cut at him with bloody hands.

The lamp quavered.

"Steady," Hugh said sharply. "Hold it steady, man."

Mrs. Torrance was calmly sponging up the flow of blood, keeping the open, deepening wound as clear as she could. Hugh's hand went into the wound. Before Broom's astonished eyes, he groped in the belly of his patient.

"God, I can't find it!"

He muttered beneath his breath and swore. There was sweat on his forehead, running down into his eyes. It was stiflingly hot but he was unaware of it.

"Ah!" His voice rose in triumph. "Give me that knife." Mrs. Torrance put the one he indicated into his hand and Hugh cut down firmly with something like a deliberate stab. Broom nearly dropped the lamp as a spurt of evil-smelling pus leaped up from the wound, spattering them with its poison. Hugh let out his breath. "Quickly, quickly!" He threw out his instructions to Mrs. Torrance, who without a word spoken, worked on with an instinctive appreciation of what he needed. As fast as he could, as thoroughly as he could, he cleaned and drained the internal abscess, pausing at one stage to order Mrs. Torrance to put a few drops more of chloroform on to the soaked cloth that covered Toms's nose and mouth.

Broom's arm was aching with the effort of holding the lamp. He felt physically sick from the smell of corruption with which the evil thing in Toms's side had infested the air. In spite of his years with Dr. Torrance, he was afraid of illness. He thought the atmosphere in the kitchen full of noxious, infectious vapours, but loyalty and discipline kept him there, holding up the lamp, watching the dreadful wound at long last being closed and padded with clean dressings and bound about with bandages till all was clean and tidy again as a swaddled baby.

A rattling breath, a groan from the patient startled him. "Dr. Radlett!"

Hugh, washing his hands for the third time, dropped the piece of cloth he was using to dry them, and came to examine Arthur Toms. He felt his pulse and listened to his breathing, he put his hand on the pale forehead and pulled back the lids to examine the eyes. The anaesthetic cloth was put away with the soiled and bloody rags for burning and all at once it was still and quiet in the kitchen.

"Get a blanket," Hugh told Broom, "and cover him. We can't move him yet."

"What is to be done next?" Mrs. Torrance asked.

"We wait." He pulled a chair from the wall and placed it close to the table. He sat down on it and wiped his forehead, still watching Toms. He looked white and strained.

"You were successful," Mrs. Torrance said. "You have saved his life. I must congratulate you, dear Hugh. You have skills and courage greater than any I have known of. How proud my husband would have been of his pupil to-night."

"It is too early to talk of success," Hugh said. He looked up at her with a brief smile. "But I'm glad of your confidence—and I could not have managed without your help." While he spoke, he put his hand to Toms's cheek, estimating the temperature of his patient.

"Do you think there might be anything to drink?" he said. "I have a great thirst."

Mrs. Toms came in, white and fearful, staring at her husband as if he were already a corpse waiting for laying-out. Mrs. Torrance made pot after pot of tea, sending Broom over to her house to fetch their own tea-caddy and a jugful of milk. Hugh waited, gulping hot tea, watching his patient. At last, Toms's eyelids fluttered, his papery lips moved. He opened his eyes and groaned. Hugh felt his pulse and cooled his forehead with damp cloths. He seemed to Broom to be taking his pulse very often.

Hugh stood up and kicked the chair away. He asked Mrs. Torrance to hold a bowl ready. Toms's head turned restlessly, seeking escape, and then he was sick. A few minutes later he was sick again.

The violence of the retching alarmed Mrs. Torrance. "Won't it break open the wound?"

"The sickness is caused by the chloroform," Hugh explained. "There is little more we can do than we are doing."

Towards morning Hugh judged they could take the risk of carrying him back to his bed.

Toms lay there limply. He was no longer sick. But the strain of it all had been too much for his weakened system. While they watched by his side, Arthur's heart fluttered and quivered and went into a violent fibrillation and stopped. Attempts to revive him were in vain. After the hours of struggle and danger, of applied skill and desperate risks, Hugh's patient lay dead.

Anne did not hear the news until later that morning. When she received the message from the Countess's butler that both her mother and Hugh had been called away, she became concerned and left the reception. She went in spite of Laszlo's casual pleas to her to stay. She could tell from the amused look in his eyes that he thought she was running away from him and she admitted to herself that perhaps she was. Or rather running away from herself, from those dangerous emotions that she had not realised lay so near the surface, waiting to entrap her in treacherous webs of delight.

It was a relief also to escape from the possibility of further encounter with Bullivant, or the prim Miss Wharton. How shocked she had looked, Anne thought, and could not help but smile at the memory. How outraged! Such experience would be so alien to Esther that she could never understand it.

It was relief indeed to leave that emotional atmosphere and be driven in the Countess's carriage towards such prosaic and impersonal matters as other people's illnesses. It was a shock of a different kind to learn from the maid Betty on arrival at Rivington that the patient was Arthur Toms. The butler had neglected to tell her that.

She picked up her shawl and ran across the street to the Toms's cottage. Her mother came out to her. At that time Toms had not yet been moved from the kitchen.

"Go home, Anne," Mrs. Torrance told her. "Go to bed. There is not room for you here."

"How is poor Arthur, Mother?"

"Hugh is looking after him wonderfully. Everything will be well. We shall tell you about it in the morning. I shall be along myself presently."

Her mother's calm manner dispelled Anne's fears. She was indeed reassured enough to feel a slight resentment at the way in which she was dismissed. No one in Rivington appeared to consider her of any importance any more. And yet she was profoundly grateful now that Hugh had ordered her to stop her own visits to Toms, and that he himself had been sent for so promptly. Her confidence in Hugh had, unknowingly, come to match her confidence in her dead father.

How dreadful if the Toms had sent for her, she thought as she went to bed, or had neglected to send for any help when the attack came. And what dangers they might have run if they had turned to Granny Lane for aid instead of to Hugh. An uneasiness stirred in her at the thought of that old woman, the first faint premonition of disaster.

It lay curled inside her as she slept and awoke with her when she awoke. The house had an unusual air. It was strangely silent, lacking its customary bustle and motion. She dressed quickly and went downstairs. In the drawing-room her mother, still in her evening gown, was dozing in a chair.

Anne's gasp woke her. She struggled upright, pushing back her hair.

"Mother! It is after eight. What has happened?"

"Oh, Anne," Her mother sighed. "I am sorry to tell you, my dear. Arthur Toms is dead." She told her the story of the night's events. She herself had been sitting with Mrs. Toms. She had been back about an hour and had intended to go straight to bed, but somehow—she broke off.

"The operation—was that not a very dangerous thing for Hugh to do?" Anne said.

"Yes, I suppose it was. And Toms proved to be too weak to survive it. But if Hugh had not attempted it, Toms would have died in a worse way. No, if any fault has to be placed it is with that poor foolish man himself for putting himself in the hands of Granny Lane."

"Where is Hugh, Mother?"

"I am sorry to say I do not know, Anne. I hope he has gone to rest. Anne . . ."

But Anne was running down the passage to Hugh's rooms. She found him sitting in her father's chair in the consulting room, staring into space.

"Hugh . . ."

He looked up at her. "Good morning, Anne. You have heard the news, I see. It was foolish of poor Toms to die, was it not, just when I had saved him."

"You did your best, I know, Hugh."

"I did more than my best, Anne. I was

brilliant. Your father would have been proud of me. Even your mother said so. All the village will applaud me, particularly Mrs. Toms."

"You are bitter. But Mrs. Toms must know that the fault lies with Granny Lane. My mother has told me——"

"Granny Lane will attack, Anne, before she can be attacked. I know old women like that. I constantly fall foul of them because I will not tolerate them. They commit murder too frequently."

"That is strongly put."

"I feel strongly. Or perhaps I say that to prevent calling myself a murderer. Was I wrong, Anne, to attempt such a radical operation? If I had decided against it, would he really have died? If I had waited might not the abscess have become more accessible? You see, it is myself I have put on trial these long dawn hours. And now, because of this death, because of my action, how many more people will run to ignorant old women for a mixture of owl droppings and cow's urine and heaven knows what useless concoctions, when they should come to me. You know what I should have done, Anne. I should have walked out of that house the moment I knew they had allowed that ignorant old woman to treat him. Toms's death would have been hers. The victory all mine."

"You could not have done that," Anne said. "You are a doctor."

He looked at her wearily. "No, I cannot escape that, can I? I am a doctor."

He held out his hand to her, as Laszlo had held out his hand to her in the gardens at Waterford; but in such a different manner, Anne thought, and for so different a reason. Hugh had never spoken to her in this way before, with such frankness and humility. For the first time, because he was tired and bitterly disappointed and weighed down with a sense of failure, he talked to Anne as freely as he was accustomed to talk to the Countess. And for the first time Anne gave, rather than received, comfort to him. For though he would never ask it, except by that one gesture, in her silence and the warm clasp of her hand as she knelt beside his chair, that was what she brought him.

6

ARTHUR TOMS'S death divided the loyalties of the villagers. As Hugh had foreseen, Granny Lane put about an elaborate story to mask the truth. In her version, Toms had been recovering under her care until Dr. Radlett heard of it, when he had come at dead of night, banished her forcibly from the bedside and proceeded to butcher the helpless man to death. Mrs. Toms, overwhelmed with bewildered grief, made no pronouncement against this. And the facts were, as anyone must admit, that Toms was alive when Granny Lane left him and dead by the time Dr. Radlett had finished with him.

Against this the villagers placed their instinctive distrust of the woman who did nothing to dispel the aura of witchcraft and ancient magic that surrounded her, and their liking for Hugh. He was not Dr. Torrance; he had been away from the village for long periods of time in foreign parts of the country, but he was Rivington born and bred and they all knew him. Besides, Mr. Carrington did not like him and the vicar was not one of them.

If Carrington had attacked Hugh on this matter, Rivington would have rallied to him as a man. At Toms's funeral, however, Mr. Carrington spoke extravagantly and unoriginally about resignation and the full span of life drawing to its close and even went so far in his sermon as to quote a line or two from "Gray's Elegy." He was concerned with the refinement and polishing of his oratorical style in confident anticipation of being called to higher office in the church, and to him a funeral was an excellent opportunity to give full range to the darker tones of his rich voice and practise the flow of his rhetoric; but the facts of death of a common labourer did not interest him.

Hugh, though he paid no attention to whatever malicious rumours reached him, could not throw off the burden of responsibility. He remembered Arthur Toms from childhood. He had never thought he would be the instrument of his death.

"How many people must we sacrifice before we know what we can do and what we dare not do?" he said to the Countess. "If

237

there had been some way in which I could have judged more closely the condition of Toms's heart. . . . As it is we are working in the dark, and too often destroy what we mean to heal."

"Would you hesitate to do such a thing again?" Sophia asked him.

"Yes I would."

She gave an impatient shake of the head. "Then you would be wrong. Hugh, you would not be talking in this faint-hearted way if other matters had not combined to depress you."

"By other matters, you mean Anne?"

"Yes. Why do you not go away for a few days? A change of scene would be beneficial to you. You see, I am become your doctor. I know what is needed for your cure. A different atmosphere. Other people, other sights, other problems. Above all, you need a pretty girl to look into your eyes and tell you how handsome and accomplished you are and how she is unable to resist you. A few tender triumphs of that sort would soon wipe out failure. You have been leading too celibate a life here in the country, Hugh."

"The gratification of the senses is the cure for all?"

"Perhaps not the cure, but it would certainly assuage some of the pain."

Hugh laughed. "My dear Countess, if Mr. Carrington could hear you speaking now, he would bar you from his church."

She leaned forward and patted him affectionately on the arm. "Ah, my dear Hugh, what a difference there is in you when that black melancholy lifts from you and those gloomy frowns are dispersed. Do not come and see me again until you have been to London. Then bring me talk of nothing but gossip and scandal. That is an order!"

Hugh was not averse to the idea of leaving Rivington for a while. He considered it as he walked back along the drive of Waterford Park. Although he and Anne were now closer than they had been since he returned to the village it was not the kind of closeness he wished for. She was friendly and sympathetic. He could say, with truth, that she cared for him. But he would have given all her sisterly concern for one such passionate glance as he had seen her exchange with Laszlo Bathory on the night of the reception.

"Dr. Radlett! Dr. Radlett!"

He turned and saw Esther Wharton hurrying towards him. She was bonneted and

239

shawled and gloved and was clearly on her way to make a visit.

"How fast you walk, Dr. Radlett," she said smoothly. "I had nearly to run to catch up with you."

"Heaven forbid that you should ever run, Miss Wharton. What may I do for you?"

"Do for me? Why, nothing. I just saw you ahead of me and thought we might walk down the drive together."

"Ah. . . ." They began strolling at a leisurely pace towards the wrought-iron gates of the park.

"It is the day of the carrier's cart," Esther explained. "I am going to Warwick to visit a friend."

"That is a long way," Hugh commented, "and a slow way of travelling. I am surprised the Countess has not sent you in a carriage."

"I am of an independent disposition, Dr. Radlett. Mrs. Wharton is very kind to me but I do not wish to trouble her about every detail of my day. I like to rely on myself."

"Very commendable."

Her pale eyes glanced at him and then away. "Dr. Radlett, you are teasing me. You are a great man for making fun, are you not. For my part, I think it a likeable quality in you, but perhaps others——" She broke off.

After these months, Hugh was beginning to know Esther Wharton. She had something to tell him; something he would not enjoy hearing, and this was the reason for her desire for his company. The interrupted sentence was intended to provoke him into asking the correct leading question.

He did not ask it. He accepted her silence. She was disconcerted but soon recovered and he was amused to find her approaching her object from another tack.

"I was sorry for that poor man who died. And how strange it was that it happened on the night of the reception. I cannot help thinking how differently some of us might have behaved had we known the struggle for life that was in progress."

"Did you behave very badly then, Miss Wharton?" Hugh asked.

She stared at him with barely repressed impatience. "No, not I, not at all."

"But some did?"

He had impeded her, and made gentle fun of her, but he had asked the right question at last. She sighed and looked away with a further show of reluctance to divulge her secrets.

"You refer to Miss Torrance, perhaps?" Hugh suggested, and very nearly smiled at the irritated jerk round of her head. But what she went on to tell him pricked him quite as much as she could have wished, though he did not let her see it.

"As I believe I once told you, Miss Wharton," he merely said, "Miss Torrance is not my fiancée. Her behaviour cannot be my concern."

"But you are her friend, Dr. Radlett, and the friend of her family. Surely you could warn her that her reputation is in grave danger?"

"Is it in danger?" Hugh asked. "What exactly have you told me, Miss Wharton. That you saw Miss Torrance and Mr. Bathory coming out of the library. That is all."

"Is it nothing that the library was in darkness and Mr. Bullivant called out to me quite vehemently not to go into the room? That, I think, speaks a great deal!"

It did indeed. It implied considerably more than Hugh wished to think about. He endeavoured to call off Miss Wharton's clamouring hounds.

"Does a private meeting between two

people who no doubt mean to marry——"

"No!" She interrupted him with unexpected brusqueness. "No, I do not think that is so. There is no marriage intended."

Hugh paused, looking at her curiously. She was a woman who looked better indoors than out. The sunlight was not kind to her. It revealed in her face faint lines marked by—what emotion, Hugh wondered. Discontent? Envy? Her eyesight seemed to suffer in bright light. She blinked and put her hand up to shade her eyes. Or was it to hide their expression from him? Hugh noticed certain things about her with the automatic observation of the doctor. She had grown thinner in the face this past month. Perhaps she found it more difficult than she let it appear to live as the poor relation in a wealthy house. How much strain and tension lay behind the meek surface? That there were unsuspected passions and rages boiling away beneath that placid exterior Hugh had long ceased to doubt. It was what would happen when they could no longer be contained that interested him.

"Why do you say there is to be no marriage?" he asked. "What do you know about Bathory?"

"Nothing," she said. "But he is a foreigner and means to go back to Hungary. I would not wish Miss Torrance to be made unhappy, and then to find also that she had lost her good name."

"There is no danger of that that I can see," Hugh remarked. "Only you and Godfrey Bullivant witnessed the incident that causes you such concern. Neither of you are gossips, I am sure."

She avoided his eyes, looking down at her dress and picking at a loose thread in a skirt seam. It snapped between her small fingers and she threw it away.

"I am grateful for your reassurance, Dr. Radlett. I shall cease to worry about it. I hope you do not think I was wrong to mention it. I felt it necessary for Miss Torrance's sake."

"It was very creditable of you, Miss Wharton. Duty and friendship I can see, are more than mere words to you."

She glanced at him with that sideways, darting look of hers, but his grave manner apparently persuaded her of his seriousness. They were approaching the road and as if their discussion was now quite closed, she asked Hugh if he knew the exact time. "I do not wish to miss the carrier."

"You are exactly on time, Miss Wharton. I can see him coming."

He waved away the lodgekeeper and opened the gate to let Esther pass through. In a few moments the cart pulled up and he helped her aboard.

"Thank you, Dr. Radlett, I am very grateful." As they drove off, she turned her head and looked back at him and there was something in her face, an unusual intensity of expression, that puzzled him. What, he wondered, was Esther Wharton really up to?

Hugh made several calls before returning home. He was, he realised, becoming almost obsessive about his care of his patients and he could see it worried the poorer ones that they could be facing a larger bill than they had planned when they first called him in. He reassured them, thinking that he was maintaining a very reasonable standard of folly by creating anxiety in the minds of the very people he wished to help, to whom his presence should have a calm and soothing effect.

He arrived back at Rivington in the early evening. As he opened the door, the sound of Anne's laughter came from the drawing-room followed by the unmistakable voice of Laszlo

Bathory. Hugh went through to his rooms and immediately sat down and wrote a letter to the colleague in the district with whom he had established an arrangement of mutual convenience asking him to be available for any emergencies that might arise in his absence. He called Broom and despatched him with the message and then went to his bedroom to pack.

The old morning-room which Mrs. Torrance had given him for his private use was adjacent to the consulting-room, a long, pleasant apartment whose two tall windows overlooked the garden. Besides the bed, wardrobe and chests of drawers, Mrs. Torrance had furnished it with a long, cushioned sofa and wing chair, the table from which Hugh ate his breakfast and any other meal he wished to take alone, a bureau, bookcase, several lamps and everything that might be needed to give him comfort and privacy.

The door opened on to a passage which ran from the front hall of the house to a glass door giving on to the garden. When Anne decided to show Laszlo the beauty of their garden on this early summer evening, it was along this passage they came. In his sudden impatience to be gone, Hugh had left his door open and Anne stopped to see the valise on the table and the jumble of shirts and socks being flung into it.

"Hugh, what are you doing?"

He came to the door. "I am going away for a few days." He saw Laszlo standing beside Anne and volunteered no further information.

"This is very sudden. Where are you going?"

"To London."

"On business, Dr. Radlett?" Laszlo inquired indifferently.

"No. On pleasure solely," Hugh remarked in a dry tone. Laszlo smiled as if he did not believe him.

"I cannot imagine you whiling away your time so carelessly, Dr. Radlett. You always seem such an earnest fellow, always so concerned with the good of your fellow men."

"Like you, Mr. Bathory," Hugh agreed. "Busy about your revolution."

Anne looked annoyed and Laszlo laughed. He seemed in a very good temper, very ready to be amused. "Do you travel to-night?"

"No. I have to see one or two patients yet. I shall leave early to-morrow."

"Then do not be surprised to have me as a travelling companion. I also am to go to London to-morrow."

247

Anne turned to him in surprise. "You did not tell me that."

"I was about to tell you in the garden, Anne, in a more private way. I have some business to attend to there that cannot wait. But I shall be back again before you have time to miss me."

As he spoke, he put his arm in a familiar, almost careless way, round her shoulder. He did not draw her closer to him, but just let his hand remain there—the wrist resting on the point of Anne's shoulder, the fingers hanging, loosely relaxed—in a way that was to Hugh more revealing, more intimate, than if he had deliberately embraced her. To Hugh, Laszlo was claiming possession, and his own unguarded reaction was mirrored in the glance he gave to Anne. She was held by it. For a long instant, she could not drop her gaze from his. There was a tension between them, a communication as eloquent as speech. She was shaken by it. Laszlo's arm on her shoulder was as heavy as lead. He, not Hugh, was at that moment the intruder. He had no place there. She felt in some way that she had wrongly allowed him to come between herself and Hugh. Then Hugh abruptly shut the door in their faces and the moment was over.

"Your doctor friend is a little discourteous," Laszlo said. "Shall we go into the garden, Anne." She sensed that he was pleased and she did not like him for it.

As they went out into the still sunlit garden, as they walked through the trees of the orchard, as Laszlo talked in an easy way about some neighbours he had recently met, Anne watched him and considered him. She had noticed since the night of the reception a change in his attitude to her. It was ridiculous to expect him not to be freer, more demonstrative towards her but she felt, and she did not know why, that there was something lacking in his behaviour. It was stupid to feel that in such affection there was calculation, or in the warmth and passion he had shown her, there had been coldness. But he seemed more and more to her to be a man whose emotions were easily controlled. Whereas Hugh, she was beginning to realise, fought many battles with his feelings.

On the night of the reception Laszlo could have been angry with her when she had insisted on leaving. He could have been apologetic, distraught, overwhelmed, persistent. He had been none of these things. He had been amused.

How deep did his feelings go, she wondered. For that matter, how shallow were her own? Perhaps it was fear of her own passions that had made her withdraw since that night; perhaps it was her own coldness she was imputing to him. She had been in the past weeks often ashamed of herself. Not of her behaviour at the reception, but of her manner since. She felt she should be one or the other, impetuous and loving, or cautious and conventional. But she was both, turn and turn about. She did not know what she was or what she wished to be. She only knew that Hugh could, with a glance, make her despise herself.

"Anne." Laszlo had stopped in front of her. "Anne, I am sorry I did not tell you before that I was to go to London to-morrow. Do not be so angry with me about it."

She looked up at him with a slightly distant expression in her eyes. He put his hands on her shoulders and kissed her.

"Do you think you would enjoy living in Hungary?" he said.

She was startled out of her self-absorption. She tilted her head back the better to read his expression. The smiling brown eyes were watching her with the amused satisfaction of someone who has presented a delightful, long-yearned-for gift to a favoured recipient, and who is waiting with pleased anticipation for the unwrapping of the parcel and the cries of appreciation.

"Perhaps you would prefer Paris?" he inquired. "It is a favourite city of mine."

"Laszlo, I——" He laughed out loud at her astonishment and kissed her again, teasing her with his lips, with light, tender, affectionate kisses.

"You will not forget me when I am away in London?"

"Laszlo, when you say—? Do you mean you are going home soon, to Hungary?"

"This will be the last visit to London, I think I shall have to make. I may be away for a week, or less, or more. When I am back, we shall have a serious talk. Yes, Anne, a serious talk." He had released her and now moved away as he spoke, glancing towards the gate in the wall.

His moods swung so fast; there was a mercurial change from the gaiety of the moment before to this obvious impatience to be off. Having achieved whatever it was he had planned, he was ready to leave. He kissed her hand in an almost absent-minded return to formality.

"Are you not dining with us?" Anne asked, and immediately wished the words unsaid. They made her seem anxious, too eager to detain him. It occurred to her how often lately she had found herself analysing the most direct and simple of her own remarks as if they might be interpreted as bearing another, hidden, meaning, part of a calculated scheme. She and Laszlo were still playing a game, she thought. They had not broken free, after all.

"Anne, I am so sorry I cannot stay," he replied. "I have many matters to see to before I go. I shall see you as soon as I come back." He paused. "Will you be faithful to me while I am away?"

Anne said nothing, merely smiled, and there was an instant when Laszlo looked puzzled, even fractionally alarmed, until he realised that she was smiling because the idea of her unfaithfulness was so ridiculous. It touched her to think that he could have been even for a moment serious in his doubt. It made him more vulnerable. How little she really knew of him, she thought. And she admitted to herself, with growing insight, that it was his handsome looks, his exotic foreignness, the flattery of his attention to her, that she had fallen in love with, as if she had caught some gorgeous bird in her net. But even knowing that, she still surrendered willingly to his charm. To be in love gave such importance to days that might be dull. It brought drama to a life that at present lacked much purpose. No, she would not easily give up such a feeling. She and Laszlo had more in common than she knew.

Hugh could never afterwards make up his mind if Laszlo had always intended to go to London on the particular day on which he himself travelled, or if it was a decision made on the spur of the moment. It seemed, later, when he realised how nearly he had stumbled on the truth, a dangerous risk for Laszlo to have taken. But he was a gambler by nature, and he had his own reasons for wishing to keep a watch on Hugh. The trouble was that like many intelligent but arrogant men he misjudged his opponent. He was too clever. By the elaborateness of the game he played on Hugh, he succeeded only in strengthening, not quenching his distrust.

Hugh had not really expected to meet him on his journey and was not surprised when he boarded the London train at Coventry without a sight of him. It would have been difficult to avoid seeing that distinctive figure at any of the early stages; from the first at the station at Warwick, from where the three and a half mile branch line, only completed five years before, crossed the Avon to Leamington. From Leamington the train took him to Coventry and the junction with the "Premier Line", the London and North Western railway to London. It was into this network that Bullivant's line would fit, extending the line from Warwick as far as Worcester. Warwick would grow further in importance with the completion of yet another railway, then under construction, to link Oxford and Birmingham via Warwick. Whether or not Bullivant felt he was in a competitive race with this railway, the pace of his building had increased. As he drove with Broom along the Warwick road, Hugh saw obvious signs of it.

"They must have brought another thousand men in," he commented. "Look at them working over there, William. There seem to be twice as many as when I last came past here."

"They're building a station there," Broom said. "Seem anxious to get it finished, I don't know why when they've a good few miles of track to lay yet. Not much more than a halting place, they say, but it'll be quite convenient for Rivington, won't it, sir? You won't need me to drive you into Warwick, then."

"I suppose not."

At Warwick station, Hugh got down and took his bag from William. "I don't think Mr. Bullivant will have finished his railway in three days, so you'd better come and meet me."

"Right you are, Doctor. Three days, you said."

"I'll let you know if I stay longer."

On the local line the carriages were crowded. Hugh, unwarily entering the least crammed, was seized upon by a patient, a wealthy magistrate with several complaints, most of them imaginary, for which he proceeded with much energy to endeavour to get some free advice. Hugh endured him stoically, managing to escape at Coventry. He had a short period of time to wait before the London train came in, long enough to observe his fellow travellers. Laszlo was not amongst them. The main line train was also busy, but Hugh found himself a seat in an uncrowded forward carriage. The only other occupants were a middle-aged Manchester businessman who was apparently sleeping his way to London, and a well-dressed young woman with a child.

At Rugby she got off the train. She had a trunk and two boxes as well as the child and her cries for a porter went unanswered. Hugh handed her down the cases from the roof of the carriage and eased the trunk on to the platform himself. He rested the trunk on its end and turned. Laszlo was at his elbow.

"Well, Doctor," he said, smiling. "Do you never stop performing your works of charity?" He turned to the woman. "Madam, I saw your difficulties. There is a porter approaching."

He was even more elegantly dressed than usual. He was carrying a small black leather case and a gold-headed cane Hugh recognised as once belonging to Sophia's husband, George Wharton. Seeing this godlike figure appearing from nowhere in the midst of Rugby station, it was hardly surprising that the woman should bestow her smiles and words of gratitude on him rather than on Hugh.

"May I join you?" Laszlo asked when she had gone on her way, and climbed nimbly aboard. He tossed the cane on to one of the other seats, but kept the black bag by his side, leaning back with his hand resting lightly on the handle. Hugh closed the door and sat down. The carriage lurched with a preliminary movement. He asked a question but his words were lost in the sudden impatient cry of the locomotive. The carriages jerked and swayed with the first pull forward of the engine. They moved, protesting with creaking wood and iron, until the engine began to gather its strength, drawing them out of the station, away from the town, into the country again, speed shaping them into one smoothly flowing entity, making one vehicle out of a series of linked boxes.

Laszlo stretched out his long legs and rested them on the edge of the opposite seat. "This is very restful, is it not? A most comfortable way to travel. What were you saying just now?"

"I was asking where you had appeared from," Hugh said. "I was surprised I had not seen you earlier."

"Ah, but I saw you," Laszlo said. He smiled. "I was not avoiding you, my dear Radlett. I was avoiding crowds. I do not like crowds. I find them dangerous."

"Full of Austrian spies."

"Yes, they could be. You may smile, but they could be. I do not think you have ever taken my mission seriously. I am not the Countess, for instance, playing at patriotism. It is a serious matter."

"Do you think the Countess insincere, then?"

"No, no, of course not, do not misunderstand me. She is deeply sincere. I could never repay her kindness to me. But she does not understand. She has lived too long in England, in a free society, to understand. Here you speak your minds, you attack your politicians, your government, your Queen. Your newspapers publish whatever opinions they choose, your people hold vast meetings, and the authorities speak of riot and act fearfully, but those crowds never attack and kill people. They set up no barricades. And why not? Because there is no need. There is always another way open to them. They can use words where we have to use knives. You do not know what it is to have your country under the control of an alien government. To know as you print an article that you will go to prison for it. That if you stand up in a street or a café and speak your mind, you may be shot. To know that you have no power, no control, over your own destiny. That is what we have been fighting. And we have won. We are a sovereign state again, did you know? Officially. Kossuth is head of state."

He had spoken all this with none of the crowd-moving vehemence he used at his meetings, but with a quietness, almost a casualness that was very convincing. It was difficult not to believe in the integrity of his opinions when they were put in this thoughtful, conversational way.

Hugh said: "And Kossuth is your friend, I understand."

"Yes, he is my friend."

"I should like to meet your other friends."

Laszlo looked puzzled.

"The ones you go to meet in London."

"Ah—! Yes. And I should like you to, but you must understand they are very wary. They have to be so careful of people they do not know."

"They might think me an Austrian spy, you mean."

Laszlo laughed with genuine amusement. "I shall never persuade you to be serious, I can see. I shall speak no more of it. Tell me your plans. Where do you stay in London?"

"A hotel I have been to often before, near the Strand."

"May I stay there too? Would you object?"

Hugh looked at him with some surprise. "Don't you stay with your friends?"

"Yes, yes, before, but now it is not so convenient for them. And they are fewer than they were. They have nearly all gone back to Hungary."

"And you?" Hugh asked him. "When do you go back to Hungary?"

Laszlo shrugged.

"Next week? Next month?" Hugh insisted. The Hungarian glanced up sharply at his persistence. He paused before replying and Hugh thought there was a guarded expression in his eyes. But he said merely: "When I've finished what I came to do."

"Is it not already finished?" Hugh said.

"No, no, it is not." And he added, by way of explanation, "The Austrians are still in Buda. We have not cleared the country of them yet." But Hugh had the feeling he had not been referring to the struggle in Hungary and had not believed Hugh to be referring to it either.

In the corner of the carriage the business man, slumped forward with head on chest, snorted himself awake. His head came up and he blinked uncomprehendingly at Hugh and Laszlo.

"Some air, sir," Laszlo said with polite concern. "Perhaps you would like some air?"

The man stared, still half-asleep. Laszlo stood up and let down the window on its heavy strap.

"There you are," he remarked cheerfully. "A fresh country breeze."

The business man nodded, an attempt at acknowledgement, but in a few moments his head sagged once more towards his chest and he was fast asleep again. Laszlo smiled at Hugh. The incident could have been seen, Hugh thought, as providing a good opportunity to change a subject that was not developing as the Hungarian wished, and he was not entirely surprised when Laszlo put a final end to their conversation by saying he intended to follow their friend's example and try to sleep. His hand still lying on the handle of the black bag, he closed his eyes and rested his head against the padding of the seat.

Hugh sat gazing out at the countryside, half-dreaming, half-dozing, soothed by the regular rhythm of the wheels over the rails. It was a warm day and the green countryside that seemed to race towards him at such speed only to flash and fade away behind him with a sigh of steam, exercised a hypnotic effect on his eyes. He shut them and leaned back, enjoying the sun on his face, and the stream of air, the motion of the train, the detachment of being carried along without possessing any control over where or how he was taken; with no responsibility, no responsibility. . . .

He was nearly asleep when the train rattled round a curve and with a shriek of warning plunged into a tunnel. It was a long tunnel, nearly half-a-mile in distance, and after a while the smoke, trapped in its confines, began to fling back soot and cinders which drifted into the carriage through the open window. Hugh got up to shut it and as he bent down in the almost total blackness his arm brushed Laszlo. There was an exclamation. His arms were gripped and he was flung violently away. Caught off balance he fell back against his seat. Astonished and wary, he said and did nothing, waiting until the point of daylight appeared and they were expelled with equal suddenness back into the open air.

He saw that Laszlo, now wide awake, was sitting upright, both hands gripping his bag. The business man slept peacefully on. Laszlo's glance went quickly round the compartment and then back to Hugh. He appeared to relax, smiling apologetically at him. "My dear Radlett, forgive me. I see it was you."

"You thought that he"—Hugh nodded towards the recumbent figure—"was attacking you?"

"I was asleep. For a moment I did not know where I was. It was an instinctive reaction. I'm sorry." He nodded at the cane thrown carelessly down out of his reach. "You can tell how little I really expected any threat when you see where I put the weapon the Countess gave me months ago for my protection."

"I am glad you did not have it by you," Hugh said, "or I might have a broken head." He glanced at the leather bag. "You guard that as if it contained the Crown Jewels."

"Oh—" Laszlo shrugged and put the case an almost symbolic few inches away from him along the seat. "That is a habit also. I am used to carrying sums of money in it."

"But you carry none to-day?"

"No." He paused, seemed about to say something further and then clearly decided against it.

"Let us forget the incident," he said briefly.

"By all means," Hugh agreed. But he sat watching the other man and wondering about him for the rest of the way. Bathory had not been acting when he thrust him away. It had been, indeed, an instinctive reaction. What was in the bag he had defended so forcefully? Was it really so unimportant?

On arrival at Euston, the two men took a cab to the hotel. There was no difficulty about obtaining rooms. The threat of cholera still kept many visitors away. When the proprietor asked if the two gentlemen would like to have rooms near to one another, it was Bathory who nodded agreement.

The two rooms allotted to them were on the first floor, facing each other. The hotel had once been a terminus for coaches and all its rooms were large and spacious, built to accommodate vast numbers of travellers. It was the airiness of the rooms which had attracted Hugh originally and the comparative quietness of the place. He had lived there during his last year in London and was welcomed back like a relative. The proprietor himself showed the two men to their rooms and stayed in Hugh's a few minutes telling him all his news, and eventually making him promise to come down directly to his private quarters for a little "spiritous refreshment."

"And bring your friend, of course, Doctor," he added.

When Hugh was ready he crossed the corridor to Laszlo's room and knocked on the door. There was no response. After a minute or so he shrugged and went on downstairs.

"Your friend went out, sir," the porter told him.

So the desire for companionship was quickly at an end. Hugh thought no more about it. After spending a half-hour or so with the hotel owner, he left and walked round to the nearby hospital to see a surgeon acquaintance of his. They talked shop, long and hard and enjoyable, for several hours, drifting about London from hospital to tavern to restaurant to the surgeon's rooms, collecting two other friends as they did so. At midnight Hugh left. He walked back to the hotel meaning to go directly to bed. He opened the door of his room and found Laszlo sitting in a chair by the window. He sprang up as soon as Hugh entered.

"What the devil are you doing in here?" Hugh asked.

"Waiting for you. The proprietor opened your door for me."

"Did he indeed?"

"I explained I had left something of mine in your room."

"And we are such good friends, he saw no harm in it, I suppose." Hugh went to the wash stand, poured water into the basin and splashed his face. "God, my head aches."

"You have been carousing about the town?" Laszlo queried. Hugh smiled at his choice of verb. Laszlo's English—so fluent, so colloquial—occasionally lapsed into endearing pomposity.

"In a mild manner," he agreed. He wiped his face dry and put down the towel. "What is it you want, Bathory?"

"We are going to a supper party. I have it all arranged."

Hugh groaned. "It is kind of you, but I have been to a party."

266

"It is my friends. I have persuaded them to meet you. They are waiting."

"No, really, I've no desire——" He broke off and slowly turned to look at Laszlo. "What do you mean by your 'friends'?"

"My fellow Hungarians." He smiled. "The ones whose existence I really believe you almost doubt."

"The ones who are so cautious about strangers?"

"I have vouched for you."

"Ah!" Hugh smiled. "I can see that would make all the difference."

Laszlo laughed. "Well?" he said. "Are you coming or aren't you?"

"Why not? How could I refuse after you have been to such lengths? Coaxing the revolutionaries out of hiding, breaking into my room. It must be a very important party!"

It was a phrase, spoken carelessly, which came back to him later that night. "A very important party." Important to whom—and why? It seemed nothing but a little theatrical and noisy at first. Laszlo hailed a cab and gave an address Hugh did not catch. They went across the river and into the maze of streets round Southwark.

"Your friends live like dock rats," Hugh observed, peering out.

"They have to," Laszlo said briefly.

The house they stopped at was badly lit. Bathory pushed open the door and they stumbled up dark steps towards the upper floor. The higher they went the louder the noise became. Music, Hugh could hear. A scraping, jigging fiddle music and singing and voices shouting. When Laszlo opened the final door there was a sudden silence. There were not, considering the noise they were making, very many people there—ten or fifteen, not more. They were drinking wine and there was a great deal of smoke and not much light. The floor was carpeted and there was another carpet hanging against one wall, hiding a little of the peeling plaster. Several divans crowded the room. Heavy curtains were drawn. It had the look, Hugh thought, of an opium den as it might be presented on the stage. And the people present might have been characters in a play.

The first man he was introduced to was enormous, six foot four with a long trailing moustache. He seized Hugh's hand and pumped it up and down, smiling fiercely. Laszlo spoke to him in German. This was the doctor, he said, a noble friend of the cause and very welcome to them all. The giant, who was called Ferenc, repeated several times that the good doctor was exceedingly welcome and they must drink a toast to him and the cause. Hugh wondered if Laszlo had discovered that he understood German.

In the centre of the room there was a table with a red velvet cloth placed over it where men had been playing cards. A chair was pulled out for Hugh and he sat down. The three men already seated at the table nodded a greeting at him. They were soberly dressed in rather shabby clothes and their ages ranged from a pale twenty to a red-veined fifty. The youngest of the men Hugh was certain was a consumptive; the eldest, sitting to his right, bore all the signs of the chronic drunkard. The third looked like a City clerk, white-faced and seemingly timid but with a sly look about the eyes. An odd assortment. Laszlo, leaning over Hugh's shoulder, said something to them in a language he did not recognise but presumed must be Magyar. They looked at him impassively, but said nothing.

"They speak no English," Laszlo said, "and as you can see I am afraid they do not entirely trust you even though it is I who has brought you here."

Ferenc touched his arm. "Bathory, a word."

"Excuse me." He went with Ferenc to the opposite corner of the room where they talked together in low voices. His three fellow-conspirators round the card-table remained staring at Hugh with the same blank indifference. He remarked in German how interested he was to meet them. He received no response. He repeated it in English and their expressions stayed as coldly vacant as before. He tilted his chair back and gazed curiously round at the rest of the company. A small group of men and women who looked considerably more animated than his companions, had turned back after the interruption of his arrival and were talking and laughing together. They spoke to the fiddler and he put the violin under his chin and began to play. He was wearing some kind of linen smock fastened at one side of the neck such as Hugh believed Russians wore. He did not play the violin very well, but with great vigour and much movement of the head and body.

"The old tunes, ah, the old gipsy tunes." A

voluptuous fair-haired woman, her cheeks reddened with patches of rouge, came up to Hugh carrying a glass of wine which she offered to him with slightly mocking graciousness. Hugh stood up, accepting the glass.

"That gentleman," he remarked, "is surely not a Hungarian gipsy?"

She laughed. She had an attractive laugh, rich and low. "No, of course not. There are no Hungarian gipsies outside Hungary. And none who can play their music. But he remembers it and he plays what he can to bring back memories for the rest of us."

Her accent was much thicker than Laszlo's but there was the same rhythm to the way she spoke. Hugh looked at her with more interest. "Do you have many memories of Hungary?"

"Ah—" She took his arm, pulling him down to sit beside her on a divan. She was wearing a heavy perfume that had gone a little stale. "I remember too much, my dear Englishman. I remember when I was a girl in Buda. Or rather just outside Buda. My father's estate was there—my father was very wealthy, you know, one of the most important people in the country. Everyone used to

271

flock out from the capital to go to the balls he held. Such nights they were! And my mother, how beautiful she was. What jewels she wore! And the lights—so many candles, a forest of candles. And the gipsies playing." She sighed. "So long ago. I become nostalgic and weep you see, like a foolish child, drinking too much wine, and listening to the music. . . ."

She was like a parody of the Countess.

"How do you come to live in England?" Hugh asked.

"Mm?" She looked up at him. "Oh, it is too long a story, you would become very bored with it. The story of my whole life——" Almost involuntarily her glance strayed towards Laszlo.

"Have you been here for months, or years? Is there a large community of Hungarians living in London? Are they all Hungarians in this room?"

He put the questions intentionally fast to her, one after the other. This time the glance she gave to Laszlo was open, and unmistakably an appeal. Hugh observed its effect. Laszlo left Ferenc. He gave an imperceptible nod to someone in the group round the violinist and then came towards Hugh and the woman.

As if in response to his signal one of the women in the group began to sing. A man joined in. The others clapped, keeping time. The violinist played faster, his face contorted with effort. His friends shouted encouragement. Even the three lay-figures at the table began to beat with their fists on the cloth. It had a rehearsed effect, Hugh felt, lacking spontaneity, but the noise grew and the singers did begin to infect themselves with some excitement. It was impossible, at any rate, for him to carry on a logical conversation. The woman beside him smiled brilliantly, professionally, at him and gestured to one of the men to bring over a bottle of wine.

"More wine, more wine." She refilled his glass again and again. The smoke was affecting his head, bringing back his headache. The long day and the long night had tired him and he put his hand to his eyes. When he looked up Bathory was before him, smiling. He was always smiling to-day. Somehow Hugh found himself on his feet, his arm round the blonde woman and she too was smiling at him. He heard Laszlo say: "And

273

what do you think of my compatriots now?"

"I wouldn't trust them with my money," Hugh said. For an instant Laszlo's expression was as guarded and wary as it had been in the train. Then Hugh smiled showing he had said it jokingly and Laszlo laughed too.

"Tell me," Hugh said, speaking more thickly than he needed. "What have you done with the money you collected from all your devoted supporters in the country?"

"We bought arms with it, sir," Ferenc boomed in his ears. "Arms, yes. Bang, bang! Dead Austrians. Powder, for explosions. Horses for the cavalry. All gone, all spent. And now victory. No more Austrians. No more Slovaks! Eh? eh?" He roared with laughter and sang out to the musician: "Go on, play, play. More! More!" He swung round and clasped Hugh in his great arms, pressing him against his chest like a jovial bear. "A toast, eh? We shall have a toast?"

"Yes," Hugh said. "I'll drink a toast. I'll do more. I'll propose one. Help me up. Come on, help me up!"

He pulled the City clerk out of his chair and jumped up on it, leaning his hand on Ferenc's shoulder. It felt as solid as a brick wall. Then bending down again he picked up

274

his glass from the table. Laszlo watched him.

"To the people of Hungary!" Hugh cried and drank. The empty glass slipped through his fingers and broke on the table. Laszlo handed up a full glass, smiling at him.

"To the noble English people!" Ferenc responded. They drank again.

"To the revolution!"

"To final victory!"

"More wine," Hugh called to Laszlo. "More wine for your fellow revolutionaries." He slipped down from the chair and as Laszlo came forward put both hands earnestly on his arm. "More money. Your friends need more money. Not just for the revolution. You cannot live like this. Whose house is it? Who lives here?"

"It is Eva's house," Laszlo said, and turned away murmuring something to the fair woman. Hugh heard her laugh. For the first time, Laszlo's answering laugh seemed genuinely relaxed. Hugh moved back from the table and let the musician hide him from Laszlo's view.

The noise they had used to mask his questions was now his servant. Under its cover he made his way unobtrusively to the door. His last doubt had been removed by the first toast he drank. He thought he had picked up his own glass, but he had taken the clerk's by mistake and found it contained wine watered down to a fraction of the potency of that which he had been given to drink. So he was the only one intended to get drunk at this riotous party. The rest had to stay relatively sober—the rest of the actors. The entire party was an elaborately staged play. Bathory had wanted to find out how much Hugh knew, how deep his suspicions really ran, and, if they were superficial, to eradicate them.

Hugh thought he had convinced them he was harmless, but if his suspicions had been proved too strong, what then? Would Ferenc perhaps have dealt with him? A drunken fall down the stairs? A stumble into the river? Laszlo must have collected a great deal of money to make this charade so necessary. Everyone there, except perhaps Ferenc, would have been paid. He wasn't even sure that Ferenc was Hungarian. German, perhaps. The violinist and his friends were possibly Russian or Jewish, the women—well, it was obvious what the women were. There were enough poor foreigners in London these days to make it a simple matter to gather a handful together for a small sum of money.

Whether or not Laszlo was a friend of Kossuth's, whether or not he had originally been sent to England by the revolutionaries, Hugh had still not decided. The one thing that was certain was that Laszlo was working to his own profit and his plans must be near fruition if he went to such lengths to avoid a possible stumbling-block, even so unlikely a one as a distrustful country doctor. But he should have remembered before trying to make Hugh drunk that he had had the experience of a medical student. The night the navvies had swept them off to celebrate, it was he, not Laszlo, who had ended the evening on his feet.

He opened the door quietly and slipped through, closing it behind him. He ran lightly down the stairs and out of the front door and turned towards the river.

When he reached the hotel he had to knock up the night porter to let him in. It was a man who had been there when Hugh was living at the hotel and it needed only a small tip to get Laszlo's room opened for him. He lighted the lamp and began a methodical search. He was looking for large sums of money, for travel documents, papers of identity, anything which would enable him to put a concrete form to his suspicions. But there was nothing, and if there was no evidence how could anyone prove that the money donated by the people of Warwickshire, and perhaps several other counties for all Hugh knew, had not been put to the use for which it had been given? It was a fraud very difficult to establish, yet there must be something, Hugh felt, that had made Bathory so anxious about his own suspicions and he thought it must be to do with his identity.

He found the black leather bag in the first ten minutes, tossed without any attempt to hide it in the back of the large wardrobe. He took it out and unfastened it. If there had been money in it, it had already been removed. There was nothing left inside but a couple of sheets of stiff paper. Hugh took them out.

"So! You grew tired of my compatriots, I see." Laszlo had come in very quietly, forewarned by the lamp in his room. "Why are you here? Did you mistake the room?"

He had arrived more quickly than Hugh expected. He must have been missed at once. At the sound of that voice, Hugh had felt his shoulders stiffen like a man who waits for a knife in the back. He forced himself to turn in a leisurely, unconcerned way and smile cheerfully at the Hungarian with a vague bonhomie. "I decided to repay the visit you made me earlier this evening. I was waiting for you. Wanted to thank you. Splendid party. I felt a bit ill. That's why I left."

"I hope you are better now."

"Yes. Quite. Quite recovered."

"What have you got there?" Laszlo took the papers from Hugh's hand, glanced at them and threw them carelessly on the bed. "Oh, those. Yes, I must not forget them. They are good, are they not? She is quite an accomplished artist."

"She?"

"Esther Wharton. She made them."

The papers were drawings of Sophia's emerald—the King's emerald; closely detailed drawings in pencil with indications of colour. They appeared to have been taken from the front and side view of the stone.

"Now where did I get those?" Hugh looked slowly round, his face puzzled. "Oh yes." He allowed himself to adopt what he trusted was a slightly guilty expression. He was aware that he was not a very good actor. "Yes, I was looking for something to drink, I'm afraid."

Laszlo smiled. "I am sorry, Radlett. I have

nothing here. It is late, isn't it? Why don't you go to bed?"

"What are they for?" Hugh asked.

"The drawings? They have two purposes." Laszlo yawned slightly and sat down on the edge of the bed. "One is to check with records in Hungary to try and establish finally whether the original owner was Mátyás Hunyadi, in which case the Countess may wish the emerald to be returned to some official keeping."

"Yes," Hugh nodded. "I know she wishes the emerald to go back to Hungary one day. And the second reason?"

He sensed Laszlo looking sharply at him and realised he had spoken in his normal sober voice.

"The second purpose is to be a surprise," Bathory said. "For that reason I have not shown the sketches to the Countess yet. I intend to get an artist to make a small 'portrait' as it were of the emerald, in as perfect detail as I may, as a present for her kindness to me." He waved a negligent hand at the drawings. "Miss Wharton did these from memory. A difficult task but she possesses an excellent memory. She wanted to be part of the secret present also."

Hugh had a sudden recollection of Esther at the reception, staying so close to Sophia's side. Observing the emerald?

"You are going to a great deal of trouble."

"It is very little trouble to me. It is Esther—Miss Wharton who has taken the trouble. But I am glad you reminded me of them. I have to go and see the artist to-morrow." He gathered the papers up and held them out to Hugh. "Put them on the table there, would you, my dear fellow?"

Hugh put the drawings down where Bathory indicated. He felt frustrated by the lack of success in searching the room. How satisfying it would have been to have confronted the Hungarian with some suitable dramatic statement such as: "The game's up, Bathory. I know everything." But he knew nothing. It was all suspicion based on mistrust—and jealousy. Even that unreal supper party to-night could have been genuine. He had no proof those people were not friends of Laszlo's, and perhaps the clerk preferred watered wine. If there had been no Anne to complicate the matter, would he not perhaps have taken Laszlo at face value? As it was he had a new suspicion now growing in the back of his mind. But his mind was too tired for him to worry it into a conclusion now.

"Good night, Bathory," he said. "I'm going to bed."

Laszlo stood up in one quick movement as if he might stop him. He touched his hand to his mouth in a gesture that was diffident, almost nervous. The charm of which he was capable was suddenly directed at Hugh in all its force.

"I know you do not like me, Radlett," he said. "I know you do not trust me and I know why."

He had managed to create an impression of complete frankness by his voice and manner. He understood, he implied, and he forgave but it was a pity he was not allowed to be a friend.

Hugh waited, half-way to the door. "Why do I dislike you?" He was curious to know what he would say.

"I do not think it is for me to mention her name," Laszlo said.

"No, I don't think it is." Hugh paused. "Who exactly is that woman I met to-night?"

"Eva?" Laszlo shrugged. "A woman of a certain kind."

"Hungarian?"

"Oh, yes. I do not know all her history,

naturally, but that is certainly true." Beneath the show of candour Hugh felt he was being shrewdly judged. "I can see it must have seemed strange company for a man such as I, but she has been useful to—us."

His reactions had been closely watched all evening. Was it because Laszlo was clever enough to know when he had underestimated a man that there was this sudden change of tune, this admittance of certain facts which might then serve to hide other, more revealing truths?

"Perhaps it is the use you make of people, Bathory, that is the root of my distrust," Hugh remarked. "Nothing more."

"Then you do me an injustice. I do use people when I must, but it is for a purpose greater than I, for a cause. I am not like a certain man we both know, greedy for his own ends."

"What do you mean?"

"You do not know? The Countess has not told you? I mean Godfrey Bullivant, of course. He has been trying to raise money all over the country. He has been to the Countess to borrow a vast sum, a very great deal of money. Do you not find that of interest? Now there is a man to be wary of."

Hugh had no wish to be drawn into any confusing blind alleys. He turned back to the door. "Good night, Bathory."

Laszlo laughed. "Good night, Doctor. I hope you have no headache in the morning."

Hugh glanced back as he left the room. Laszlo had swung his feet up on the bed and was lying back, arms under his head, looking at the ceiling. He appeared to have forgotten Hugh. Or would the right word have been "dismissed"? Hugh thought. He shut the door and went to bed.

7

HUGH slept late. When he awoke he found Laszlo had already gone out. His door had been left ajar. Pushing it open Hugh saw the gold-topped cane lying tossed on to the counterpane of the bed as if Bathory had decided at the last minute not to take it with him. Hugh would have preferred to know what he was doing but as long as the Hungarian was still in London, there was no immediate need for action. Though he did not know what he meant by "action". What action could he take?

Restlessness and a vague sense of urgency led him to retrace his steps to the house in Southwark. When he reached the street he found he could not be certain which of the row of houses confronting him was the one he had been brought to the previous night. And then again, what would he achieve by entering it? Laszlo was a man who enjoyed detail. There would be nothing of interest remaining in Eva's house to-day. He turned away and went back across the river.

Hugh's father, Charles Radlett, had a brother who like him was also a solicitor, with offices in Holborn. Hugh went there next. John Radlett was delighted to see his nephew and insisted he should go with him to his house for a family luncheon. Before they left the office Hugh asked his uncle, on an impulse of curiosity, if he knew anything about the Warwick and Worcester railway company and its directors. Mr. Radlett had never heard of it. Hugh wondered if the head office was in London. A clerk was summoned and instructed to find out. When they returned from their luncheon about four o'clock, the address had been obtained. Nobody knew anything about the company however, either to its credit or its disadvantage. If they had longer time to make inquiries . . .

They were not to trouble themselves, Hugh replied. It was of no importance. He put the piece of paper in his pocket and said his good-byes.

The address he had been given turned out to be on the third floor of a respectable office building in the City. A clerk scrambled off his stool to greet him. It was a small room with one window overlooking an area. A second door apparently led to another room. There was a large map on one wall showing the railway system of Great Britain as it had existed in 1840. There was another large chart showing in detail the network of lines in the Midlands. It was of more recent date but Bullivant's railway had not been marked on it.

"What can I do for you, sir?" asked the clerk.

"Are you in charge here?" Hugh asked.

"I am at the moment, sir. Mr. Smeaton's out."

"Who is Mr. Smeaton?"

"He is the manager of this office, sir."

Hugh nodded. He looked round the room. From a table in the darker corner he picked up a brochure, shaking it to dislodge a layer of dust. It had been printed in 1844. It was an invitation to subscribers to support a projected railway running from Worcester . . . etc. etc. He put it down. The clerk was watching him patiently.

"You don't seem to be very busy," Hugh said.

"No, sir."

"What exactly do you do?"

"General duties, sir." He was a young

man, barely eighteen. Hugh liked him.

"Don't you find it very dull?" he asked.

The boy gave him a half-smile. "A bit, sir. But it's steady employment."

"Are there just you and Mr. Smeaton working here?"

"Just the two of us, sir. At present."

"Do you ever see the directors of the company?"

"I haven't ever, no."

"Mr. Bullivant?"

"Oh yes, I know him. He's been here."

"Have you a list of directors?"

"Yes, sir." He rummaged in a drawer and eventually produced a copy of the brochure that Hugh had already seen. There were eight names listed as directors, none of which was Bullivant's.

"Have you nothing more recent?"

"I don't know, sir. Mr. Smeaton might know. If you care to wait."

Hugh agreed to wait. He was shown into the inner office. It was even smaller than the other and contained a roll-top desk securely locked, two chairs, a cupboard also locked, and a chart identical with the one in the other room of the British railway system. Hugh sat down in one chair, hooked the other one over to rest his feet on and went to sleep. Twenty minutes later he was awakened by the sound of voices outside. Mr. Smeaton had returned.

It was obvious as soon as Hugh saw him that he was not a person of any great authority in the company. He was no more than a senior clerk. His coat was of the same rusty black cloth as his junior's, his face looked as worn and patched as his linen. But time had erased in him the joyful optimism that sustained the boy in the other room, the conviction that his day of wealth and success approached ever nearer with each week, each year. The time of promise for him had gone. The moment of achievement had somehow inexplicably missed him and now receded even further into the distance. He was left in a state of perpetual irritation, filled with a nagging resentment that embraced everyone he came into contact with, including Hugh. He was angry with the clerk for allowing a stranger into his office and his annoyance spilled over pettishly.

No, he told Hugh, he could give no information about the company. The gentleman would have to write a letter to the company, when all his inquiries would be fully answered. He could not possibly stay to answer any questions now, the office was about to be closed. Hugh announced that he was a shareholder. He wished to know how the building of his railway was progressing. A full report would be made, said Mr. Smeaton, edging him out of his office with sweeping movements of his hands. There would be a shareholders' meeting in due course. Hugh mentioned Mr. Bullivant's name. He said he was acquainted with him.

"Mr. Bullivant can give you information direct if he wishes," Smeaton said. "I have no authority to do so."

It was impossible to tell if he had anything to hide or if this was merely his usual manner. From the sympathetic smile he received from the young boy, Hugh guessed it was the latter. He thanked the junior clerk for his courtesy, nodded to Smeaton and left.

He had arranged with his friends to go to a theatre that night. Afterwards they ate supper and appeared to have every intention of making it a long night. Hugh left before midnight, carrying with him the cheerful insults of his friends and went back to the hotel. Laszlo's room was still deserted, the cane still resting where he had thrown it. Hugh shut his own door with a feeling of a plague upon all their houses and went to bed.

The next morning Bathory's bed remained unslept in, the cane undisturbed. Hugh decided his own level of intelligence was very low. The night porter was still up. Hugh questioned him. Laszlo had gone out again on the night of the party, about half-an-hour or so after his return. He must have left the hotel as soon as Hugh had gone back to his own room. No one had seen him since. As far as Hugh could gather he had never slept in the room at all. He went to see the proprietor and told him he thought it likely his friend had been called away. He paid for both rooms and told the man to keep the cane until someone called for it. He then caught a train back to Warwickshire.

The first person he saw when he left the station at Warwick was Esther Wharton. She was walking slowly along the opposite side of the road. As he watched she paused, gazing towards the railway station from which a small group of travellers was emerging. Her face looked stiff and white as if cut from paper. William Broom was waiting with the trap. He had been there in time for the previous train. He told Hugh Miss Wharton had already been there when he arrived.

"She's been walking up and down like that all the time."

Hugh crossed the road and went up to Esther. She started when he spoke to her and looked at him almost wildly for a moment. Then her face fixed into its normal cool expression.

"Dr. Radlett, how pleasant to see you again. Have you just returned from London?"

"Yes. Are you waiting for someone, Miss Wharton, or would you care to drive back to Rivington with me. Broom has met me with the trap."

She seemed undecided. "When is the next train due in, do you know?"

"From London?"

She hesitated. "No—I—from anywhere."

"There will not be another one that has made the connection with a London train for quite a while. As to a local train, I'm afraid I don't know. Would you like me to find out?"

"No, no! There's no need." She gave him a thin smile. "I was expecting to meet a friend from my home village. I understood she was to be passing through Warwick to-day. But either she or I have mistaken the day, that is clear. I shall not wait any longer." She gave one last glance at the station, the smile leaving her face as soon as she turned from him. She murmured: "It would be pointless to wait."

Hugh escorted her to the carriage. The seat was narrow and they were forced closely together. Esther's feet touched Hugh's and he was conscious of her small, aware body next to his. A nervousness communicated itself to him, leaping from her to him like an electric spark. He glanced at her face and saw the plain profile beneath the bonnet, as pale and seemingly as self possessed as ever.

"I met Laszlo Bathory in London," he said. "He showed me your drawings of the emerald."

Her head turned sharply. "He showed them to you?"

"Don't worry, Miss Wharton. He explained to me that they are to remain a secret for the time being. I shall not mention them to the Countess."

"How did you happen to meet Mr. Bathory? Was it by arrangement?"

"By his arrangement, I imagine," Hugh said drily. "We met on the journey."

She said nothing more, but Hugh had the impression she was suppressing a great many questions which she was in a fever to know the answers to. He looked at her again, more deliberately this time, and felt a sudden unexpected compassion for her. Poor woman, he thought. Poor woman. Her life runs so contrary to her desires.

At Waterford Park, Esther slipped away upstairs as soon as Sophia came out to welcome Hugh. She thought he looked much better, she told him, more himself, more "concentrated".

"Yes, I am concentrated. You might very well put it so," Hugh agreed. "Before we do anything else, Countess, I should like you to go and look at your emerald."

"The emerald? Why?"

"Because I believe it may have been stolen."

She scrutinised his face closely and saw that he was not joking. She said quietly: "Come with me. It is upstairs, in my bedroom."

He followed her up the stairs and along wide corridors into her sunlit bedroom. She opened the door to her dressing-room. It was furnished with two large wardrobes, chests of drawers, a dressing-table and a looking glass. She opened one wardrobe. On its top shelf were stored three leather hat boxes. With the aid of the dressing-table stool, she climbed up and pulled down the first of these. She removed the hats, putting them carefully to one side.

"Do you mean to say that this is where you keep the emerald?" Hugh asked.

"No, of course not." She had taken something from the bottom of the box. "Just the key." She held it up. "Who would think of looking for a key in a hatbox. The emerald is in my bedroom, as I said."

There was a small bureau in the corner of her bedroom. She unlocked it and drew down the top, revealing the ranks of small drawers and compartments.

She suddenly smiled at Hugh, with the mischievous expression of a small child. "It is a toy my husband gave me. He knew I would be intrigued by this." She removed one of the drawers. "There is a secret compartment, here at the back. And here is the emerald." She brought out the wooden casket and laid it on the top of the bureau. "Now we shall see."

She opened it. The emerald lay in its white velvet bed, its gold chain coiled round it like a serpent protecting an egg. It seemed to Hugh as he looked down at it to possess a secret life of its own. It lay there heavy with the weight of its history, waiting, waiting for the times it was allowed to come out into the air to reveal its sullen green beauty and to lie for a while against the fragile flesh of those who could never outlive it.

The Countess let a little sigh of relief escape her. "I was concerned, Hugh. You do not joke about such things. Why did you think it had been stolen?"

"It was one possibility. There were others. I am glad I was mistaken." He paused. "Does anyone know where the emerald is hidden?"

"I have told no one."

"Your maid?"

"It is possible that over the years the servants may have come to know vaguely where it is kept. But I am sure no one knows where the key to the bureau is hidden for the reason that I occasionally change the place. Do you think I should put the emerald somewhere else?"

"No." Hugh shook his head. "No. I think it is safe. Tell me, have you discussed with Laszlo Bathory the possibility of the emerald being returned to Hungary?"

Sophia was engaged in replacing the stone in the bureau. She locked it. "Yes. We have decided that he shall take a drawing of it back to Hungary when he returns to see if he can trace its history."

Hugh nodded. So Bathory had been telling the truth about that at least. He should have been glad that his imagination had proved too overheated. Down here in the country the intense sense of intrigue and danger which he had experienced in Laszlo's company in London was gone. He was convinced however that Laszlo had taken the money he had collected over the past months and left the country. But he did not feel he should be the one to say so. As long as the emerald was safe, as long as the Countess believed so implicitly in the Hungarian's integrity, Hugh did not intend to shatter any illusions. Let him go.

Rivington, like any other village, possessed its full share of keen-eyed observers who saw to it that every variation in the behaviour of its inhabitants was noted and publicised with the smallest possible delay. Before Hugh had returned to the house from Waterford Park Anne had learned that he had driven back from Warwick with Esther Wharton. She had previously heard that they had been seen together on the day Esther caught the carrier's cart. The village began almost automatically spinning a love affair between the two.

Anne decided to tease Hugh about it, and then when she saw him decided not to. She did not want to associate him with Esther. It was ridiculous to think he could be romantically interested in such a dull, plain woman who must be at least twenty-five if not nearly thirty.

She met him at the doorstep. "Did you enjoy your holiday?"

"Very much." He seemed off hand and she responded with an equal coolness of tone.

"There is a man waiting for you in the surgery. He had heard you were back so he decided to wait. A railway worker. Someone collapsed there to-day."

"Oh? Where is the ill man?"

"He is still down there. They put him in one of the sheds."

Hugh went to his room and changed his clothes, then collected the navvy. They walked down to the workings together while the man answered his questions about his friend's illness. Before he had even seen the man, Hugh had a good idea of what was wrong with him.

He made them carry him out into the air so that he could examine him carefully. He stood up wiping his hands on his handkerchief and asked if any other men had been ill lately. Two other men had been away from the workings during the past week. They were still away. They were all lodged in the same place, the camp on the hill.

Hugh sent a man to fetch Simpson to him. The contractor arrived in his usual bad temper at any interruption. He had felt humiliated at being sent for by the doctor and had wanted to refuse, but had not quite got the courage. The men had heard the message. They stopped working and waited to see what he would do, leaning on the handles of their picks, their weatherbeaten faces impassive.

Simpson glared round at them. "Who sent for the doctor?"

No one bothered to reply. They merely watched; a circle of watchers round him. One cleared his throat and spat, a foot away. At such moments Simpson felt as if he was in charge of a pack of wolves. Unpredictable, vicious, casually ready to destroy him. He pushed past them and walked down the line.

He was afraid of Hugh also, but in a different way. Hugh was a doctor, but he was gentry too. He wasn't a kind of superior tradesman, with a shop in the town high street with a stuffed crocodile and bottles of coloured water in the window. He was the other kind of doctor, who had been to a university and worked in hospitals, and should be restricting himself to a carriage practice alone. Simpson, who had never met Dr. Torrance, couldn't think what Hugh was doing burying himself in the country and treating scum like his navvies. He didn't fit into the social pattern.

Hugh was sitting on a pile of timber talking to one of the men.

"Well, Doctor, this is a waste of all our time." Simpson covered up his uncertainty with a show of truculence.

Hugh disarmed him by the quiet gravity of his manner. "I am sorry to have to tell you this, Mr. Simpson, but you will have to stop work for the time being. This man has typhoid."

Simpson looked down at the sick man, lying covered in his comrades' coat. His eyes were open, bright as a bird's. "Nonsense. He's had too much to drink and working in the sun's knocked him out. He's all right

300

now. He's conscious. He'll sweat it out working."

"He's running a fever."

"Maybe he is, but that doesn't mean it's typhoid."

"He has typhoid," Hugh repeated calmly, "and so probably have two other men. You've got to stop the work."

"I can't."

"If the disease spreads——"

Simpson was becoming more aggressive. "If it spreads then I'll have to stop, I quite agree, because I'll have no more workers, will I? But it won't."

"Mr. Simpson, I must insist——"

"You can't insist, Doctor. You can't tell me what to do. If the man is ill he can go off. I don't want any invalids here. But we're behind schedule and I need every man. I'm stopping nothing. If you want any alteration here you'll have to see Mr. Bullivant about it. Get him to order it stopped and I will."

"Very well. I'll go and see him at once."

"He's away." Simpson couldn't resist a little smirk of triumph. "You'll have to wait till he gets back, Doctor."

Hugh looked at him for a moment in silence. "Very well, I'll wait. How many of your men come from the camp on the hill?"

"I don't know where they live. Fifty or a hundred. I don't know."

"Well, keep them away from the others. And if any more fall down under the over-powering effects of our sun, let me know at once."

After he had arranged for the sick man to be taken to a hospital, Hugh went up to the camp on the hill to see what the situation was. On this pleasant July day, the pungent smells rising from the crowded shacks and hovels rushed to meet him. There was no sanitation in the camp and the only fresh water was from a stream half-a-mile away. All around, the refuse of human habitation lay piled in heaps and trampled into the flattened muddy grass. Dogs rooted among the rubbish, flies and fat bluebottles crawled and hovered over it with sluggish, glutted deliberation. Children played obliviously, every now and again brushing the flies away from their eyes and mouths.

Most of the navvies lived eight or so to a dwelling, looked after by some ancient hag who cooked their food and kept the key to the beer. Some of those with families had come to the hill too, camping out in tents or lean-to's with their women and children. The camp had been in existence for a year. There had been a coming and going of its population and fights and deaths and a couple of births. When the railroad was finished, when the men moved on, it would vanish in a night, leaving its stinking detritus behind it, until the grass grew over it and the hill returned to itself.

At this time of day it was empty except for the women and children. Hugh was known there. He was accepted. He asked his way to the lodgings of the two ill men and confirmed to his own satisfaction that they were suffering from typhoid. So were two of the children; a girl of two and a baby boy. The mother refused to let him take them away to hospital and Hugh did not insist. The boy was dying and there was little he or a hospital could do to help him. He died that evening.

The mother wanted a church burial for the baby. She wanted it, Hugh could see, with a superstitious desperation that saw a funeral and a service and a cross over the child as a protection for it, lost in the dark so soon. He was the fourth son she had had, she told Hugh, and they had all died within a year but they'd all been buried in a churchyard. They were all safe. Hugh went round to the vicarage the following day and tackled Carrington on her behalf. He met the same rigid refusal as he had almost a year before over the navvy killed in an accident.

"They are not Christian," Carrington said. "They have had nothing to do with the Church. I am quite certain the child was never baptised. They cannot expect to make use of the Church merely when it seems convenient for them to do so."

"Did not Christ say: 'Suffer little children to come unto me'?" Hugh observed.

Carrington's lips snapped. "Do not preach the gospel to me, Dr. Radlett. I know my Christian duty. When those people rejected me, they rejected the Church. They must learn humility and repentance before they can be accepted." His voice was almost quivering with repressed feeling. The farcical business of his venture up to the camp and his forcible expulsion from it was burned too deep for forgiveness. Hugh did not trouble to discuss it further.

"Good day, Carrington." He was half-way to the door of Carrington's study when the vicar recalled him.

"Dr. Radlett——" Carrington was hesitating. Hugh's capitulation had unsettled him. His long face lost its put-upon expression and looked curiously puzzled; and his fingers which he had been pressing together in a pulpit gesture, fiddled somewhat nervously with the buttons of his coat.

"What will happen?" he asked.

Hugh had lost his patience. "No doubt they will bury the child in a dung heap where it belongs."

"That is unjust of you——"

"No, you are quite right. These people are none of your business. They do not belong to your parish or to anyone's parish. What is more they are ungrateful and uncivilised. As you say, when you nobly attempted to evangelise them they repelled you. So stick to your principles, Mr. Carrington. If you allow them to slip, God knows what might become of you."

He left the vicarage, both relieved and slightly ashamed of his outburst and took the short-cut to the village street through the churchyard. He paused at Dr. Torrance's grave, remembering the day of the funeral and his first glimpse of Anne after two years of endeavouring to forget her. It had been a day like this, warmer than this. A year had passed; the grass was as green, and the trees in their summer leaf threw the same shadows on the ground. Nothing changed, everything renewed itself. That was what he had come back to the country to remember. In a city hospital he had seemed at times cut off from everything but the process of decay and death. Here, unimpeded by the efforts of medicine, the land died and was reborn, withered and flourished, as it had always done, with a magnificent indifference to the skills and opinions of Hugh Radlett.

As he passed through the lychgate he saw Anne coming to meet him from the house. She was wearing a dress of soft apple green and her skin was faintly coloured by the sun. Hugh stopped to let her come to him for the pleasure of seeing her walk towards him.

"Hugh, you wanted to speak to Godfrey Bullivant," she said as she came up to him. "He has been here."

Nothing about Anne escaped Hugh. He said: "What is the matter?"

"The matter?"

"Yes! The matter with you."

"Oh!" She turned her head away. "I don't like Bullivant, that is all. He offends me. He is too gross. Bull-like. I don't know."

"I suppose he is a little like the minotaur with those massive shoulders. His hair curls too in a sinister manner above his ears, have you noticed? Perhaps it conceals horns."

"Hugh——" She smiled affectionately, putting her hand on his arm. He captured it immediately, covering it with his own hand.

"What did he have to say?"

"Nothing very much."

"I mean," Hugh remarked patiently, "why did he come?"

"No reason. To pass the time of day." He noticed that she blushed and he wondered why.

"I told him about the case of typhoid," she went on, "and that you wanted to talk to him and he said he would be at the Wharton Arms for the rest of the day." She did not say that Bullivant had wished to wait and she had refused to let him. It had been a strange meeting. She had received the impression that Bullivant had not wanted to come, that he had been drawn to the house almost against his will. She had found his expression, his manner—odd. When she had told him it was not convenient for him to wait for Hugh he had shrugged, showing no surprise at her attitude and had left at once.

307

Anne had never behaved with such abrupt rudeness to anyone before. In spite of her ambiguous relationship with Bullivant she had no real excuse for it. That was why she had blushed.

"Come for a walk," Hugh said suddenly.

"Why?"

"Why not? Do you need a reason?"

She was suddenly delighted by the idea. To walk with Hugh on this summer day appeared the one thing in the world that she wished to do. She said: "I have no hat. I shall spoil my complexion."

"Don't be so vain." They were passing the house. "I shall give you one minute to fetch a hat. And let it be that straw one. It makes delicious patterns on your face."

He was foolishly pleased, when she did return, to see she was wearing that very hat. He felt it was a good omen. He seized her hand and swung it gently as they walked away from the village.

"Do you remember the walks I took you when you were a child?" he said. "Your favourite one was through the fields to the mill pond. Do you remember?"

"No," she said. "Not at all."

"We turned off the road here, down this

lane and then across the fields there. Now you remember."

"Nothing," she said laughing. She pulled her hand from his and ran ahead, running down the narrow lane to a stile that opened the way to a footpath through the trees. "I remember nothing of this, not this stile, nor that field full of buttercups where you held one under my chin to see if I liked butter, nor the time the cows chased you and I rescued you . . ."

"*You* rescued *me*!"

She swung up on to the stile, perching on the top, laughing down at him. He put his hands on her waist and lifted her down and she was close to him smelling of the freshness of the sun, warm and sweet-smelling like the July day, her eyes mysterious in the shadow of her hat, her lips smiling, half open, close to his—He kissed her. He kissed her with a year's longing and with no pretence of anything but loving her; loving her and no longer caring to hide it; loving her and no longer wishing to pretend he could ever overcome it.

The straw hat, tied by ribbons round her throat, slipped from her head, forming a frame for the dark hair. Anne felt the sun strike her bare head, falling on her with midday heat. She felt enveloped in sunlight, held so in Hugh's arms, and her response was as to sunlight, open, generous, smiling. She was aware of an intense happiness, as unexpected as it was overwhelming; like an explosion of light.

Hugh said: "Marry me."

He sensed the change in her as he spoke and knew he had reminded her of Bathory. She moved away from him without replying, into the shadow of the trees. A branch brushed against her face and she put her hand up and caught it, turning as she did so to look back at Hugh, with something regretful in her face.

"Marry me," Hugh repeated. "You love me, Anne."

"I don't think I am certain what love is." She turned, walking deeper into the trees and Hugh followed her, keeping a little distance, as if he had to win the confidence of some wild animal.

Anne could not decide what kind of person she was who could believe she loved two men equally. She could not face the idea that the feeling she had had for Laszlo all these past months could fade. She realised but would not accept that each time he went away his influence over her had grown less. At first when he had gone her days had been spent in thinking about him, waiting for his return; that had become less and less true. It needed the magnetism of his presence to revive in her each time the emotion that had once governed her life. She preferred to think that her feeling for Hugh was the lesser. Was it not old affection, the bright day, her high spirits, that had combined to bring about this moment? Yes, her happiness was the cause, not the result.

She raised her head and looked at Hugh. She thought: But I am possessive about him. I do not want him to think of any other woman. I want to hold him bound to me. She said out loud, a harsher edge to her voice: "I want to keep you enslaved to me, Hugh. Did you know that? That is not very loving of me, is it?"

"As he wishes to keep you enslaved, you mean, Anne?"

"He?"

"Don't pretend you do not know. Who else were we talking about? You know he has gone?"

"Gone? Where?"

311

He shrugged. "Back to Hungary, perhaps."

She came quickly back to him, looking into his face. "I don't believe it. He spoke of taking me to Hungary."

"He has been using you. As a diversion. A pleasant way of passing the time he has been forced to spend here in the dull country."

"Is this your jealousy speaking, Hugh?"

"Partly. But it is true. He makes use of anyone, man or woman, who can serve his purpose, but he finds women more easily amenable."

She was growing angry. She would have walked past him, but he grasped her wrist, forcing her close to him. "He won't marry you, Anne."

She jerked her arm, trying to free herself. "He merely intends to seduce me, I suppose?"

"If he has not already done so."

They were held rigid, in a tense silence. He had told her what he believed to be the truth. He had spoken deliberately to force her to choose. He was tired of being an onlooker. He had decided to fight.

He was pleased to see the contempt in her eyes. "I'm surprised you still wish to marry me, Hugh, if you believe that."

"I don't merely wish to marry you, Anne. I shall marry you."

"I am marrying Laszlo Bathory!"

He released her, so suddenly she almost stumbled. "Find him, then," he said. And walked away.

Anne, more shaken than she cared to admit, waited for him to come back. But he did not. He did not even look back.

The Wharton Arms, a square red-brick building, standing at a junction of roads on the other side of Waterford Park, had to all practical purposes been taken over by the railway company for the past six months. The line of the railroad ran so close to it that to reach the inn yard Hugh, who had walked over the fields from Rivington, had to negotiate a maze of planks thrown in a series of precarious bridges across ditches and raw diggings.

Bullivant had taken possession of two large rooms at the back of the house. When Hugh asked for him he felt as if he were being shown into the presence of a general on the field of battle. There was an air of a campaign headquarters about the place: the turmoil, the

313

apparent disorganisation, the makeshift living arrangements. He was almost surprised to glimpse through the communicating door of Bullivant's two rooms, a normal brass bedstead instead of a soldier's collapsible affair.

Bullivant was seated at a large table studying a column of figures. He had just finished a meal. Plates and cutlery were pushed to one side among the untidy mass of papers that littered the table top. When Hugh walked in there was an interval of some seconds before Bullivant raised his head from the papers before him. Hugh, who had not seen him since the night of the reception, was struck at once by some indefinable change in him. He could only describe it to himself as a state of tension, as if beneath that stolid surface, those ponderous slow movements and deliberate speech, nerves stretched as taut as wires were held in tenuous control.

"Dr. Radlett." Bullivant finally acknowledged his presence. "You received my message, I see."

"Yes. I have just come from Anne Torrance."

Bullivant nodded. He fell silent again, his gaze veering away from Hugh. He stared towards the window, only arousing himself to

314

say: "Sit down, Doctor. Sit down."

Hugh drew a chair near to the table and sat down. He waited until Bullivant, with an almost visible effort, brought his concentration to bear on him. Bullivant said with a return to his more usual businesslike manner: "Typhoid, I was told. Is it true?"

"Yes."

"Many cases?"

"Three so far among your men. There will undoubtedly be more."

Bullivant frowned. "What do you want me to do?"

"I am satisfied the disease originated in the hill camp. So far it is confined to the men living there. I want you to halt work on all sections where the men from the camp are employed."

"That is quite impossible."

"To prevent the possibility of an epidemic," Hugh explained patiently, "it is necessary to try and isolate the danger."

"If I dismiss the men, Doctor, they will simply go on the tramp to find other work."

"I am not asking you to dismiss them."

Bullivant stared at him uncomprehendingly. "You mean me to keep them on the payroll? To pay them for not working?" He thrust himself away from the table in an angry movement and stood up. He began to walk up and down the room, hands clasped behind his back, glancing every now and then at Hugh with an expression both puzzled and considering.

"Dr. Radlett," he said at last, "have you any idea what it costs to build a railway?"

"No," Hugh said.

"Would you be surprised if I told you that a modest estimate would be in the sphere of fifteen thousand pounds a mile?"

"That is a great deal of money."

"It is a great deal of money and what is more to the point, any delay, any trouble, increases the cost to a degree that even you, Dr. Radlett, would find alarming."

Hugh ignored his heavy sarcasm. "Presumably," he remarked blandly, "the company had raised sufficient capital when it was formed or it would never have received Parliamentary consent to begin the railway. Mr. Smeaton, at any rate, appears to think there is no problem."

While Bullivant had been talking, Hugh's attention had been attracted by what appeared to be a printed brochure lying among the papers on the table. What had caught his eye had been a name. Stretching out a hand, he picked up the document.

"Smeaton?" Bullivant said. "What do you mean?"

"I met him when I called at your office," Hugh said. "At least I presume it to be the same Smeaton. I see he is named here as a director of your company. You have changed your directors since the early days, I notice."

"You have been to the company's offices in London?" Bullivant said. "Why, Doctor? For what purpose did you go there?"

"To be perfectly frank with you," Hugh said, "it was because of a remark made by Laszlo Bathory when I met him in London. He said you were looking for money, that you had even asked the Countess for a loan."

"So . . ." Bullivant shrugged. His massive body seemed to sag. He sat down again, spreading his hands open upon the table in a gesture of resignation. "So . . . it is becoming public knowledge."

Hugh watched him for a moment. He said quietly, "Bathory has vanished and I don't believe he intends to return here. And I have no reason to spread rumours. I know, after all, nothing of the facts."

"Then you might as well know them,"

Bullivant said. "You have certainly guessed most of the story. If I tell you the rest, the true situation, perhaps you will appreciate my position a little better. You will understand why I take certain decisions. Confidence, Dr. Radlett. That is what I am living on. I am balanced on it, with an abyss waiting under my feet. That is a dramatic way of stating it, perhaps, but it is true. I am a gambler, Doctor. This is my greatest gamble. And I intend to win."

He faced Hugh across the table. As he spoke his hands clenched into fists. His colour was high—too high, Hugh noticed. A vein at the side of his temple was distended. It throbbed visibly to the beat of his blood.

"You should know," he went on, "that when the Warwick and Worcester railway company was first established I was not a director. I was not even a shareholder. My relationship with the company was that of contractor."

"Like Simpson, you mean."

"Not at all like Simpson, Dr. Radlett. He is a sub-contractor and not a very efficient one. No, I was the man above the Simpsons. The man who let out sections of the proposed line to such men as he. He is responsible for his few miles of line only. I was and am responsible for the whole."

"I see. And you are now unable to fulfil your contract, is that it?"

"You run ahead too fast, Doctor. Two years ago, like so many other companies, the Warwick and Worcester fell into financial difficulties. A certain number of those concerned, to put it bluntly, panicked. There was a suggestion of abandoning the whole scheme. The engineer resigned. But I knew this line, Dr. Radlett, I believed in it. I knew how much work had already been done. In some sections we were so far advanced it would have been criminally foolish to abandon it. I had made a personal fortune through my contracting business. I invested it all. I acquired control of the company."

"Smeaton and these others—" Hugh tapped the paper with a finger—"being your nominees."

"Not all of them. But most I admit. It was something I did not wish too publicly known, that one man, in fact, now bore all the burden of the company. That matter of confidence I mentioned. I needed working capital and I knew that the more names that could be put forward, the more people it was believed were

319

involved in the company, the safer and happier investors would feel. Naturally I anticipated some difficulty in raising a loan but——" He paused. "Confidence has taken a long time to be restored and we have had problems, as you know, weather, accidents, illness. Now you tell me to stop work on a whole section of the line because of three workmen. It is not possible, Dr. Radlett. There is too much at stake here. I cannot afford not to finish this railway and at this stage every day of delay increases the risk of disaster."

He leaned forward across the table. "I shall not allow it to fail. For the first time for a year I have hopes of raising sufficient capital to complete it. I have succeeded in interesting certain parties in the City and the railway world. They are shortly coming down here on a visit of inspection. They must see, they will see, a line so capably managed, so far advanced towards completion that to allow it to be brought to a halt for lack of ready money for labour and materials would be nothing short of folly. They must not find work at a standstill, a labour force idle. I cannot allow that. I don't intend, understand this, Dr. Radlett, to lose everything I have worked for all my life."

As he spoke he appeared to gain in confidence, as if the very fact of repeating his story convinced him of his own invulnerability.

"Don't you think you might be exaggerating the effect of stopping work," Hugh said, "and underestimating the risk if you don't? A labour force decimated by disease seems a high price to pay."

"I think you are the one exaggerating the risk, Dr. Radlett."

"So you refuse to stop work?"

"Yes."

"And you will not temporarily remove from the workings the men living in the camp."

"I see no reason to."

"Very well." Hugh got up. "I presume you will have no objection to my arranging for any future cases of typhoid to be removed to hospital."

"I shall be happy to provide the means of transport." Bullivant also stood up with a heavy courtesy. "Dr. Radlett, I am sure you will be gratified to know that as soon as I heard of your report from Mr. Simpson, I notified the parish authorities of my earnest desire to co-operate in preventing an epidemic."

"And what was their reaction?"

"They were pleased with my suggestion that I take responsibility for my own men. Any decision regarding the workings remains, and will remain, in my hands."

"In that case, I have been wasting my time. Good day, Mr. Bullivant."

"Dr. Radlett . . ."

Hugh paused.

"You spoke of talking to the Hungarian. Did he say when he intended to return?"

"No. I doubt if he will return. You are not expecting money from him, I trust?"

Bullivant gave him a grim smile. "My opinion of that gentleman is, I believe, the same as yours. We are among the few who were never deceived by him. I could wish there had been more. I have no wish ever to see him again. And now good-day to you. I may rely on your discretion, may I not, Doctor?"

"You may rely on me for nothing, Mr. Bullivant," Hugh said pleasantly.

He shut the door on the other man's startled grunt of protest. It gave him a certain minor satisfaction to do so. As he left the inn, some of the men working nearby called out a greeting to him. Dr. Radlett was a name becoming known in the freemasonry of the navvies.

8

WANDERING through green meadows, through fields waist high with bowing, swaying, delicate gold-fringed heads of wheat and barley; fields studded with poppies like flecks of blood, murmuring with growth, so warm beneath the high sun, it was possible, Anne discovered, to lose identity, to lose the painful insistent necessity to think, to analyse. Thoughts and feelings blurred into the immediate sensations of the moment—the faint sibilant rustle of her skirts, clinging, disengaging, moving as she moved; the rough prickled touch of her wrist as she brushed against a hedgerow; the singing, climbing, hovering spirals of flies above drowsing cattle, the flickering butterflies that darted on the edge of her vision, the languorous self-absorption of the instinctive, natural world.

She took off her straw hat and carried it, shaking her hair loose. She carried the hat carelessly, dangling by its ribbons from the tips of her fingers, and as she threaded her way along a path through a cornfield it slipped away from her hand. Stooping to pick it up, she noticed a movement, a small brown speck of life creeping over the dried hummocks of soil; an insect making a voyage through the giant forest of wheat stalks. It reached the plateau of her hat and, struggling, climbed upon it.

Anne lifted up the hat and the alarmed insect began a desperate circle of escape. Anne tilted the brim and let it slip safely on to a blade of wheat. She felt as pleased to see it go as if she had performed some act of great importance. She was possessed by a feeling of enormous contentment and turning round, looking up at the sky and towards the thick trees and the hedges aflower with dog roses and honeysuckle, she suddenly stretched out her arms in an impulsive gesture of delight, standing alone in her green dress in the middle of the wheat field.

Not until clouds began to gather and the first warning chill touched the air did she turn towards home. Coming back along the road to Rivington she saw the railroad and in the distance a light working engine rollicking along the line. She was becoming used to seeing the railway, she realised; even the great embankment, its sides covered with an ebullient riot of weeds luxuriating in the new-turned soil, was acquiring familiarity, as if it were just another hill, another natural line on the horizon.

A boy was sitting on the wall opposite the Torrance house, swinging his legs. When he saw Anne he jumped down and ran to her. He was one of the boys who hung about the navvies. Anne, assuming he was begging, and having no money with her, walked past him. He ran round her and stood in front, blocking the way.

"What is it?" she said.

"Got a message for you," he said. "From the foreigner."

"What foreigner?"

"He said you'd know. He said to say it was from Lasly."

"Laszlo!" she cried. "You mean Laszlo." He nodded.

"Well, what is it?" she asked impatiently. "What is the message?"

"He wants you to meet him at the birch copse on the path to Waterford Park at ten o'clock to-night and is sorry he cannot come earlier." He rattled it off as if learned by rote, without punctuation.

Anne could have hugged him. Laszlo was back! He had come back! She was full of questions. "When did you see Mr. Bathory? When did he return? Where is he now? What else did he say?"

The boy shrugged. He had delivered his message. He had no more interest in it.

Anne wanted to give him something in return for what he had given her. She felt that this was the resolution of all her doubts. She knew now the reason for her happiness. She had had a presentiment. She had known that Hugh was wrong. "Find him!" he had challenged her and as if in answer the message had come. She seized the boy by the hand and rushed him down the lane to the kitchen door of the house. Sweeping aside the cook's cry of protest, she took half a cooked chicken from the larder and some pie and a loaf of bread and crammed them all into the child's arms.

"If you see the foreigner again," she said, "tell him I shall be there."

Her exuberance, the gaiety of her smile, her impetuous generosity overwhelmed the boy. Grinning and nodding he ran off, clutching his treasures.

"What on earth are you up to, Miss Anne?" the cook demanded.

"I was sorry for him," Anne said airily. "He looked half-starved." She slipped out of the kitchen before she became any more involved.

Hugh dined with Anne and her mother that evening. He was his calm, pleasant self, but Mrs. Torrance noticed that he was more silent than usual. Whereas Anne, who had been in such a conflict of moods lately, seemed to be borne up by some inner excitement.

After the meal, Hugh left them to visit a patient he was concerned about. Soon afterwards Anne excused herself. Mrs. Torrance heard her for a while moving up and down in her room; then there was silence. Mrs. Torrance would have liked to have had her daughter's company a little longer; not to pry or question her, just to talk about nothing in particular—village matters, but she presumed Anne had gone to bed, and decided not to disturb her.

About twenty minutes to ten Anne opened her bedroom door and moved quietly down the stairs. She was half-way when she heard a knocking at the front door. She hesitated as the maid went to answer it, retreating a little way up the stairs. She heard the maid talking, then footsteps, her mother's voice, a strange woman's voice. She wondered what she should do if her mother called for her, but no one came near her and after a while the murmur of talk ceased and Mrs. Torrance returned to the drawing-room, shutting the door behind her in what seemed a final way.

Quickly Anne ran down to the hall, along the passage and out of the garden door. Keeping to the edge of the lawn, she found the gate in the wall and let herself into the lane. As she did so, she found herself remembering the night when Godfrey Bullivant had prowled the dark garden and stood watching the house—an action he had never explained.

The visitor, whoever it had been, had delayed her and she began to hurry, pulling the shawl she had put on against the night air, closer about her. It was almost dark, the long summer dusk providing just enough light for her to see her way. She walked down towards the railroad and then along it, this being the quickest route. She felt no uneasiness at walking alone at night. She knew the way

329

well and her mind was wholly concerned with the man she was to meet.

She was aware that this meeting would be a test for her; for she would know when she saw Laszlo again how much her feeling for him was genuine, and how much imagination or the intoxication of the romantic, adventurous quality he seemed to impart to everything and everyone he was involved with. She was not prepared to fail her own test, however. The scene with Hugh had aroused all the stubbornness in her character. She was determined to love Laszlo, to marry him, to go to Hungary or wherever he wished with him. He was exonerated from any accusation of indifference in her eyes. He had not left her, as Hugh had tried to make her believe. He had not used her. He had come back to her.

She crossed the line by the temporary wooden footbridge the navvies had thrown over it and walked on, moving away from the railway workings. Ahead of her rose the hill of the navvies' camp, the faint blur of their fires becoming sharper and redder as the evening faded slowly into night. It was with a growing sense of excitement that Anne opened a gate and leaving the cart track she had been following, began to cross a wide field of pasture. She was now on the direct path to Waterford Park, with the birch copse already visible at the far end of the field. It was very quiet. She was away from the road, away from the railway line, on the most isolated part of her journey. And there was something about the shape and atmosphere of the trees ahead of her that made her suddenly nervous. The light wind shivered through them, so that they seemed to be chattering and murmuring together. She hesitated, disconcerted by an odd intuition of danger. She walked on again and again stopped, some way away from the birches, reluctant to go any farther. Then she saw a man come out from the trees and stand waiting for her.

The relief of seeing him after her stupid fears made her run to him. She had almost flung herself into his arms before she realised the man was not Laszlo; before she realised who it was.

"Mr. Bullivant . . ." She stepped back. "What are you doing here?"

"Waiting for you." He spoke in a level, unalarming tone. He appeared to be quite calm. To any other person, in fact, that stolid, square figure, with the heavily handsome face, and thick spade beard, might have been a reassuring presence in such a lonely place.

"Why should you be waiting for me?" Anne said. "How did you know I would be coming along this path?"

"You received my message. I knew you would come."

"*Your* message?"

"I knew you would not come to me. But you would come to him. And you have, haven't you?" There was a faint emphasis, a bitter edge to his voice.

"Where is Laszlo?" Anne demanded. "What has happened to him?"

"I have no idea. Gone to the devil, I trust."

"He is not back at Waterford?"

"No, no. He's gone. For good. He is not coming back." The words came more slowly, with a careful deliberation. He swayed slightly on his feet and for the first time Anne realised that he was drunk. She began to move away. He said at once: "Where are you going?"

"Home."

"No, no." He blundered forward, coming close to her. She could smell the whisky on his breath.

"Anne . . ." he said and again, "Anne . . ." staring at her almost helplessly.

"Mr. Bullivant, I have nothing to say to you," she said gently. "Let me pass."

"I love you," he said thickly. "Love you."

"I am sorry."

"Sorry! That's ironic. Sorry! It is not enough to be sorry, Anne. You have tormented me for so long. Too long. You gave smiles and promises with your eyes and then you turn away and smile at another. Knowing I am watching, knowing how I feel."

"That is untrue," she said. "I have never behaved like that to you."

"Never teased me, made fun of me? Never provoked me, amused yourself at my expense? Never?"

There was enough truth in the accusation to silence her.

"It has gone on too long, Anne," he said. "I cannot endure it any longer. I had to see you, to make you see. . . ."

She was aware of the danger. She felt as if she faced a powerful animal, irrational, unpredictable, whose mood could change in an instant. She tried to keep her voice quiet, her manner calm. "I am sorry," she said again, "but we cannot talk here. Come back with me now, to the house."

She turned away but he caught her by the arm, pulling her against him. He drew his hand over her face, tenderly, his fingers trembling, like a blind man learning the face of a stranger. He cupped his hand round her chin, imprisoning her, and kissed her mouth, his lips hard and seeking, his beard rough against her skin.

In spite of herself, in spite of the common sense that told her to bear this, bear it and hope to calm him, the physical repulsion she felt for him made her instinctively struggle to turn her head, endeavouring to twist away from his searching mouth. He grew rougher, holding her to him in a grip that hurt.

"Let me go!" She pushed against him with all the force she was capable of and managed to wrench herself free, her shawl slipping to the ground.

She paused, catching her breath. Bullivant was standing still, watching her. He looked obsessed. His eyes had a vague, lost expression. She still did not believe what was happening or that she could not control the situation. His stupid drunken manner deceived her into thinking he was manageable. She

334

must try and stay cool and composed—at least until she could slip away into the refuge of the trees and escape from him.

He spoke to her in a reproachful voice. "I saw you together, you know, that night. I know you, Anne. I know what you are. And I love you more than he did."

She took a step sideways thinking he would not notice, but he moved at once in the same direction. She retreated and he followed, stopping when she stopped.

"Don't refuse me, Anne," he begged. "Please——"

The combination of that quiet pleading voice with the threat of his physical presence had the elements of a nightmare. It seemed to go on so long. Every time she moved he was there, his implacable figure blocking every way. Anne realised he did not intend to let her go whatever she said to him, whatever she promised. He was content to wait another minute, another five minutes. . . .

In the end it was her nerve that broke. She gathered her skirts up in one hand and ran towards the trees. He caught her at the edge. She screamed and his hand came across her mouth to blot out the sound. She bit at the hand and when he jerked it away screamed

again as loud as she could and Bullivant hit
her with the back of the hand across her face.
The blow half-stunned her and she became
terror-stricken. She felt he no longer knew or
cared who she was, that it was some blind
brutal revenge he was taking on her. There
were no more words, no more talk of love or
need, but the collapse of his self-control that
was like the breaking of a dam. He lost
identity to her; he became nothing but a force
that would overwhelm her. She fought against
him as she would fight an animal that
attacked her and when the voice came and the
shouting that rang through the darkness she
did not hear it. But suddenly Bullivant was
gone, stumbling and crashing away through
the trees, and she was alone.

She struggled to her knees and, hunched
over, her arms crossed over her breast, she
wept. She abandoned herself to her tears like
a child. It was there that Hugh found her,
crouched upon the ground.

When Hugh realised that the woman he had
rescued was Anne he was horrified. He had
had no idea that the screams he had turned
his horse off the track to investigate were

hers. His first reaction was a blind anger.

"Anne, for God's sake, what are you doing here? What were you doing here at this time of night?" He drew her up into his arms and she clung to him desperately. She was shaking. "Has he harmed you? Who was it? Some navvy? If he's harmed you I'll kill him. I heard the screams. I never thought it could be you. What could you expect wandering about alone? The stupidity of it. You idiot. Idiot child."

He stroked her hair and wiped her face, soothing her. It was impossible now to distinguish shapes more than a few yards away. Anne's attacker might be anywhere. It would be pointless to search for him.

"Would you know him again?" he asked. "Could you give a description, do you think?"

She raised her head. "A description?"

"So he can be found and punished."

She gazed into his face for a moment, saying nothing. Then she pulled herself erect and stepped away from him. She seemed quite calm again. In silence she combed the hair back from her face with her fingers, securing it in a knot at the nape of her neck. The bodice of her dress was torn. She found her shawl where it had fallen on the ground and wrapped it round her, knotting the ends together.

"He was drunk," she said at last. "I would not recognise him again."

"You must have seen his face."

"No. It was too dark." She glanced at Hugh. "No harm has been done. I am perfectly all right, Hugh, only frightened and a little bruised. It was my own fault. I deserved it."

He was puzzled by the change in her. He asked again: "What were you doing here?"

"I was walking to Waterford Park. I thought—well, it doesn't matter."

"Were you going to meet Bathory? Has he returned?"

When she did not reply he said: "It was a foolish thing to do even if you were expecting Bathory to be here to protect you. It was not Bathory you were struggling with, I presume."

"No!"

"Well, then——" he paused. "Come along, Anne, I'll take you home."

She did not move. "How did you happen to be here, Hugh? Where were you going?"

"I was on my way to the camp. Someone came to the house while I was out, asking for me. Apparently there is a young girl having a difficult labour. They asked if I would see her."

Anne was surprised. Doctors did not usually attend the confinements of that class of woman, except in very unusual circumstances; nor did the women often seek their help.

"Why did they not send for a midwife?" she asked.

He shrugged. "They seemed to think I would come."

"Yes," Anne said. "They trust you, don't they? Hugh, let me come with you."

"Don't be foolish, Anne."

"Why is it foolish? How do you know any delay might not prove fatal for that girl? You cannot waste time escorting me back to the house."

"It will not take long. I shall waste very little time."

"Can't you see!" she burst out. "I cannot go home yet. If I go like this——" She broke off. "I must have time to recover, Hugh. Please."

"You mean to keep this attack on you a secret?"

"Yes, yes!"

"Why?"

"Because I wish it!"

"It was an attempted rape," he said bluntly. "Do you think it right to keep quiet about it? Don't you think you should warn other women about this man? Suppose he should attack someone else—more successfully?"

"He won't," Anne said.

"Are you sure you don't know him, Anne?"

"No! He was just a man who had had too much to drink and acted on impulse. It was not a deliberate, planned attack. If I had not been here, by chance, nothing would have happened. Please, Hugh, my mother would be so distressed if you made this public knowledge and no good would come of it, I assure you."

He considered it, not, as Anne could tell, in the light of anything she desired, but in the view of his own judgement of what should be done. It was very rarely that she was able to influence him against his own opinion.

"Perhaps you are right," he said. "If you cannot identify the man there is no point in inflicting on you and your mother the unpleasantness that is bound to ensue—the talk, the questions and so on. But I am adamant about not taking you to the camp with me. You have never been there, Anne. This is not the moment for you to pay a social visit."

"That is a cruel thing to say. I suppose I deserve it."

"I don't mean to be cruel, only realistic. Apart from other considerations, have you forgotten that there is typhoid in the camp?"

"Then be realistic." She had recovered a slightly arrogant note to her voice. "I am a doctor's daughter. I am not totally ignorant of the medical facts of life and death. I might even be of use to you. I am not afraid of typhoid, and in any case you have removed the only sufferers to hospital."

Hugh wondered about her motives for this insistence. They must be based on fear. He was not convinced that the man who attacked her was a stranger. It might have been someone who lived in or near Rivington, whom she might expect to meet at any time; who might indeed be waiting for her to return home. If Hugh took her back to the house and left her he would not be easy in his mind. He could protect her best by keeping her with him, and it was true that he could guard against coming into contact with any case of typhoid which might have developed since his last visit. The risk of infection would be small or great depending on the length of time they spent there.

As he stood, still undecided, Anne came up to him and quite unexpectedly, in the darkness that made it difficult for him to discern the expression on her face, put her hand into his. It was an action so contrary to the proud independence of her speech, such a childlike, trusting gesture, asking for protection and friendship, that he found, as so often with Anne, all his opposition melting before it.

He put his arm round her shoulders. "How my poor horse will sustain our combined weight, I cannot imagine, but as I, for one, am not prepared to walk all the way to the camp we had better try it. Come along."

They rode up to the camp in silence, the horse picking its way slowly up the hill with no more than a gentle guidance from Hugh. As they drew near the top the black mounds that crowned it, that had from a distance looked like clumps of bushes or the curved barrows of primitive dead separated into a conglomeration of shanties and shacks and turf-roofed hovels. In daylight some of the huts had a look of permanence, constructed of wood and bricks, weatherproof and stoutly built; others seemed no more than overnight shelters, flung together from bits of tarpaulin, a couple of planks, a wall of earth. The more sophisticated had proper hearths for the cooking fires; the inhabitants of the others cooked in the open on the fires that Anne had seen from her bedroom window for so many months. The dwellings were set higgledy-piggledy where the builders chose, without reference to their neighbours. The paths between them, consisting in this weather of dried mud, ridged and uneven, were turned into streams whenever it rained, the water draining from the highest points and seeping into the lower-lying huts, turning their earth floors into dank mud.

As Hugh and Anne approached, the noise from the camp increased from a first faint hum like a soughing wind to the clattering, changing, roaring confusion of a city. Children crying, women shouting, men singing and laughing and talking, the incessant barking of the dogs they had brought there, a fiddle playing somewhere, a scream—it seemed impossible that all this vigorous life should not have spilled over and swamped the quiet valley beneath it and all the sleeping villages below. Anne wondered how they would find anyone in this world of deep black shadow and flickering firelight, but they had been watched for and as Hugh dismounted and helped Anne down, a man stepped forward holding a torch of wood dipped in pitch. He led them, a straggling band of children soon gathered at their heels, to a hut in the centre of the camp. Anne followed Hugh closely, thinking it ironic that because of Bullivant she should feel safer up here tonight, among the people she had feared and despised, than in her own home fields.

At the entrance to the hut, the guide held aside the blanket that served as a door and gestured them to go inside; sending the children, with a wave of his torch and a shout, scattering like chickens.

Anne stood quietly inside the hut, blinking to accustom her eyes to the light. It was one of the larger shanties, about twenty feet long. At one end the fire, over which heavy iron cooking pots were suspended, had burned low but was still sufficient, despite the evening chill, to keep the temperature at a clinging summer heat. Two sides of the walls were lined with rough wooden bunks, one row above another, in several of which men lay sleeping. The landlady of the hut, who was also the mother of the girl Hugh had come to see, had cleared the rest of the men out. In one corner her other children, huddled like fledgelings in the nest, wide-eyed and curious, watched everything that happened.

It was the landlady who had come down to the Torrance house to ask for Hugh's help. Anne recognised the voice as that of the woman who had talked to her mother. She had taken great care with her appearance before taking such a drastic step and in her respectable dress, her greying hair neatly plaited round her head, she looked very little different in Anne's eyes from some of the village women.

Her daughter lay on a mattress near the doorway in the coolest part of the room. Candles stood fixed in their own wax on an upright box and there was one oil lamp whose smoking wick filled the room with acrid fumes. The girl, Anne learned later, was sixteen but she might have been any age. Her thin hair, dark with sweat, clung to her head, her face was pinched and grey, beaded with moisture, the eyes sunk deep in the sockets like a victim of fever. Her arms, pitifully thin and childlike in contrast to her swollen body, lay outside the rough blanket that covered her, her fingers clenching feebly like the aimlessly clutching fingers of a baby. She was too exhausted by the hours of fruitless labour to respond to their presence.

Anne stood to one side of the bed while Hugh examined the girl. Nobody had so far paid her any attention. Hugh was the focus of their interest. They assumed he had brought Anne with him to assist him.

"I reckon the child's dead," the mother of the girl said unemotionally. "And she'll be an' all. I thought mebbe you could cut the babe out, Doctor, and give her a chance. They say you can do anything. They say you put people to sleep so they don't feel no pain."

"How long has she been in labour?" he asked.

"Near two days. It's not moving, you can see that. It's killing her. I want you to cut it out."

"If I perform a Caesarean section," Hugh said quietly, "I might save the child but I should certainly kill your daughter. It is very rarely indeed that a woman survives that operation. But don't worry. We shall manage, I am sure."

He patted the girl's shoulder gently, stooping down to talk to her. When a pain seized her she reached out and clung to his hand, panting, her eyes filled with blank agony. Moved, Anne wrung out a handkerchief in a pail of cold water, and cooled the girl's forehead with it. As she stood up again, Hugh smiled encouragingly at her and she found herself so pleased to have his approval that she realised how out of joint everything was when they were at odds with each other. She smiled back at him.

"Hold her hand," he said. "Let her grip you when she is in pain."

Anne knelt on the earth floor by the side of the mattress, holding the girl's hand and wiping her forehead while Hugh made his preparations. He made the mother banish the watching children to bed and got one of the navvies to rig up another blanket to give the area round the bed more privacy.

"Where's the father?" he asked as he worked.

The landlady snorted. "Out drowning his sorrows. He couldn't stand the row she were making. He won't be back for a while, if ever."

Hugh glanced up at the man who had met them with the torch and who was now tying up the rope to hang the blanket from. "Is he your husband?"

"My husband's dead. Killed last year. Tip-truck killed him. If the old woman that had this shanty hadn't dropped dead one night I don't know what I should have done. But the men let me take it over. My husband and I lodged here you see. I'd nowhere else to go. Spent all me married life on the railways." She gestured at the figure of her daughter. "It's no life for a woman but you get trapped, you know. Where can you go? What can you do else? Now she's trapped too. What can you expect, though? They're young. What can you expect?"

Hugh observed the progress of the labour. The girl had an unusually narrow pelvis which, though not deformed, would always make childbirth difficult for her. In this case the child's large head was blocking the birth canal and would not move forward. It seemed to Hugh that the only chance of saving the child would be to turn it, but he waited for a while in case natural delivery still proved possible.

After half-an-hour the baby's head had not moved forward an inch and it was clear that there was no chance of a natural birth. For the sake of both mother and child it would be dangerous to delay any longer. Hugh decided to give the girl chloroform and attempt to turn and deliver the child with instruments and by manipulation.

He bent down over the girl, speaking gently to her while he placed the cloth over her mouth and nose and administered the chloroform. The sickly sweet smell of the anaesthetic filled the air and Anne watched amazed at the speed with which the girl's groans subsided and her breathing calmed. Soon she was lying quite still.

"Now, Anne," Hugh said. "I want your help."

She nodded, outwardly calm but full of apprehension. Contrary to her brave words to Hugh about being a doctor's daughter, she was ignorant of a great deal about the process of birth and had never witnessed it even in an animal; but the trust he was putting in her and her pity for the girl overcame any irresolution. She forgot herself, her anxieties, her confusion, and became utterly absorbed in the medical problem Hugh was faced with. She was fascinated to see that the chloroform had no effect on the movement of the uterus. The girl's unconscious body continued to strive for its release in collaboration with Hugh's skill and gentleness. With the complete relaxation of tension in the girl he could work without hesitation to turn the baby and to assist in its expulsion into the world without danger to its mother.

He worked with complete concentration. When he wanted her to do anything for him, he gave her her instructions quickly but so clearly that she had no difficulty in following them. Seeing him at his most professional she became aware, more clearly than ever before, of the qualities he had in common with her father; the qualities that had made them both, though of such different personalities, such good doctors. She did not realise that the circumstances were revealing in her similar qualities. When Hugh announced that the most important stage was over, that he had succeeded in turning the child, she gave no exclamation or comment but waited as calmly as before for her next order.

She found that such a fundamental situation as childbirth broke down all barriers whether of class or of false modesty. She did everything she was asked whether by Hugh or by the girl's mother, carrying herself the heavy pots of hot water from the hearth, helping the older woman remove soiled cloths for burning, trimming the wick of the lamp. But when the child was at last safely born she could not maintain her mask of composure. She gazed in something like awe at the frail infant lying in Hugh's hands.

"He's alive," he said. "That's something to be thankful for."

He cut the cord and was about to hand the child to Anne, but seeing her expression in which amazement and wonder were combined, he changed his mind.

"I wouldn't wish you to drop him," he remarked with a smile, "after all this," and gave the child to its grandmother while he turned back to the young mother.

The afterbirth was delivered and the girl began to regain consciousness. When she realised her agony was over, when Hugh showed her her baby, a boy and alive, the smile with which she greeted them touched Anne to tears.

When every last task had been completed

and all was put in order, Anne asked if she might hold the baby for a moment. The grandmother handed him to her. She took the tightly-wrapped bundle with great care. The baby's head, thinly covered with black hair, was slightly misshapen by the experience of its birth, the face wrinkled and blind like a kitten. The simple astonishing fact of the new being she held against her breast, the tiny whisper of breath, no more than a sigh, with which it clung to life, moved Anne more than anything she had experienced.

"What will you call him?" she asked the girl.

The girl smiled and shook her head, too weak to answer.

They were all filled with such relief, such satisfaction at the safe delivery, that they smiled constantly and foolishly at each other. The navvy who had been guarding the door was allowed in and with him came four others, lodgers in the hut. They brought out jars of gin and water and insisted on Hugh joining them to wet the baby's head. Anne sat on a low stool by the girl's bed, watching while in the group round the trestle table at the end of the room Hugh drank and laughed and listened to the men as cheerfully as if it were one in the afternoon and not one in the morning. He escaped at last and came across the room to collect Anne.

"You must be tired," he said. "Come along home."

"Hugh," she said, "I believe you are quite an extraordinary man."

"I am glad you are beginning to appreciate me." He took her arm. "But the pretty speeches must wait until later. If we do not leave now, I am afraid we shall be here till dawn."

Going back to Rivington, he insisted on Anne riding while he led the horse. He said it was safer. They travelled down in a very different mood from the one they had been in on the journey up to the camp. Both were filled with a sense of elation which blotted out their weariness. Hugh was thinking about Arthur Toms. By saving the child, he felt he had repaid a debt. In each case he had been called on as a last resort. One failure, one success. It evened itself out.

Anne asked suddenly: "What would have happened if you had performed a Caesarean operation?"

"The girl would probably have bled to death. No one has yet discovered a way of successfully stopping the bleeding or the infection that results. When it is successful it is a matter of luck. That is why it is only resorted to when it is certain the mother will die in any case."

"It is a dangerous life being a woman."

"It is dangerous to be alive."

At the house she waited while he stabled the horse. They walked across to the door of the house, entering through the consulting rooms.

"You looked very dignified to-night," Hugh said to her, "and very competent. Your father would have been proud of you." And as he saw the tears start to her eyes he bent forward and kissed her gently. "Good night, Anne."

"Good night, Hugh."

It was not until Anne saw her face in the mirror in her bedroom, saw the bruise on her cheek, that she thought again about Bullivant and his assault upon her. And then it was as something unimportant. The events of the night had wiped out its significance for her.

During the next week Hugh spent many hours up at the camp. The baby was sickly and the young mother developed a fever which, though not as dangerous as Hugh at first feared, was still cause enough for him to keep a constant watch on her. Then, in the space of three days, ten new cases of typhoid appeared. And the fine weather broke up in a series of shattering thunderstorms that turned tracks into rivers and hampered all movement about the countryside. Hugh would often arrive back at the house at the end of a day filthy, drenched and exhausted.

"There is one consolation," he told Anne. "Parts of the line are flooded and work has been halted. I think the epidemic may be contained."

On Sunday morning Anne and Mrs. Torrance went to church as usual. Hugh sometimes accompanied them to morning service but on this occasion Mrs. Torrance had given instructions to the maid the night before not to awaken him.

"He will be ill himself," she said, "if he does not get more rest."

He got up about eleven and was drinking a cup of coffee in the drawing-room when they returned, a good quarter of an hour earlier than was customary. It was clear at once that something had happened. Anne came sweeping into the room, her eyes bright with indignation.

"It is not to be borne," she declared. "He has gone too far. It is intolerable."

"Who are you talking about?"

"Carrington! You must defend yourself, Hugh. You must go and tell him what a bigoted fool he is."

"I do that regularly, about once a month," he observed.

He stood up as Mrs. Torrance entered, unpinning her hat. He appealed to her. "What is this about?"

She laid the hat carefully on a small round table, placing her gloves beside it. "Anaesthesia," she explained. "Mr. Carrington believes it to be against the will of God."

"He has taken his time in protesting. It is long enough since I operated on poor Toms."

Anne swung round. "It is not your use of chloroform on Toms he spoke of. I do not believe he has any objection to it for such a purpose. Dear me, no. A man may be shielded from pain by all means. But not a woman in labour. That is going a little too far for Mr. Carrington."

"Stop pacing up and down, Anne," Mrs. Torrance said. "You are making me dizzy.

He was speaking about the girl in the camp, Hugh."

Though not about my part in it, Anne thought. If he had known about that he would have been doubly shocked. Everything that had happened to her that night had remained a secret. She had not returned to the camp since though she longed to see the baby once more. Hugh had said the risk of infection was too great and she had accepted his verdict with a new humility.

"So he has heard about that poor child," Hugh was saying. "And he preached a sermon about it?"

"He did indeed."

"On the text: In sorrow shalt thou bring forth children and so on and so forth, and that God in his heavenly wisdom having seen fit to inflict the pain of childbirth on women, it amounts to blasphemy to attempt to alleviate it."

Anne sank down in a chair. "How did you know?"

He shrugged. "It has been a common reaction from many of the clergy. They have referred to chloroform, I understand, as 'the fruit of the Devil'. Did Carrington attack me by name?"

"No. He avoided that," Mrs. Torrance said. "But it was obvious who he meant. His sermon was a general attack on the snares and delusions of modern so-called progress which is leading our country, in Mr. Carrington's view, towards shame and decay—not to mention corruption, the evils of Sodom and Gomorrah and many other Biblical matters."

Hugh smiled at her. "What was the reaction?"

"We did not feel he had won outright the support of the mothers of the congregation," Mrs. Torrance remarked drily. "There was a certain amount of murmuring." She glanced at Anne. "Anne rose to her feet and walked majestically out of the church, so naturally I followed."

"When I remember the dinners he has consumed," Anne cried, "the hours of boredom we have endured! Well, he will not be welcome here again."

"There is no need to be childish," Mrs. Torrance said. "I suppose he is entitled to his opinion."

Anne seemed to feel this revealed her mother as lacking in all strength of character.

"There is a simple Biblical reply to his objections which could be quoted back at him the next time you meet," Hugh remarked. "As far as I remember, it goes like this: 'And the Lord God caused a deep sleep to fall upon Adam and he slept: and He took one of his ribs and closed up the flesh thereof.' If that is not a description of anaesthesia, what is?"

"Ah," said Mrs. Torrance. "He will say that was before the Fall."

"Yes, of course, and that was a woman's fault, was it not. It has been a long punishment for eating an apple."

"You take this so lightly, both of you," Anne protested. "Hugh may be used to it, but Mother, you were there, you heard the vindictiveness in Carrington's voice. You cannot believe others will remain uninfluenced by his hostility. It could cause Hugh great harm."

"I shall wait and see before I act," Hugh said. "I have better things to do than squabble with Carrington."

It soon appeared that Anne was right. Others had been strongly influenced by Carrington's sermon, but in a way quite contrary to her expectations. She came down to breakfast on Tuesday morning to find the servants in a flurry of gossip.

"What is the matter?"

"Oh, Miss Anne, William Broom has been in and he says he came past the church and there were people standing there and he went in and it's as if a whirlwind had struck it. He says you never saw nothing like it. . . ."

Anne took her shawl and ran up the road to the church. There was a small knot of people crowded round the entrance, their faces agog with the morbid excitement any kind of disaster engenders. She pushed past them and into the church. For a moment she saw nothing wrong and then as she began to walk down the central aisle her foot slipped and she looked down to see that she was walking on mud and that mud and filth and pools of dirty water were everywhere. Then she noticed the dark wooden pews had been splashed indiscriminately with whitewash, and saw that the altar cloth had been torn down, and the crucifix and the tall candlesticks and even the communion goblet had been thrown to the floor and lay scattered and tarnished.

In the middle of this desolation Carrington was standing. His shoulders drooped like an old man's.

"Come and see," he said. "Come and see what barbarism has done." There were tears in his eyes. "Desecration." He said, "Desecration."

It was as if a mob of malicious children had run riot through the church. Nothing had been stolen, nothing had been damaged beyond repair, but the deliberateness of the vandalism chilled Anne.

"Who could do such a thing?" she said. "And why?"

"Is there any doubt?" he said bitterly. "Those pagan devils who have invaded our countryside. Dr. Radlett's friends. They wish to destroy everything virtuous and good. But I shall not be defeated. No, never defeated." He pulled himself straighter, gazing round his church with a martyr's passion. "I speak God's truth, Miss Torrance. I speak out too clearly and truly and that is why they attempt to stop me. But I shall not be stopped. They may burn my church to the ground and I shall defy them."

Anne said nothing. She saw he had been imbued with a sense of mission and that now it would be open war between him and the navvies, between him and everything that Hugh represented. She was struck by the senselessness of it; sick at heart at the thought of the pattern that was emerging in the life of

361

the village. She saw how each act, beginning with the vicar's refusal to bury the man killed in the tipping accident, had led in turn to this. How in the end violent speech had led inevitably to violent action. All was lost then.

"I was part of it too," she said aloud.

Carrington misunderstood her. "No, I cannot believe that, Miss Torrance. Mistaken and foolish, perhaps, in some of your views. But I know who is responsible and they will be made to pay for it in the end."

She wanted to say: "You are responsible, quite as much as they." But she did not. She left him gazing round his church with the warming fire of vengeance newly alight in him, and went out of the ancient wooden door as the men began to arrive with stiff twig brooms to sweep the floor clean.

Hugh, Anne discovered when she sought him out on her return, was not unduly surprised by what had happened.

"I am sorry for it," he said. "I would go to help but I imagine Carrington would attempt to fling me bodily from the church."

"How can he link you with the people responsible for this! It is so unjust. Do you believe it was the navvies?"

He nodded. "Yes."

"What puzzles me is why it should follow on his sermon. How did they hear of it? I saw no navvies in the church."

"I have heard about the sermon from six different people," Hugh said, "excluding you. These things spread very quickly——"

He broke off. They had been standing by the window of the living-room as they talked, looking at the church. Now something had caught his attention. He said abruptly: "Excuse me, Anne," and to her astonishment left the room almost at a run. She heard the house door open and shut and saw Hugh walking quickly towards the church. When he reached the lane that led down to Mrs. Toms's cottage, he halted. A woman had come out of the lane and seemed to be hesitating which way to go, perhaps disconcerted by the unusual number of people gathered outside the church so early in the morning. Anne saw Hugh go up to the woman. She turned her head and her face previously hidden by her bonnet became visible. It was Esther Wharton. Hugh was saying something to her. Esther put her hand to her face and turned away. Hugh took her arm and spoke again to her. He seemed to be insisting.

Esther shrugged. Slowly they began to walk to the house.

To Anne's surprise they did not come to the front door but disappeared down the side lane that led to the entrance to Hugh's part of the house. After a moment Anne went out into the hall and a little way along the corridor. She could hear the murmur of voices in Hugh's room. She considered knocking on the door on some pretext or other and breaking in upon them but she was ashamed of the idea as soon as it formed, and after a minute or two of hovering uncertainty, she went, considerably disturbed by the incident, to join her mother at breakfast.

9

THERE was another visitor to the house that day. Godfrey Bullivant came to call on Anne. He asked to see her alone. When she entered the room he was standing by the fireplace, hat in hand, facing the door. She had the impression that he had not moved since the maid left the room to fetch her. She was glad he had come. She no longer felt any fear of him. He had lost his power to exercise any dominance over her.

They regarded each other across the room in silence. At length Anne spoke. "Why have you come?"

"Do you need to ask that?" he said in a low voice. "To apologise for my behaviour at our last meeting."

"I have forgotten it."

Her reply seemed to affect him. He looked away. She realised he was holding himself under rigid restraint and asked herself what it must have cost him to come here. When he glanced back at her his expression was one almost of grim amusement.

"Did you know that that was the worst thing you could say to me?"

"Why so?"

"To be so easily forgotten. Even after such an outrage. I would have expected a little hatred. That would have been infinitely more solacing."

"Mr. Bullivant, I am sorry you are so unhappy."

"Anne, don't be kind to me."

"I don't intend——"

"I know, I know."

"Are you ill? You don't look well."

"I have been waiting to be arrested. Then I realised that you must have said nothing. But I wondered about the man who came——"

"That was Hugh Radlett," Anne said. "I told him my attacker was a drunken navvy."

"An accurate enough description," Bullivant said. "I have learned that I am little better than the lowest of my men." He paused. "I must tell you that I never intended you harm. Do you believe me?"

"Yes."

"Then that is that." He spoke with a forced briskness. "I don't intend to visit this house again. Perhaps you will make some excuse to your mother, if explanations are needed. I will say good-bye, Anne."

"Good-bye, Mr. Bullivant."

She stood aside to let him pass. He turned, gripping the edge of the door with one hand. "Your lover is back. I have seen him walking with Miss Wharton."

"Miss Wharton? Are you sure that was not Hugh?"

Bullivant did not reply. He looked at her once more, with the same bleak expression in his eyes, and then was gone, closing the door behind him with infinite gentleness, like a man careful of an injury, as if to shut it firmly would cause him pain.

Deciding that she was justified by Hugh's abrupt departure from her that morning, Anne asked him about Esther Wharton. He would not be drawn.

"Is she ill?" Anne persisted. She could almost hope Esther was ill; it would be an explanation more satisfactory to her than any other.

"No," Hugh said. "She is not ill." And when he saw she was about to pursue the matter further, he interrupted her. "I can say nothing about Esther, Anne. It is a private matter."

"Did she mention Laszlo?"

There was a moment's hesitation. "In what connection?"

"Godfrey Bullivant told me he had returned. But I believe he mistook you for him. He said he saw him with Esther."

"She said nothing to me about Bathory's return." The cold statement sounded unfriendly, and when Hugh, making an excuse of work, left her then, obviously avoiding more questions, Anne had a disquieting sense of desolation, as if everyone was abandoning her.

The following day she walked over to Waterford Park with the faint hope that the Countess might have news of Laszlo. It did not occur to her to question the servants so that when she was shown into the Countess's small study, the sight of Laszlo seated in a high-backed winged chair as if he had been settled there a fortnight, shocked her into immobility.

"Anne!" He rose to his feet somewhat apathetically. "My dear Anne." He kissed her hand. "I was about to come and look for you."

"I have been here, all this time, in Rivington, Laszlo," she replied. "Where have you been?"

"Here and there, here and there."

He was, she saw at once, at his most Hungarian. He had not even smiled as he greeted her. He seemed sunk in gloom.

Coming farther into the room she saw the Countess sitting in a chair by her late husband's desk. "Anne, we are delighted to see you, but I fear you will soon be driven away by our misery. We are hiding in here like victims of war. You must forgive Laszlo for not riding over at once to see you. He did not want to distress you with his grief."

"What is the matter? What has happened?"

Laszlo shook his head. "It is all over. All over."

Anne looked from one to the other in bewilderment. "What does he mean?" she appealed to Sophia. "What is all over?"

"The revolution!" Laszlo cried. "The tyrants have sunk all their differences in order to slaughter us."

"But I thought your armies had defeated the Austrians? I thought you had won?"

"We defeated the Austrians. We cannot expect to defeat the Russians as well."

"The Russians have sent their armies into Hungary," Sophia explained. "The Czar has made an alliance with the Emperor to crush the revolution."

"He was fearful of Poland." Laszlo was bitterly scornful. "He was afraid his vassal state might catch fire from our flame. They have combined armies of nearly four hundred thousand men against us. Twelve hundred guns. We have four hundred and fifty guns. They marched into Hungary in June. We are being driven back every day. Buda has already fallen to the butcher Haynau. We cannot survive. Hungary has always been Europe's bastion against the East and now its so-called emperor and protector has invited the barbarian hordes in to murder us. And no one helps us. No one. Not one country to whom Kossuth has appealed for help, not one country of those who profess to love freedom has raised a finger to help us." He bowed his head. "I am an exile for ever, Anne. I dare not go back. They will execute every patriot they capture. The country will run with blood."

"But have they really surrendered?" Anne asked. "Is it really all over?"

"It is a matter of time. What can they fight

with? They are outnumbered by men, by guns, by everything. We have been fighting a long time, on small resources. Without help——"

"But what of all the men like you, Laszlo? All the men who have been asking for money and help. You were so successful——"

He took her hand, clasping it between his hands. "I have found true friends here in England. I have thanked God for it."

"You foresaw this," Anne said. "I remember a day in winter when you told me the revolution would not survive."

"Liberty is a delicate plant," the Countess observed, "much disliked by governments. But it always survives somewhere. It can be destroyed in one country; it appears in another. I think we should not allow ourselves to despair, Laszlo."

"You take the long view, Countess," he said. "I feel my life is too short to be satisfied with the consolations of history. Of the hopes of the past year, what is left? We were the last hope of Europe and when we are suppressed, what will be left of freedom?"

"I have a very simple definition," Sophia said. "Liberty to me is one individual speaking his mind without fear of unjust punishment. When they silence the individual, that is the end of freedom. Hungary had just learned to speak. Now her voice is to be silenced. Her poets and writers will be dumb. That is the tragedy."

"Those limits are too narrow for me," Laszlo said. "It is not merely a question of speech. To me freedom should give the power to rule and not be ruled."

"My father used to say," Anne said, "that liberty depended on the rule of law."

"Law is corruptible, Anne," Laszlo said. "Unjust governments make unjust laws. The railway you dislike so much is imposed on you by act of Parliament. Is that not so?"

"But we are free to change the laws."

"Perhaps the only definition one can make of freedom is that you know when you live in its atmosphere and when you do not. My country has breathed that heady air. They will never entirely forget it."

They sat on, talking endlessly, returning each time to the disastrous events of the past two months in Hungary. Anne felt her personal anxieties, her emotional confusions, were of trivial importance in the face of the calamity that had struck Laszlo's countrymen after so much struggle, so much gallant endeavour. He was quite sure that final defeat was now inevitable. When Anne tried to ask him what he would do, he seemed unable even to bear to think of his future, except to repeat that he could never go back to Hungary.

She stayed to eat with them, and with the food and the wine, Laszlo's mercurial spirits began to rise. Esther Wharton did not dine with them. She was, Sophia said, feeling unwell, at which Anne's spirits too, in a reprehensible manner, began to rise. By the end of the meal, Laszlo was almost cheerful. He began to argue that all might not yet be lost, after all. The great powers might yet intervene.

Later, he accompanied Anne home in the Countess's carriage and kissed her with passion, but did not seem to wish to stay with her. He declined to come into the house. "I have so much to do, so many plans to make."

Anne looked at him in silence. She had waited so long and so hopefully for his return. She had been confident that to see him again would be to resolve everything, but now she knew it was not to be so simple. She had thought at first that he must have changed towards her. Otherwise why had he not come straight to her, or at the least sent a messenger? But perhaps it was she who had changed, who after this long absence, was seeing him more clearly than before.

She studied his face, the fine profile, the fair hair, the long elegant hands; even in despair, he had dressed to perfection. He was made of such contrasts, like quicksilver, unknowable. To love him, she realised now, would be to put trust in the unknown. There would always be uncertainty, and doubts. She would always be the one to give. He would hold her in dependence because he appeared to need so little from a woman, relying perhaps on their need of him. She did not see that he could ever commit himself to another person. Yet he had been capable of committing his life to an ideal, to his country's freedom. It was the contradiction which kept her from breaking free. That and the attraction that flared between them, as when his hand brushed hers; the attraction that was so difficult to resist. Is this love, she wondered, and felt too confused to want to follow the thought farther.

He had told her he would call for her early the following day. When he did not appear she waited, and when she was tired of waiting she set out to walk to meet him along the road. There had been all morning an unusual number of men about the village and it puzzled her until Hugh remarked that it was the day the navvies were paid. A month's wages.

"They pay them off at the Fox and Grapes. I believe Simpson lodges there."

She walked quickly, still after this time, a little fearful of the men, but they did not seem to notice her. They were walking down through the village in groups of four or five, purposeful and silent.

It was a sullen sort of day, depressing in its humidity and its greyness. It was hot, without the pleasantness of sunshine, damp without the freshness of rain. Anne found the walk tiring. She was aware of a sense of unease, a prickling along the nerves as before a thunderstorm. She blamed it on the heat but was afraid that what might be disturbing her was the gathering of another kind of storm. Since the episode of the desecration of the church, there had been an unpleasant air about the village. A sense of disintegration. She had a weird prescience of everything rushing to disaster, a presentiment she now tried to attribute to her feelings about the

Hungarian collapse; but in honesty she had to admit to herself that she was not so involved in that country's affairs as to make it natural for her to be so distraught.

"It is a feeling like Doomsday," she tried to explain to Sophia.

The Countess nodded sympathetically. "It is an affliction of youth to think the world is coming to an end. It will pass."

They were in Sophia's bedroom at Waterford Park. It was with a sense of inevitability that Anne had learned on arrival that she had missed Laszlo somewhere along the way.

"He was up and off very early, the servants tell me," Sophia said. "I am afraid I do not know where. He is in a strange mood, as you know."

Sophia was still in bed, sipping chocolate. Her hair, however, had been dressed and in her deshabille she looked as feminine as ever and rather more fragile and vulnerable. She rang for more chocolate and told Anne to sit down.

"I must apologise for this sluggardly behaviour," she said. "I am getting old, you see, Anne. I need my rest."

"I am sorry, Countess," Anne said. "I

know what a terrible blow the news from Hungary has been to you."

Sophia shrugged. "I should be lying if I said I had not expected it. The whole affair, the remarkable success they achieved, somehow always seemed too good to be true, too right and just to last. In this wicked world, Anne, old men with guns usually defeat young men with ideals. And by the time the young men have acquired the guns and achieved the power, they have become as old and selfish as their predecessors. A vicious circle. It is better to cultivate one's garden."

"You feel it a wasteful tragedy," Anne remarked.

"No, you misunderstand me, Anne. For all my cynicism, I know that such events are never in vain. Laszlo cannot take the long view of history. But I am older, and I can. What happened in Hungary was like a lightning flash that for a few seconds illuminates a dark landscape which is then plunged deeper into darkness. What you see, in that flash, remains imprinted on your eyes. That episode of romantic heroism, as your Hugh would call it, cannot be wiped off the records. It will always be there to inspire others; and the tyranny is recorded also."

"It seems so simple when I hear you and Laszlo talk. Everything appears a matter of clearcut right and wrong. I cannot help feeling that life is easier to live if you can see it in such terms. In the ordinary problems of my own life, everything merges into confusion."

"My poor Anne." Sophia patted the bed beside her. "Come and sit here and let me look at you." Obediently Anne went up to the bedside. Sophia studied her. "I had not realised before how much you have changed in the past year."

"Grown older, you mean," Anne smiled.

"Yes, I do mean that and it is a compliment. Youth need not be tied to immaturity. You were a beautiful, foolish girl last year. Now you look like a woman."

Inexplicably, Anne's eyes filled with tears. She turned away. "I do not feel mature. I feel a foolish schoolgirl who has been too ready to play with other people's lives."

The Countess laughed and patted her hand. "But that is what I have been saying. To know you are a fool is the first sign of maturity. Now I must say something else. Marry Hugh. Do not marry Laszlo Bathory."

Anne looked at her in some surprise. "I thought you admired Laszlo. You have always seemed to like him and defend him against Hugh."

"What has that to do with it! We are talking about you. You will make Hugh happy. Laszlo I do not think will make you happy. Your temperament needs a strong man to balance it."

"You do not think Laszlo has a strong character?"

The Countess answered the question obliquely. "With Laszlo your life would be a matter of fireworks and cavalry charges and dazzle and glitter—and long hours of loneliness." She paused, looking at Anne with an expression of great affection. "I speak not entirely without experience. My first husband, who as you know was Hungarian, was very like Laszlo." She smiled at some recollection. "Very like. . . ."

They were both silent, both lost in thought, and in the silence came a soft knocking at the door, very quiet and tentative. Then the door moved open and Esther Wharton slipped into the room. She paused, perhaps disconcerted to see Anne there.

"What did you want, Esther?" Sophia asked sharply.

Esther stood by the door, saying nothing.

She seemed to Anne to have been drained of what vitality she had. She looked as plain as ever, but the one quality she had possessed, that of her stillness and serenity, seemed to be lost. There was an air of nervous tension about her. Her pale eyes glanced from one woman to the other. She licked her lips.

"There is rioting in the village," she said. "Did you know that, Miss Torrance?"

"No! What do you mean, Miss Wharton? Who is rioting?"

"The servants have just heard. The navvies are rioting, they say."

Anne stood up. "My mother. . . . Hugh is usually out at this time. I must go."

"No one will harm your mother, Anne."

"I must go. She may need me."

"Then I shall come with you." Sophia swept aside the covers. "I shall be dressed in a quarter of an hour. You may ring the bell for my maid, Esther. I can be quick when I need to be. We shall drive over in the carriage. I cannot possibly allow you to walk alone about the country with that sort of nonsense going on. I expect it is greatly exaggerated. Servants love to invent murders and robbers and such-like violence. The excitement pleases them. Do you wish to come with us, Esther? Or perhaps you would prefer to rest in your room?" There was, Anne thought, a sardonic note in her voice. "You look tired."

Esther did not reply. She went away as quietly as she had come.

The household aroused by the Countess's ringing bells, swarmed into activity like an alarmed colony of ants. Within twenty minutes, Anne, to her mild surprise, was in the carriage rattling down the drive with the Countess, dressed in what she considered suitable clothes for riots, alertly poised beside her. Suddenly, Sophia called out for them to stop, the driver obeying with such alacrity that Anne was flung back against the seat. Sophia lowered the window and leaned out, calling, and Anne saw what had taken her attention. Laszlo had entered the gates and was riding past them. At Sophia's beckoning he dismounted and came to speak to them. He seemed to Anne to be avoiding her eyes.

"Did you not see us?" Sophia cried. "Where are you going?"

"To the house."

"Turn round, turn round, you shall escort us."

"Where to?" he asked.

381

"Have you not been to the village? They say the railway workers are running amok."

"I have heard nothing. I would hardly believe it." He glanced past the Countess at Anne and away again and Anne felt a coldness in the pit of her stomach.

She wanted to say: "If you had forgotten you were to see me, say so. Why this slyness? Admit it, it does not matter." She looked away from him, saying nothing.

"I'll follow you," Laszlo said. "Do not wait." He left abruptly.

The Countess looked at Anne and made a clicking noise with her tongue. She called to the driver to go on.

The trouble with the navvies had begun in a small way. Bullivant maintained that it could have been avoided if Simpson had obeyed his instructions and not acted like a fool. Simpson swore nothing could have prevented it in the mood the men were in. They were looking for trouble, he said.

It had begun when the gangers gathered at the Fox and Grapes to collect the wages for their teams. They had been working in teams of five or six men. Some Simpson had hired as gangs, fixing a price for the team with the ganger. Others had been hired separately and formed themselves into teams during the work, deputing one of them to act as leader. The Fox and Grapes, which had been one of Arthur Toms's haunts, was little more than an ale house, but it had a couple of upper rooms that suited Simpson and it was convenient to the workings. He made the pay-off as usual in the bar of the inn seated at a table. What he knew and what made him nervous and tight-lipped before any of the men appeared was that there was not enough money. Bullivant had dismissed it as a matter of little importance that could be settled next time.

"What do they want money for except drink and they can get that at the tally-shop along with anything else on credit. Divide it up so they each get a bit. That'll keep them happy."

The first of the men came in and lined up at the table. With a clerk at his elbow to mark off the list, Simpson began handing out the money.

Simpson usually quite enjoyed the pay-out. He liked being in the position of the one who sat while men twice his size and half his age,

383

men who could knock him flying with one blow and often looked as if they wanted to, stood and took what he was prepared to hand out. He liked the proof it gave him that he'd climbed up above the herd. That was how he liked to think of the navvies—as cattle. Stupid, ignorant, brainless—commodities to be bought and sold. He could think of them like that when he was in command, when he had them shuffling along in front of him in their heavy work-boots, their great dirt-encrusted hands held out to him. If they didn't take their caps off to him in the respectful manner that was owed to him, he didn't let it bother him. He didn't worry about such niceties. He was the master in this situation, however much they might ignore him or disobey him or jeer at him behind his back, out on the workings.

But it was different to-day. Crowded into the small room, they looked enormous and powerful and threatening, the smell of their unwashed clothes, the stale dirt, the stale beer, the tobacco, the foul clay pipes, the coughing and spitting, things he never noticed before, made him feel stifled and sick. And the murmur of the men waiting outside seemed all the more menacing because he knew what they did not—that they had cause for anger. Trouble had already arrived in his own mind.

The men, in fact, were not particularly looking for trouble. They wanted to pick up their money and be off. They didn't give a damn about Simpson. They weren't thinking about him. It was pay-day so they were, at the beginning anyway, in a fair good-humour. They weren't thinking about trouble and were slow to start.

The first ganger in the line was a man of about twenty-seven, with a square, fleshy intelligent face. He looked down at the money Simpson handed him and frowned. "What's this then?" he said.

"What do you think it is?" Simpson said. "It's your pay."

"It don't look enough," the ganger said.

"You'll get the rest next time." Simpson called the next man and went on with the paying out. He ignored the first man, who stood there with the money in his hand laboriously counting it over again. Then he came back and stood in front of the table.

"I want it now," he said stubbornly. "It's not enough."

The palms of Simpson's hands began to sweat.

"Look, Jack," he said. "I've told you. That's all there is. Any that's coming, you'll get it. The rest hasn't arrived yet. That's all that's the matter. You'll get all that's owing. Now stand out of the light. You're holding others up."

The navvy put both fists on the table and leaned down to Simpson.

"Now look you here, Mr. Simpson," he said. "We've worked for that money and that money we're going to have. All of it. Now." And before Simpson could prevent him he snatched up a handful of coins from the table.

Bullivant told Simpson later: "That's the moment you should have stopped it. If you'd had half the authority over your men you were supposed to, you would have stopped it then."

"You didn't see them," Simpson said. "You can hear them now outside, can't you? Well, I had thirty of them in here, all round me. You couldn't have stopped them, Mr. Bullivant. I don't care what you say."

Simpson had made an effort. He had told the ganger he would be doing the rest of his mates out of their money. He appealed to the others. Smelling a swindle, they crowded round saying they weren't going till they got all they were entitled to.

"It's little enough once you take off all you say we owe you in credit."

"You've had the goods, you know," Simpson said placatingly. "It's right you should pay."

"But proper prices. Not mucked up prices for tommyrot."

"I can't help that. That's not my affair."

"No, you're just here to pay us our money, aren't you, Mr. Simpson? And we're here to see we get it."

They stood round him threateningly. He looked up at the circle of faces. Behind him the clerk stood frozen as if to draw attention to himself would be to invite disaster. Simpson wiped his damp hands along the seams of his trousers.

"There's not enough to go round," he said.

"There's enough to go round us, isn't there?"

"Yes—but what about the others? If I give you this, there'll be none at all for most of them."

"That's your worry. It's not ours. We'll have ours now and thank you very much."

He gave in. It wasn't in his interest or the railway's to get beaten up by his men, he told Bullivant.

"You might have guessed what would happen next," Bullivant said. "Stupidity. You should have cleared them all out. Paid none of them."

But Simpson had paid the thirty or so men who had happened to be the first to arrive. He paid them all they were due. And they took it and being in an inn, they proceeded to spend some of it on drink and then they went outside and waited to tell every one who came that Simpson had stolen the money and was saying there was none. The men had been waiting outside for their share-out. Those that had it came into the inn and began spending it in the traditional way. Those without came in and demanded theirs. The crowd inside and out grew bigger. It grew more restless too and noisier. There were shouts—"to get the bloody money out here!"—and yells to know why they were waiting, and whistles and stamping feet and men calling to their mates in front to know what the devil was going on. The crowd moved and surged and jostled and coalesced and separated, still fluid, still manageable, but beginning to boil, like water on a stove, with whispers of impatience, bubbling and swirling with rumour and argument.

When Simpson had no more money left he folded up the table and sent the clerk out the back way to fetch Godfrey Bullivant. The clerk returned in a minute saying he couldn't get out. There were two men outside the back entrance and they thought he was sloping off with the money. Simpson called one of the gangers and told him he'd have to get Mr. Bullivant if they wanted any more money that day, and the clerk was allowed to go through. They sat and waited and stood and waited and drank and waited. Rumours spread through the crowd, growing with each new bunch of men arriving. The rumour that Bullivant had gone with the money was equal favourite with the rumour that there was no money left at all to finish the railway and they'd do better to start tramping right away.

"Not without my money!" came a reply and it was taken up in a shout that brought the villagers to their doors and windows and sent the first news that the navvies were running wild down through the lanes to Waterford.

By the time Bullivant arrived he had to

push his way through a surly mob in an edgy, ugly mood. He harangued them into some sort of silence and because they respected him they listened, but once they found out he'd brought no money with him he was shouting into the air. The more they drank the worse their tempers got. They'd come for the celebration every pay day brought, the one holiday of the working month. Now they were angry and bored and frustrated. And beneath the anger was fear: fear of the typhoid, fear of being out of work if the railway stopped building. It hadn't been a good workings and some had felt it was doomed. Now they all felt it.

The undercurrent of violence that was always present whenever a bunch of navvies was on the loose, the violence that came with the pay-outs and the randies, that was fed with whisky and prejudice and old scores to settle and hatreds and uncertainties and the release after weeks of humping and digging and carrying and tunnelling and seeing mates killed or hurt or fall ill or be dismissed, the violence that ended sometimes with pitched battles between gangs fought till the blood flowed and the combatants fell unconscious or dead drunk or dead, the violence that was the terror of the countryside and the source of all the stories that ran ahead of the railroad like a poisonous mist souring the air before the navvies ever arrived, that undercurrent was beginning to come to the surface and both Simpson and Bullivant knew it.

"Where's the money?" the cry came. "Let's have it!"

"There'll be money," Bullivant promised them. "There's men coming down to-day who'll provide more money than anyone can want. They're coming to see what you've done and what you're going to do. I'm going to tell them I've got the best navvies in the country, the only ones who can finish a road ahead of time. So you stand by me, lads, and I'll stand by you. If you put a bit of a spurt on I'll double the wages. You'll be the richest navvies ever to ride a railroad!"

He got a cheer and a laugh for that from those who'd been paid, but that only incensed the others further.

Bullivant turned and pushed his way into the inn. By this time Simpson had retreated upstairs.

"Stop serving," Bullivant told the landlord. "You'll get your place broken up otherwise."

The landlord disagreed. He thought he'd get his place broken up if he did stop serving. Bullivant turned to go but this time he was stopped at the door.

"You ain't going nowhere," they told him. "Not till we've got our money."

He swore at them and threatened them but it was no use. They barred the door. Uncertain what to do and getting drunker and more muddled with every drink they clung to one idea. No one was moving till they were paid and that was that.

Bullivant went upstairs to find Simpson and discover exactly what had been going on. When five minutes later he came down again with the idea of talking to the more sensible and sober of the men he found that the bottom of the staircase had been blocked by a trestle table tipped over on its end like a door. It enclosed the staircase and he could not move it. The navvies had effectively imprisoned them.

Bullivant rejoined Simpson in his room and sat down to wait. After a while they noticed that the shouts of the men outside had begun to take on a more ominous note. The situation had become reversed in rumour and now those at the back of the crowd had the

idea that Bullivant and Simpson had barri-
caded themselves in to stop the navvies
getting at the money. They shouted insults,
threats, calls to action. Someone threw a half-
brick and shattered the window of the
upstairs room. Simpson cowered back, his
face white.

"Don't look so frightened, man," Bullivant
said. "They're only making a bit of a noise.
We'll soon get ourselves released from this
place. I sent the clerk to fetch the constable
before I came."

"You should have brought the militia,"
Simpson cried. "For God's sake, why did you
come alone? It's soldiers we'll need to get out
of this! Can't you hear them, Mr. Bullivant?
They're after us. They're after our blood!"

The Countess's carriage came into
Rivington along the Warwick road, which
entered the village at the opposite end to the
Fox and Grapes. Here was the raggle-taggle
end of the crowd, a fringe of loungers and
watchers and late-comers that hung round the
edge of the denser mass centred on the inn.
The carriage moved slowly through them
until the knots of men in its path grew more
numerous and less ready to stand aside, and
the noise, like a wall of sound, seemed to

block the way. The driver stopped and asked the Countess what she wished him to do.

"Can you get into the lane by Miss Torrance's house?"

"I think so."

"Then that is what we shall do. We can enter the house by the back way."

They went on a little farther up the street. Opposite the church they halted again. There was a swirl of movement round them and some men ran past. The shouting grew nearer. There was a whistle and then, astonishingly hoots of laughter. Anne lowered the window on her side of the carriage and looked out.

"It might be a scene from the French Revolution," the Countess remarked. "What are those men doing?"

Anne sat back. She looked pale. "It's Mr. Carrington," she said. "I think he believes they have come to attack his church."

Mr. Carrington, returning from a parish visit, had found the village street full of a rabble of drunken navvies. It was at once clear to him that his hour had come. He gathered together his dignity and his courage, and brandishing his umbrella above his head he advanced upon them, a fine flow of Old

Testament abuse rolling off his tongue. With superb oratory he condemned them for the desecration of his church, he condemned them for their loose living and impious dying, he chastised them for their drunkenness and denounced the sinful harlots they lived with in defiance of God's laws. Like a black angel of retribution he advanced upon his enemies alone, with nothing to sustain him but his umbrella and his principles. The navvies, at first bewildered, began to be amused. Most of them, at this straggling end of the crowd, had no idea who he was or why he was in such a rage. They gathered round him and jostled him, ducking as he struck out with his umbrella and cheering him on. But as one or two of his blows struck home, they became a little angrier; and those pressing forward to the inn turned back to see what was happening and among them were some who knew him. A new cry went up, with a jeering edge to it, and then another. Anne could not identify them. She heard "Hypocrite!" shouted, and then what sounded like; "Witch-lover" and then a name, "Granny Lane" called over and over again, and a sound like a cat miaouwing taken up and repeated louder and louder until it was like the howling of a hundred cats.

"What on earth is that terrible noise?" demanded the Countess.

"They are imitating cats," Anne said.

"What on earth for? Have they all gone mad?"

"I can't imagine why——" And then Anne did remember. Granny Lane and the dead cat and the trick she played on the vicar to get him to bury it. Anne had told Laszlo about it as a joke. And Laszlo, that night he went drinking with the navvies—had he retold it, a good story against the vicar? Surely other people must have known? No, she would have heard it herself. It would have come back to her through the servants if it were common knowledge. So Granny Lane had told no one, and Mr. Carrington certainly would not have done so. Only she, only she had told it. It was her fault, hers and Laszlo's. And poor prejudiced, stupid, intolerable Mr. Carrington was being subjected to ridicule he did not deserve. If the navvies had knocked him down, beaten him, he could have been a martyr as he wished, but not this, not this derision. . . . She pulled open the carriage door and jumped out.

"Anne," Sophia called, "what are you doing? Are you mad? You will be trampled!" And when Anne would not stop, she said quietly to the driver: "Joseph, go after her."

Anne made her way through the crowd towards Carrington's tall figure. She was angry, angry with a deep bitterness because there was not one person in this affair who was devoid of blame. Neither the navvies, nor Carrington, nor herself. Stupid, stupid people, all of them. Blind and intolerant and hateful, all of them, including herself, including Laszlo. There were tears of rage in her eyes as she pulled at arms and pushed at backs that gave way with surprise as the men saw who it was struggling to pass them, and suddenly she came to him. "Mr. Carrington——"

She had no time to say more, for Joseph, as big as any of the navvies and more purposeful, following close behind her—a fact that had eased her passage more than she knew—took Carrington firmly by the arm while he was still amazed into inaction by Anne's appearance before him, and began guiding him across the street to the Torrances' house.

The men fell away. They let them go the short distance without hindrance. Anne had been recognised and they had no quarrel with her. Carrington, recovered from the shock of seeing her in the midst of that crowd, was under the impression that she had gone to him for help and hurried her to her door grasping her arm as firmly as Joseph was holding his. Only once inside the house did he seem to become aware of Joseph for the first time and realise that they had rescued him. He was overcome, he protested then, by Anne's courage.

"You should not have to witness such scenes," he cried. "Animals. I am afraid they are animals, Miss Torrance. How noble of you to brave them for my sake. I am quite ashamed."

"I think you were very courageous, Mr. Carrington," she said quietly, "to do what you did."

"It was my duty," he said, and for once his pomposity did not irritate her.

Mrs. Torrance drew them into a room away from the street. "It was not the church they were attacking," she explained to the vicar. "They have trapped Mr. Bullivant and Mr. Simpson in the inn. They say they are going to keep them there until they get paid some money. That is what we can gather——"

She broke off as there was a sudden roar and the sound of breaking glass.

"Where is Hugh?" Anne asked her mother.

Mrs. Torrance looked at her steadily. "He went up to the inn five minutes ago. He had met the constable on the road and called in to say he was going with him. Anne—you are not to go out there again."

"No," Anne said, "I won't, Mother. I won't interfere. I was going to suggest to Joseph that he should bring the Countess in here. I am sure no one will prevent them."

She put her hand on her mother's. "I was worried about you," she said, and quickly kissed her cheek.

Hugh stood outside the Fox and Grapes and watched the faces of the men while the constable struggled to make himself heard. They had made their way to the inn along the backs of the houses, avoiding the worst of the crowd, but they had found the building quite surrounded and any hope they had had of quietly extracting the two trapped men from their prison faded. There was nothing for it, the constable, Mr. Cready, announced but to try and talk some sense into them. A big man, broadly built and slow-moving, he had not the imagination to visualise any danger to himself in the situation he was attempting to control. In his own eyes he embodied authority, as the young doctor, in his own way, also did, and he simply acted accordingly. They forced a passage fairly easily round the side of the inn and took up a position by the front door. Their sudden emergence in front of the crowd brought them the attention they needed. There was a lull in the noise and the constable, standing up on the mounting block, seized his opportunity.

"Now come along, men," he cried. "This isn't doing any good, you know."

He got the answer he might have expected to that beginning, Hugh thought. When he could hear him again, he was reproving them for the broken window. "No good comes of destroying property," he warned them.

"What about stealing property?" he was challenged. "What about that then?"

There was a roar of assent. The constable swayed as men pressed round him. Hugh took a step forward so that he could protect Cready's back.

"Settle down, settle down!" Nothing

disturbed Cready's majestic manner. "You're creating a disturbance. You don't want me to call the militia, do you? You don't want us to have to read the Riot Act, do you? There's nothing you can do here. Nothing's going to happen while you've got those gentlemen shut up in there. Now let's get them out and get this sorted out like sensible men."

His voice growing hoarse with shouting, he went on chiding and bullying them like a nurse upbraiding children and because he was taking so positive, so calm a stand, because he was so supremely confident of his own immunity, nobody somewhat to Hugh's surprise, knocked him down or pushed him aside or entirely ignored him. The crowd did, in fact, begin to quieten. They were at a moment of balance, when the scales might tip either way and it was beginning to seem they might come down on the side of order, with men starting to drift away and others sullen and silent, when a new element was introduced which completely reversed the situation.

In the room upstairs, while Bullivant watched the scene, standing a discreet distance back from the window, Simpson had been pacing nervously up and down, wincing at each swell of noise. Suddenly unable to bear the tension a second longer, he went into his bedroom. When he came back he was carrying a shotgun. He went up to the broken window and before Bullivant could prevent him, thrust the barrel of the gun through the hole in the glass and fired a burst of shot over the heads of the crowd. There was a startled silence and then pandemonium broke loose. It was impossible to tell at first who was fighting to get away out of range of the next burst and who was fighting to get to Simpson. Enraged, terrified, cheated, baulked, they swept past Cready, knocking him against the wall of the house and flooded into the already crowded bar of the inn, carrying Hugh with them.

In the upper room, Bullivant snatched the gun and pulled Simpson away from the window with a violence that sent him crashing against the table. "You bloody fool, what the devil do you think you're doing? Do you want to be killed?"

Below, they were pulling at the table they had used to block the stairs, rocking it back and forwards. Hugh heard the sound of bottles being broken for weapons and saw a man approaching with one in his hand, the

402

jagged edge towards him. It was a navvy he knew. He knocked the arm up and away from his own face, yelling the man's name. The navvy's face cleared to recognition and he dropped his arm. "Doctor——"

Hugh edged past him towards the stairs. With a final swing the table crashed over on to its side. But in the way it had fallen it still half-blocked the entrance to the stairs. Hugh pushed through the gap and leaping out of reach up the narrow staircase, swung round, his hands touching each wall, barring the way.

"Don't be fools!" he shouted at them. "D'you want to get yourselves hanged? If there's no money, there's no money. The redress isn't murder. You'll get nothing by coming up here except a face full of shot or a rope round your necks."

He caught the eye of the navvy he knew and flung the question at him. "I'm right, aren't I, Ben? Aren't I, Ben Redhead? There's nothing for you up here but the gallows."

The appeal made them turn to Ben, the interruption made them hesitate. From the back of the room came a new call. "If we get no money, they get no railroad. Let's tear it up." And it got taken up and carried outside and spread through the crowd till there was a chant: "No money, no railway, no money, no railway," that could be heard in the Torrance house. The great unresolved urge for action, to do something, anything, that hesitated at killing, yet burned with frustration, was channelled into a new purpose. The lead was given, the first man turned to run, and like a mob of stampeding cattle they surged after him. Within minutes the inn was empty.

Bullivant saw them streaming away down the road and turned with raised eyebrows as Hugh burst into the room. "Where are they going?"

"Are you all right?"

"Of course we're all right. Where are they going?"

Simpson, crouched on a chair with his head in his hands, looked up at Bullivant with something like hatred. "They're going to tear up your railroad, Mr. Bullivant. Didn't you hear them shouting it? All that work, all that money. It'll all be gone. Didn't you hear them?"

Bullivant ignored him. He said to Hugh, "Do you think they mean it?"

"Yes, I think they do."

"Then we must stop them," he said. "There's a train on that line."

Three miles away, a light engine was pulling a train of two coaches up the first approaches to the long embankment. Seated in the carriages were six men, four in the first coach, two in the second. Three of the men were the important visitors whom Bullivant had at last persuaded to consider interesting themselves financially in his railway. The fourth man in the first carriage was the engineer Bullivant had engaged after the one originally employed had resigned. The two men in the second coach were the sub-contractors for the two sections before Rivington.

To ride along the temporary line in this manner was the simplest way of allowing the visitors to inspect its progress. At the small halt built on the other side of Rivington, Bullivant had arranged to meet them. From there they were to be taken by road to the Wharton Arms for a meal and for the serious discussion of the business. It was a satisfactory and sensible arrangement and it was all going extremely well, except for the fact that Bullivant had only just been released from the upper room at the Fox and Grapes, and that a throng of half-drunk and exhilarated navvies, wielding their hammers and picks with abandon, were beginning to tear up the track they had laid only a few months before at the other end of the embankment.

Because it was pulling so light a train the engine could go fast. It climbed the gradient with ease. It rattled along the top of the embankment, while the passengers admired both the view and the technical achievement and the engineer explained the difficulties they had had to solve.

It was at this point that the train was seen for the first time from Rivington: the little working engine, smoke pluming from its funnel, the black boxes of its coaches rocketing gaily behind it, were outlined with nightmarish clarity against the sky, perched up on the embankment.

The train seemed to Hugh, running across the fields with Bullivant, Cready and Simpson at his heels, to be moving intolerably fast. He stopped, catching Bullivant by the arm. "Is there no way of stopping it?"

Bullivant shook his head. His gaze was fixed on the embankment.

"If the men have seen it, it won't be too late," Hugh insisted. "They can't have done much damage in this short time, surely."

"In one minute they can have done enough damage to wreck a train."

Simpson said: "It's useless, useless. Even if they knew about the train, they wouldn't care, not now."

They none of them moved. They could see the men, a mass of navvies spread out along the line. They could see the train approaching. They stayed, paralysed, too far away to shout or help or take any part in the action unfolding before them.

On the embankment the train had reached the downward slope and began to descend, swaying lightly on the rails and gathering speed. The engine driver suddenly saw men running towards him shouting and waving their arms. The guard saw them too and began to apply the brakes. Looking along the line they could see ahead of them the broken end of the rails and a group of men clustered about it. The crew went on trying to slow the train, exerting as much effort and will power as if they could stop it with their bare hands.

But they had been going too fast, they had had too little warning. The engine wheels, speeding along the rail, ran into the twisted torn metal, and like a toy tossed up into the air by a child's bored hand, the train jack-knifed. It seemed to hang in space for an interminable moment, then it fell back upon itself, one coach on top of the other, crashing across the line and over the edge of the embankment in a tangle of smashed metal and wood and broken glass, the fractured boiler of the engine emitting the burning steam that scalded the trapped crewmen to death.

When Hugh and the others reached the scene of the wreck, the navvies, working like demons, had already levered the top coach free and toppled it back on its side. They looked up as Bullivant and Simpson appeared, but said nothing. There was nothing for anyone to say.

There were two survivors—the two men in the rear carriage. One was pinned by the legs and had to be cut free, the other had been thrown clear and suffered nothing more than cuts and bruises.

The four men in the first carriage were all dead. If they had survived the first impact they must have been crushed when the second coach fell on them. The men worked for two hours before they got the bodies out and all that time Bullivant stood beside them, watching, his face impassive. When the last man was out, he looked at the bodies lying in a careful row along the grassy bank, looked down at the death of his last hopes, and then walked away along the line. No one stopped him. Few people saw him go.

10

IT was late afternoon before Hugh came back to the house. He had sent one of the men earlier on to fetch instruments, bandages and so on and Anne working with quiet efficiency had packed a case with everything she thought he might need. She had questioned the man about the crash, but he was not communicative and she did not press him. Though all the men of the village had gone up to the scene neither she nor any of the women did. It was not a business for people who could not offer immediate practical help. It was not a place to go merely to stare. Over them all the tragedy hung like a heavy weight. The village street, so recently in uproar, was unnaturally still. The navvy who took Hugh's case avoided Anne's eyes.

Hugh came in silently, his face grim, and went to wash. Anne asked the cook to make some tea and took it in to him herself. He drank the tea standing, gulping it down as if it might wash away the taste of what he had seen.

"Carrington was up there," he said.

"What was he doing?" Anne asked.

"I thought perhaps he had come to preach but he behaved in quite a human way. He may have felt it a judgement but he didn't say so. I asked him to let the bodies rest in the church. He's agreed to it."

"Hugh, I don't want to trouble you, but there has been a message from the Countess."

He glanced up inquiringly.

"She left about an hour ago," Anne went on. "A messenger has just come from her. She asks you to go to Waterford as soon as it is convenient."

He shrugged. "I might as well go at once. There is nothing more I can do for the two survivors of the crash. One will be quite recovered after a night's rest. The other has been taken to hospital and is no longer under my care."

"Hugh, I want to come with you. I may, mayn't I?"

He paused, looking down at her. "Of course, if you wish. Is this something to do with Bathory?"

"I don't know. He said he would follow us from Waterford Park this morning. He never arrived."

"So naturally you are worried." He spoke quite matter-of-factly, refusing to allow his emotions to colour his reaction. "You think something has happened to him."

Anne struggled to express to him the exact nature of her feelings. She felt it was very important to do so. "I am not worried. I am—puzzled. I know there is something wrong. I do not know in what way."

"Very well." He picked up his coat. "Let us not waste time in finding out."

They had both expected, following the normal pattern of unusual events at Waterford, to find the place in confusion. Instead they entered a silent house and were shown directly into the Ivory drawing-room where a regal Sophia, straight-backed and coldly dignified, awaited them. Seated opposite her was Esther Wharton. It was obvious she had been weeping.

Sophia regarded her with distaste. "You had better tell them your story at once, as you told me, then we shall decide what to do."

Esther shuddered. She drew her arms about her body, clutching herself as if she were cold. She seemed unable to speak.

Sophia clicked her tongue in disgust. "You were full enough of it all a while ago—"

"Sophia." Hugh stopped her. "I know most of her story."

"Perhaps you do, but I doubt if you know the worst."

Anne could not prevent herself from interrupting. "What is it? What is going on? Where is Laszlo?"

The sound of her voice seemed to put a little spirit into Esther. She sat up, looking at Anne with spiteful eyes. "He has gone. He is on his way to France. He has gone without you. He never intended to take you. He was going to take me. Me, not you!"

Sophia said coldly: "She tells me she is to have his child, Anne."

Anne stared at her. She thought at first she must have misheard. She looked from one to the other, from Sophia, too angry, she realised, to speak other than bluntly, to Esther's white intensity, to Hugh's silent acceptance. She said; "Laszlo's child? Esther? I do not believe it."

"Why not?" Esther almost spat the words. "Why not? Do you think because men admire you, they do not admire me? Am I so plain, so insignificant, so unimportant? Not to him! Not to——"

"Be quiet," Sophia snapped. "You behaved

like a servant girl and he treated you like one." She turned to Hugh. "She says he has taken the emerald. It has certainly gone. She said they had a plan which she has only betrayed because he would not take her with him once he knew about the child. She has said I would never have discovered the loss, at least until they were out of the country, and she may be right. You shall see for yourself. I have left the case on the bureau in my bedroom. I will get the maid to fetch it."

The maid was rung for and received her instructions. They waited, Hugh leaning against the mantelpiece, his expression grave; Sophia so unusually still that Anne could only guess how deeply she had been hurt by what seemed a double treachery by two people she had welcomed so generously to her house.

Anne sat down at the end of the sofa and looked at Esther. She could not believe her story. She was lying for some purpose of her own. She studied the small round face, the pale eyes, the greyish complexion, blotched and unhealthy. She did not doubt that she was pregnant. What possible reason could she have for saying so, if she was not? But that Laszlo was the father . . . She thought of

414

Laszlo's elegance, his fastidiousness—and remembered his readiness to go drinking with the navvies. She thought of his kisses, the expressions of love—and remembered his many unexplained absences, the casualness as well as the passion of his love-making. She closed her eyes. So many memories, and her imagination was already colouring, adding, destroying. The night of the reception, had he left her arms to go to Esther's? I cannot believe it, she thought, and the names— Laszlo and Esther, Laszlo and Esther—beat behind her eyes like a drum.

But what was the alternative—Hugh? There had been his concern for Esther, the meeting in the lane, the secret conversations, the refusal to explain them. His saying a moment ago: "I know most of her story." No! Not Hugh! The vehemence of her reaction shook Anne. She could not bear that it should be Hugh who had made love to Esther Wharton, who had given her a child. That would be betrayal indeed. But that it should be Laszlo, no, she realised, that was not betrayal because there had been, in spite of their protestations, their extravagant emotions, no real bond of love between them. She felt hurt and shocked and angry by

415

Esther's revelation, both her vanity and her pride suffered, but beneath these surface reactions the deepest core of her feelings remained untouched.

She opened her eyes and found Hugh watching her. He met her gaze steadily, his expression giving nothing away, neither of guilt nor pity nor love. And she thought, I love him. If I lose him, I shall die. If it is too late, if I have already lost his love, I shall want to die.

There was a knock on the door and the maid re-entered carrying the ancient wooden box that had been made in Hungary those long centuries ago. She set it down on the table in front of Sophia and was dismissed. Sophia unfastened the case and opened it. At first Anne could see no difference. Inside lay a dark green emerald with an ornate gold chain. It was the same size, the same shape, it fitted exactly the hollow in the white velvet as the one she had seen before. It was only when Sophia picked it up and held it to the light that they could tell that it was not the King's emerald but nothing more than carved green glass.

"A substitute," Hugh said. "That was what the drawings of the emerald were for.

That was the purpose of that last visit to London. Bathory knew you very rarely did more than look at the emerald, Sophia. You had to be persuaded to take it out of its case or show it to anyone. By replacing it with a copy, he hoped the deception would last long enough for him to make his escape." He turned to Esther. "You did not tell me this part of the story. Bathory had not yet left then, I suppose."

Esther was endeavouring to recover her poise. "If you remember, Doctor," she said smoothly, "I did not wish to tell you anything. You made me do so."

"Made you?" The Countess looked inquiringly at Hugh. "When was this?"

"A day or so ago. I suspected Miss Wharton's condition. I noticed it last time we met, when I came back from London. I hoped, for her sake, that I was mistaken. Then when I saw her coming away from Granny Lane's cottage, I was certain. She had gone to buy one of Granny Lane's notorious potions for girls in her situation."

"If you had only let me take it and be rid of the child, he would have taken me with him for certain! It is because of you he has left me."

"You might have destroyed yourself," Hugh said. His voice was gentle. "Don't you understand that? Isn't your life more important to you? If you care nothing for your child, don't you care about yourself? One girl has already died from these famous infallible remedies. I could not allow you to be another."

Esther buried her head in her hands and began to cry.

"He would not have taken you with him under any circumstances, Esther," Sophia said. She sounded tired. "Don't waste your tears on him. Presumably he needed your help to steal my emerald and so used the simplest and most effective way of gaining your co-operation and your silence. The prize was worth anything he had to do to acquire it. The emerald is priceless. He does not even need to sell it. He need only own it to get sufficient credit to live as he desires." She glanced at Hugh. "Is there anything to be done?"

He nodded. "I think there might be, if I act quickly. Esther—" He sat beside her. "Did Bathory know you were going to tell the Countess about the emerald? Does he know he has been discovered?"

She shook her head. "I don't know. I do not think so." She would not look up. She spoke slowly, her gaze fixed down at the floor. "When he came back from London he had brought the copy of the emerald with him. He had not planned which day to go. It was to be this week. But—" she paused, "when I told him about the child, I think he decided then to leave as soon as possible, before I could become a danger to him. He was merely waiting for an opportunity. When Mrs. Wharton and Miss Torrance left the house this morning he went straight to Mrs. Wharton's room and took the emerald. When I realised what he intended to do I pleaded with him to take me, but he would not. He did not even pretend that he would send for me later. He went about three hours ago. As soon as Mrs. Wharton returned I told her what had happened. But I do not think he expected me to tell. No, he would not expect it. He would not think me capable of it."

"He was going to London first, before he left for France?"

She nodded.

"He may have to collect papers or money first," Hugh said. "I may be able to find him. I think it is worth trying."

"Hugh——" Anne stood up, involuntarily drawn to protest. She was afraid for him.

"Yes?" The word was cold and flat. She realised Hugh believed her to be distressed because Laszlo had deceived and deserted her. She turned away and walked over to the window, feeling in her own way as defeated as Esther.

The Countess spoke Anne's thoughts for her. "I think it a very dangerous manœuvre." The old briskness was back in her voice.

"You don't want him to escape with Hunyadi's emerald?"

"I confess I do not feel any tender inclinations towards him, but there is no inanimate piece of history worth a man's life. Bathory has shown himself to be both unscrupulous and greedy and that is a dangerous combination."

"I'll take care not to turn my back if I happen to run him to earth." He nodded at Esther. "You had better put her to bed to rest—that is, if you do not intend to turn her out of the house."

"What do you think me? A monster?" Sophia shrugged. "It is such an old story it is almost tedious to hear its repetition. It is always the plain girls who allow themselves to be seduced. They become desperate for the attentions of a man and decide to equate love-making with love. They have an infinite capacity for self-deception. But you are more sensible, Esther, are you not?" She poked the girl's shoulder with a long forefinger. "You never for one moment believed this man to be in love with you?"

Esther slowly raised a tear-stained face. She met the shrewd glance of the Countess and her mouth tightened upon itself in a familiar thin line.

"No," she said. "I knew he was not in love with me. He used me, perhaps, but I used him. If it were not for the child I might have succeeded in getting what I wanted."

"And what do you want?" Sophia inquired.

"Freedom." She spoke the word with an intense bitterness. "Independence. Escape from the slavery of being an unmarried female dependent. You do not know what I mean, Mrs. Wharton, and neither does Miss Torrance, but I had had too many years of it in my father's vicarage and too many years lay ahead. I would have done anything, *anything*, to escape. Now—" She shrugged. "Do you wonder I weep? My tears are not for

Laszlo Bathory, Mrs. Wharton, they are for myself."

Sophia gave a snort of approval. "For that answer I shall not turn you over to the mercy of your father and aunt, at least until you wish it. You have behaved stupidly and selfishly and immorally, but you are not a fool. Now you had better go to your room before I change my mind."

Esther stood up and without looking any of them in the face again, glided out of the room. Already there was a slight lift to her shoulders. She recovered her wits and her confidence very quickly.

"A natural adventuress," Sophia commented. "If she had had the looks, she would have made her fortune."

"Well," Hugh sighed. "What will you do with her?"

"My dear Hugh, I have not the remotest idea. Something will come to me, no doubt. It is such a large house, an infant need be no trouble. It can be practically invisible, if not inaudible. I may let her stay. I shall see." She paused. "It is interesting to think that the child will be part Hungarian."

Anne, who had been listening to them from the other side of the salon, came forward again. "Are you really going to London to look for Laszlo?" she asked Hugh.

"Yes, Anne."

"Then take care of yourself, for my sake."

She said no more, but the manner in which she spoke those quiet words, the expression in her eyes as she looked at him, gave them so clear a meaning that Hugh stared, startled into silence.

"Here is another who has come to her senses," Sophia said drily. "If you wish to embrace each other pray do so. It will be far less than what has apparently been taking place under my roof."

Hugh smiled. "I shall be back, I hope, tomorrow. I shall save any rewards either of you may wish to give me until then." He saw Anne's face and said: "Anne, my dearest Anne, allow me my pride. Let me get rid of him first. Let me slay the dragon before I claim the princess. I have the need to win by conquest, not by default."

It was dark when Hugh arrived in London. He went first to the hotel where he had taken Laszlo, where they had had what was, in retrospect, that revealing conversation about Esther's drawings of the emerald.

The landlord thought he had called to collect the cane Bathory had left there.

"I've been keeping it safe." He brought it out of a cupboard. "Very fine gold head it has on it. Nearly as heavy as iron." He weighed it in his hand. "Must be worth something, Doctor."

"My Hungarian friend has not been back at all?"

"No sight nor sound of him since that day. Why, were you expecting to find him here?"

"No." Hugh picked up the cane. "Not really. I'll say good night."

The landlord followed him to the door. "Don't you want a room for the night then, Doctor?"

Hugh paused. "Now you mention it, perhaps I shall. I may be back later."

"I'll tell the porter. Very pleased to have you here again, sir."

Hugh wondered why he should be suddenly so comforted by the thought of having a room in the inn waiting for him, as if he had established a base in enemy country.

He took a cab over the bridge to Southwark. The river water moved sluggishly. It looked oily and sinister in the light of the lamps; a smell rose from it, the heavy, rotting smell of a city in summer. Hugh found himself considering the diseases endemic in a city of this size, and pondering the problems of municipal sanitation. A defensive reaction by his mind, he decided, to the situation he was about to involve himself in. He had a disturbing feeling that it might be dangerous.

The cab stopped at the end of a narrow ill-lit street. "Third street off on the right, you said you thought it was, sir," the driver said. "Is this the one you want?"

Hugh got out and looked about him. "Yes, this is the one. I remember it."

The difficulty was going to be, he realised, in remembering the house. They all looked much the same.

The cab driver gave him a knowing, sly look as Hugh paid him off. On impulse, Hugh said to him: "Do you know which house it is?"

The driver nodded, satisfied. "I thought you'd come here for that. I asked myself what other reason would he want to come here for. It's that one there, fourth along."

"Thank you."

"Enjoy yourself," the cabbie said laconically. "I don't suppose you want me to wait."

"As a matter of fact," Hugh said, "I think I do." He reached into his pocket and gave him another coin. "Wait on this corner, will you? I'll double your fare."

"I'll wait all night, if you want me to, guv. I'm in no hurry."

Hugh walked along the street to the fourth house. All the front windows were close curtained, blank as a wall. Whatever Eva's house was, it was discreet. He lifted the knocker to rap on the door and found it ajar. He entered the dark hall he remembered from his first visit. Only this time the door to the room on the left was open.

The room, he saw, was lit by pink-shaded lamps on which had been sprinkled some incense-like powder. Its scent rose to meet Hugh, mingled with the odours of musk and cologne, of cigar smoke and the sweet floury smell of face powder. Settees lined the walls and on them several bored girls were lounging, idly chatting, yawning, playing with ringlets of hair, staring into space. At a table by the door, two men were playing cards. On seeing Hugh, one got up and came out to him.

"I want to speak to Eva." Hugh put on his

most authoritative voice, at the same time turning a coin between the fingers of one hand. The door-keeper looked him up and down, summing him up with a practised eye. Then, his face expressionless, he crossed the hall to the door on the right, plucking the coin from Hugh's hand as he passed with the dexterity of a pickpocket. He knocked on the door and waited. A voice answered. The man nodded to Hugh and opened the door, indicating that he should go in. He closed the door quietly behind him.

The room Hugh now entered was furnished like the comfortable living-room of a bourgeois shopkeeper. There were a great many rugs on the floor, and a great deal of heavy materials about. The curtains that silenced all noise were of thick plush. The chairs were deep and crowded with fringed cushions, the thick wallpaper was encrusted with a gilt pattern, there were two tall gilt containers sprouting sprays of palm. The woman Hugh knew only as Eva was seated in an enormous armchair. Her hair was elaborately dressed and her evening gown was hung with imitation diamonds. Her face, like the faces of the women in the other room, was heavily painted.

She smiled as she saw him. "It is the young Englishman who came to our little Hungarian party. How delightful! You have remembered us."

"I want to see Bathory," Hugh said.

"Bathory? He is not here."

"I have got something for him."

"He is not here. I have told you. Why should you think he is?"

"Would he have told me to meet him here, if he were not coming?" Hugh remarked calmly. "I should be glad if you fetched him quickly. I have not much time."

She looked at him. He had made her uncertain. He met her regard with a completely blank face. After a moment she stood up in a rustle of satin skirts.

"Wait here," she said peremptorily.

She went out into the hall, shutting the door behind her. Hugh waited a count of three seconds and then opened it and slipped outside. He was just in time to see the train of her dress disappearing round the turn of the stairs. The hall was empty. The men in the room opposite had their backs to him. He followed Eva, avoiding the centre of the stairs, moving like a shadow behind her. As he climbed up through the house he became

428

aware of a sense of furtive occupancy. From the rooms he passed came soft sounds, a murmur of voices, music, a man laughing. Eva, he thought, must have a rich and well-behaved clientele.

She went right to the top of the house, to the very room Laszlo had brought him to that other night. She knocked at the door bending her head and whispering urgently. After an interval of some moments there was the sound of a key turning and the unlocked door was pulled open. Eva went inside. Hugh leaped the last four steps and without allowing her time to speak, was through the door and locking it behind him, the key smooth and cold in his hand. Standing with his back to the door, he withdrew the key and slipped it into his pocket. The two occupants of the room had swung round at his entrance. The man was, as Hugh had hoped, Bathory.

"So . . . it is my friend the doctor," Laszlo said. "I must confess I never expected this." He had obviously been sleeping. There was a day bed in one corner. He was dressed in his shirt and trousers, with no shoes.

Eva shook her head and said something in Magyar.

"She is reproaching herself for leaving you

alone," Laszlo explained. "But it is not her fault. I did not take her fully into my confidence about you. I did not warn her. Why should I? I never considered you two meeting again." He sank down on the bed and ran his hand through his hair. "Don't tell me Esther betrayed me." He shrugged, smiling at Eva. "But she must have, why else are you here."

"I have very little time to talk before the police come," Hugh said. "I want the emerald, Bathory."

"The emerald, the emerald! Why should you have the emerald, or the Countess have the emerald, rather than I, or any other. It was stolen from Hungary. It should go back to Hungary. Your notions of property are deceiving. It does not belong to dear Sophia. Her family stole it. As she asked me to at one time or another, I am returning the precious heirloom to Hungary."

"You are not going back to Hungary. You are going to France."

"How do you know that? You cannot prove it. And let me tell you if the police come here with accusations of robbery, I shall deny it vigorously and claim I am acting as an agent of the Hungarian government. I shall also create a great deal of unpleasantness for the Countess. I shall make her look a fool in the eyes of her local society."

"There is no Hungarian government. And the Austrian authorities would no doubt be pleased to learn of your rebellious activities. They have representatives in this country. I think they would find some means of taking action against you."

"You would not do that to a patriot, a fighter for freedom."

"No, I would not do that to a patriot," Hugh said contemptuously. "I would do it to you."

"What do you mean by that?"

"You care nothing for your country. You have used its struggle in the most cynical way, to get money for yourself. No Hungarian would allow you to be called by that name."

"Watch what you are saying, Doctor. You have insulted me before. Do you think because I took money for myself, that none of it went to Hungary? Do you think because I take a priceless jewel from a woman who does not need it, that I do not know what its history means, or cannot imagine the man for whom it was cut? Do you think when the

Russians stormed my country I did not wish to be there to kill them? I am going back to France, indeed, but only because it is not safe for me to go back to Hungary."

"And Anne," Hugh said, "were you going to take Anne?"

For a moment Laszlo said nothing. Then he shrugged expressively. "My beautiful Anne, how could I ask her, with that emerald burning in my pocket? She would have wanted me to return it. She would have caused me a great deal of trouble in the end. It was wiser not to begin. Though I confess—" a smile crossed his face, "I was tempted. A beautiful, passionate, loving woman, my Anne. Almost like a Hungarian. I hope she will miss me."

"And Esther Wharton," Hugh snapped the name out. "What about her? What about her child?"

"Was I the only one?" Laszlo said. "I am surprised. She was a companion, was she not? I thought she was one of the amenities of the house." Eva laughed and Laszlo turned to her, smiling at his own joke.

Hugh tightened his fingers round the knob of the cane but he did not move from the door. He knew that Bathory was goading him, trying to make him attack him, come forward so that his back was unprotected. He said: "If you wish to have time to leave the house before the police enter it, you had better talk reasonably."

"Ah, you have a bargain to suggest. That is not like an honourable Englishman, surely?"

"I'll take the emerald and give you twenty minutes to escape. You can lose yourself in London in that time. You can get your boat to France and safety. The Countess is not vindictive. I don't think she wants you put on trial. She wants the emerald."

Laszlo studied his face. He said: "I do not believe there are any police coming. You have not had time to arrange it."

"Look out of the window if you don't believe me."

Laszlo nodded to Eva. She went over to the window and moved the curtain aside. After a moment she let it drop. "There is some sort of vehicle waiting at the corner of the street. I can't quite make it out."

"So you have been telling the truth. Well, I must congratulate you." As he spoke he was unfastening his shirt; round his neck hung the gold chain and the glowing pendant emerald. He drew it out and over his head.

"The safest way to carry it," he remarked. He turned it in his hand. "Beautiful stone, don't you think so, Doctor. Here, catch it." With a flick of the wrist he tossed it to Hugh, so fast that Hugh instinctively moved forward. He caught it in one hand and looked up just in time to see Eva handing Laszlo a pistol.

"Thank you, my dear," he said quietly. "And now fetch Ferenc. Radlett, stand aside from the door." He smiled. "The pistol is loaded." He cocked the trigger. "And I am quite prepared to use it. I have wanted that emerald for a very long time. I came to England to get it. I am not going to let you stand in my way. Now, I repeat, get away from the door."

Hugh obediently stepped away from the door. It was not a large room and it brought him quite near to Laszlo. Eva went past him and tried to open the door.

"He has the key," she said.

"Give her the key," Laszlo said. "No, on second thoughts, give me the emerald first."

Hugh took out the key and handed it to Eva. As she bent to insert it in the lock, Laszlo snapped his fingers impatiently. "The emerald. Give it back to me at once, Radlett."

Hugh waited. He heard the key turn. Eva's back was to him. He held his left hand out holding the emerald and as Laszlo took a step forward to take it, he brought the cane down on his wrist in a blow which sent the pistol clattering to the floor. Turning in the same movement, he pulled Eva from the open door, flinging her back into the room on to Laszlo, and was down the stairs in a series of running leaps. Eva's shouts brought the doorkeeper out as Hugh reached the ground floor. As the man rushed him, Hugh jumped aside, bringing the gold head of the cane hard down on the back of his neck. The man grunted and collapsed and in the time gained Hugh was out of the house and running down the road to the cab.

"Get going, get going!" he shouted.

"My God, what have you done, robbed the place?"

The cab rattled off down the street. There was no pursuit. Whether it was fear of the police they believed were waiting outside, or fear of disturbing the business of Eva's house, no one followed them. Of course, Laszlo would be delayed by his lack of shoes, and by what might prove to be a broken wrist. Or he might already have left by some back entrance and be several streets away by now.

Hugh sat back in the cab, breathing heavily, feeling the reaction to danger coming over him like a sickness. He held the emerald in his hand, the chain twined about his fingers. It felt heavy in his hand and cold. A man had come a thousand miles for this. He had lied and cheated and been prepared to murder for it. It would be better not to underestimate the strength of his desire to repossess it. Laszlo knew the hotel, he knew the station from which Hugh must go back to Warwickshire. In daylight he would not risk anything, but at night— It would be better to spend the next few hours in some quiet place where Bathory and his men would never think of looking.

Hugh spent the night walking the wards of his old hospital. He had gone to one of his friends, a dresser to a surgeon, learned he was at the hospital and asked to accompany him on his rounds. And he found as he walked through the familiar corridors with him, as he observed and talked to patients, as he discussed cases and asked questions, that something had happened to him during his year away. He had regained his sense of proportion. Where, in his last months at the hospital rage and disquiet and deep despair had constantly haunted him, now nothing remained of those feelings but compassion. He was able to believe that things would change, that conditions would improve, patients survive the most radical operations, women be saved from the murderous aftermath of childbirth, hospitals become places where sufferers were cured, not as in so many cases, mere staging posts for the dying. His year in the country had given him back his optimism.

He caught the first train that would take him on his way to Warwick, arriving, without incident or interruption, at Waterford Park. He was shown up to Sophia's room where she was still breakfasting and when they were alone he placed Hunyadi's emerald in her hand. She listened while he told her how he had won it back for her.

"I suppose," she said thoughtfully, "it is possible a thief can also be a patriot. It may not all have been lies." She stretched out her beautiful white hands, the emerald held in one, the glass copy in the other, and sighed.

"Hugh, I have become a very foolish old woman."

"Why do you say that? Because you liked a very likeable young man who was determined to charm you?"

"Not only me!" she cried. "Everyone! And he succeeded. Only you, wise Hugh, were not deceived."

"That was not acumen, that was jealousy."

She laughed and patted his hand. "If I were twenty years younger I should marry you myself. Now go home and marry Anne." She held up the emerald. "This is all that endures, Hugh. Don't waste a moment of your youth. Everything moves so fast. We grow old before we have accustomed ourselves to living, we die just as we begin to appreciate it. In three hundred years time this stone will lie, beautiful and unchanging, in another woman's hand, while we, like the men who first admired it, will be nothing but bones crumbling into dust."

"What has happened?" Hugh said. "Something is wrong. You are never usually as morbid as this. Is it the train wreck that has affected you?"

"No, Hugh. I am afraid it is something

else." She raised her eyes. "Godfrey Bullivant has shot himself."

"Bullivant! But how? When?" Even as he spoke Hugh was thinking, I should have foreseen it. I should have prevented it. He saw in his mind's eye, in a flash of memory, the figure of Bullivant walking away from the train wreck along the line. Hugh had been too busy to pay any attention to him, but he knew now that some part of him had recognised and known what Bullivant was going to do.

"It was some time yesterday afternoon," Sophia was saying. "Apparently he went back to the Fox and Grapes, took up Simpson's gun and shot himself. The house was empty, everyone was at the wreck. Simpson discovered his body later."

"Poor Bullivant. Poor man. I am very sorry indeed. It was money, of course, that made him do it."

"I suppose so. Unless he felt responsible for the deaths of those men. He was a strange man. He seemed so ruthless, so insensitive. Who would have thought he would have committed such a deliberate and drastic act?"

Hugh stood up. "I had better get to Anne."

"Yes, my dear, go to her." She paused—"And thank you for my emerald."

"What will you do with the false one?" He flicked it with a nail.

"I shall probably give it to Esther Wharton as a souvenir."

He smiled slightly, returning for an instant to the light mood of their usual encounters. "How extremely cruel of you, Countess."

"I thought I was being kind. After all, it was her design!"

When Hugh had gone, Sophia lay back in her chair with her eyes closed, her long white hands resting limply in her lap. After a while, she stirred. She put the emerald back in its case and hid it in its accustomed place. The imitation she dropped into her jewel case. The key to the bureau she kept with her on a thin chain. She might as well, she thought, learn one lesson from the adventure. Only a fool thought events never repeated themselves. Then she went to visit Esther.

Anne was in the study at the vicarage talking to Mr. Carrington. She was endeavouring to persuade him to do something against his will.

He sat, considerably disturbed, looked down at his desk. "It was suicide, Miss

Torrance. How can I possibly do as you ask? How can I possibly bury him in consecrated ground?"

"You may not need to. He may have relatives to claim him. But somehow," she added, "I think no one will come. I believe he was a man alone."

"That does not solve the problem. Suicide . . ."

"We do not know it was suicide," Anne pressed. "It could have been an accident. After the episode at the inn when Mr. Simpson fired the gun, he may have thought he should unload it. How do we know, Mr. Carrington? How can we judge?"

He sat looking at her, genuinely troubled. The distresses and deaths and troubles of the navvies had never impinged on his mind. But this did. He had known Bullivant. He had been rather afraid of him and for this reason he had allowed his petulant dislike to be directed solely at the men who were building the railway, not the man responsible for it. He had recognised and kept away from the power, the suppressed force of the man's personality.

A man like that to shoot himself. He knew it was a death that should not have happened.

It was, like the wreck of the train, yesterday, an unnecessary, a futile tragedy . . . He had not expected when he had prayed for revenge in his desecrated church, when he had sought his martyr's crown in the face of the riotous crowd, to evoke such a terrible response. The crushed bodies of the men in the train, the sight of Bullivant's head——

Carrington had had to go to the inn. Simpson, near hysterical, finding Hugh Radlett away, had come to him. It had been his duty to go. He had looked down at the man lying in his clumsy, ugly, bloody death and he had caught a glimpse of a world so removed from his own well-planned progress to a bishopric, with its comfortable order and unquestioned opinions, that the conventional phrases of acceptance so useful at death-beds had frozen on his lips. He had seen for a brief instance the gap between his mind, his neat thoughts and regulated emotions, and that of a man like Bullivant. He had looked into an abyss of inner despair such as he could never envisage and he had been frightened into silence. The moment, like the wreck, the riots, everything that had happened during that terrible day had shaken him profoundly.

He said: "If the inquest decides it was suicide . . ."

"But if they decide it was an accident?"

He nodded. "Very well, Miss Torrance. If Godfrey Bullivant's death is stated to be the result of accidental causes, if no relatives come to claim his body, I will bury him here in my churchyard."

"Thank you," Anne said.

"But you and I and everyone else know that it was really suicide. Why are you doing this? Why are you so concerned? I thought you disliked him and his railway."

Anne got up to leave. "It is the only thing I can do for him now." She paused at the door. "I feel responsible, Mr. Carrington. Don't you?"

Hugh saw her walking through the lychgate. He stood waiting for her to come to him, as he had so many times. As she approached he held out his arms to her and she came into them. He held her tightly, neither of them speaking; then, his arm still round her shoulders, they walked together to the house.

September came. The last of the harvest and

443

the smell of autumn. The nipping edge of frost at night. The sky a different blue than a summer sky. The trees burdened with papery, curling leaves flaming with the last fires of life. A time for endings and beginnings.

The coroner's jury, moved perhaps to sympathy by the tragedy, had brought in a verdict of misadventure on Bullivant. No one had claimed his body, though many creditors had appeared to claim whatever goods and money he had left. Carrington held a service and buried him in a corner of the churchyard, near enough to the boundary wall to make a compromise and satisfy his conscience.

Esther Wharton remained at Waterford Park, growing large with her child, and wearing the self-satisfied air of a cat who has schemed her way into a comfortable home. Her father had barred her from his doors for life, and returned all letters concerning her that were sent to him. Apart from sending her out to beg her bread there was little Sophia could have done to be rid of her, even if she had wished to. But she did not seem to wish to. She seemed pleased at the prospect of entertaining a new presence in her house.

"I like children," she remarked. "They

have such possibilities. I am exceedingly curious to see what this one will be like. It will be such an odd combination of vices."

In Hungary, the revolution was over. Kossuth escaped to Turkey, burying before he fled, the holy crown of St. Stephen on the banks of the Danube. Görgey and his army surrendered to the Russians. The Austrian Baron Haynau began a policy of brutal repression, boasting that he would see to it that there should be no more revolution in Hungary for a hundred years. The firing squads and the prisons engulfed the nation's leaders and the long night of oppression settled over the land.

Of Laszlo Bathory there was no news. When Hugh on a visit to London went out of curiosity to the house in Southwark, he found it deserted. Eva and her girls had gone. No one knew what had happened to her or to Laszlo, but he did not feel that either of them would ever starve.

The railway had been abandoned. Whether or not another company would be found to finish it, no one knew. The navvies were packing up and going. The camp on the hill was empty.

But Anne walking home across the fields on

a bright sunny day found a reminder of it. A girl was sitting on the edge of a field in the sunlight, playing with her young baby. There was something about her that seemed familiar to Anne, and, because to-day she felt like smiling at everybody, she smiled at her.

The girl sat up, returning the smile shyly. Anne praised the baby and asked his name.

"Hugh," the girl said. "After the doctor."

Anne stared and then laughed. "Why, you are the girl, the girl at the camp whose baby he delivered. I was there."

"Yes, miss, I know you."

She was married, the girl said. She was living nearby with her husband. He had become a farm labourer and they had a cottage to live in and she had never been happier in her life.

"We've escaped the railways, that's what my mother says. She says we've escaped and no matter how poor we be, we are safe."

"You must come to my wedding," Anne said impulsively. "I am to be married to-morrow."

"Yes, miss, I know. To the doctor. Everyone knows."

"Everyone?" Anne cried, and they laughed.

Hugh had come out from Rivington to meet Anne. He saw her sitting with the girl in the golden stubble of the wheatfield, holding a flower up to the baby. She was wearing a russet-coloured dress and her hair gleamed as she moved her head. She looked up and saw him and smiled.

"My most satisfactory patient," Hugh remarked, allowing his finger to be clasped by the baby. "I wish they all looked as plump and well."

"But then you'd get no money, would you, Doctor," the girl said, "and then you'd fall away in your turn!"

"He will have to be doubly grasping now," Anne said. "Now that he has to keep me."

"I was thinking," Hugh remarked, as they said good-bye to the girl and started to walk home, "that from to-morrow I may order you about."

"Only because I shall have consented to it."

"My chattel," he said affectionately, and kissed her nose.

"Husband is quite a pleasant word," Anne said. "To husband is to look after, is it not? To take care of."

"Lover is a more interesting word."

"Yes," she said. "The verb to love is best of all."

The girl watched them as they wandered away from her through the fields, their arms entwined, their progress slow as they stopped each yard or so to kiss. Then, as the baby pulled at her and gave a few impatient cries, she unfastened her bodice and began to feed her child.

THE END

GUIDE
TO THE COLOUR CODING
OF
ULVERSCROFT BOOKS

Many of our readers have written to us expressing their appreciation for the way in which our colour coding has assisted them in selecting the Ulverscroft books of their choice.

To remind everyone of our colour coding—this is as follows:

BLACK COVERS
Mysteries

⋆

BLUE COVERS
Romances

⋆

RED COVERS
Adventure Suspense and General Fiction

⋆

ORANGE COVERS
Westerns

⋆

GREEN COVERS
Non-Fiction

THE SHADOWS
OF THE CROWN TITLES
in the
Ulverscroft Large Print Series

ROMANCE TITLES
in the
Ulverscroft Large Print Series